FOR THE RECORD

"Going on tour with Chelsea and the Melbourne guys made me feel like I was on the best summer break of my life. Once you start reading *For the Record,* you won't want to stop!"
—Leila Sales, author of *This Song Will Save Your Life*

"I adored hanging out with Chelsea and the boys of Melbourne—when they felt the music, I felt it, and when they were off their game, so was I. Fun, fast, and colorful, this book isn't just for music lovers, it's for anyone who ever looked at a band onstage and thought, 'I wonder what that would be like.'"   —Francesca Zappia, author of *Made You Up*

"Pitch-perfect and utterly addictive."
—Michelle Krys, author of *Hexed*

"For teens who dream of a glamorous lifestyle."
—*Kirkus Reviews*

"An absorbing behind-the-scenes look at life on tour."   —*PW*

"Original and fresh."   —*SLJ*

"There's a lot to enjoy."   —*Booklist*

Praise for

Insane *Clutch*

CHARLOTTE HUANG

FOR THE RECORD

EMBER

For Andrew

Text copyright © 2015 by Charlotte Huang
Cover photograph copyright © 2015 by Getty/Brand New Images

randomhouseteens.com

Educators and librarians, for a variety of teaching tools, visit us at RHTeachersLibrarians.com

Library of Congress Cataloging-in-Publication Data
Huang, Charlotte.
For the record / Charlotte Huang. — First edition.
pages cm.
Summary: As the new lead singer of the band Melbourne, Chelsea has only the summer tour to make the band—and their fans—love her, or it is back to boring high school.
ISBN 978-0-553-51182-6 (hc) — ISBN 978-0-553-51183-3 (glb) — ISBN 978-0-553-51184-0 (ebook) [1. Rock groups—Fiction. 2. Bands (Music)—Fiction. 3. Fame—Fiction. 4. Dating (Social customs)—Fiction.] I. Title.
PZ7.1.H74Fo 2015
[Fic]—dc23
2014029972

ISBN 978-0-553-51185-7 (trade pbk.)

Printed in the United States of America
10 9 8 7 6 5 4 3 2 1
First Ember Edition 2016

1

As far as stupid mistakes go, failing to get to the stage when your band is making a major announcement probably ranks pretty high. But I was lost in the fog of an unlikely makeout session in the bathroom of the Roxy when I heard Pem take the mike. "We want to say a big thank-you to everyone for coming out tonight. Come on up here, guys. Thanks to everyone at Pacific for supporting Melbourne and believing in our record. And thanks to the folks at AEA, we have some exciting news."

Oh crap. I tore my lips away from Lucas Rivers in a total panic. "I have to go." I slammed out of the stall, fixing my shirt as I went.

"Um, anyone seen Chelsea? Okay, she'll get up here in a minute. Anyway—" Pem stalled, waiting for me to get my butt onstage.

"I'll call you," Lucas drawled to my back.

I checked the mirror to make sure I didn't have lipstick smeared all over my face, then turned to look at him. He shot me his trademark smile, eyes bright with mischief. God, that face. No wonder it was plastered on every billboard and bus shelter in the country. "You don't have my number," I said, and banged out of the bathroom.

In my rush, I plowed right into a wall. Only it wasn't a wall. It was a mountain wearing a black double-breasted blazer over a T-shirt, with sunglasses perched on his head even though it was nighttime. "Excuse me." I checked my irritation. It wasn't his fault I'd missed my cue.

He didn't acknowledge me but reached behind me and used one of his treelike arms to prop open the door. "Yo!" he said into the bathroom.

"Yeah, coming," Lucas called back as I ran off.

Sneaking onstage at the Roxy in front of five hundred people was idiotic, but I had no choice. I dodged spotlights, acting like my late entrance was planned. When I reached Pem's side, he covered his mike with his hand. "Nice of you to join us," he muttered, eyes flashing so hard they could have lit my head on fire.

Malcolm and Beckett avoided looking at me, not wanting any part of the trouble I was in.

Pem turned back to the crowd. "We're completely stoked for our tour this summer. Come out and see us!"

Malcolm grabbed the mike, interrupting the applause. "We're hitting thirty cities! Coming soon to a club near you!" He pointed dramatically at the audience, then dropped the mike and walked offstage. Pem suppressed a laugh. For reasons I hadn't figured out yet, Malcolm could get away with things Beckett and I couldn't.

We followed Malcolm up to the dressing room, where we collapsed on sunken couches. The place was shabby, with stains on the carpet, fluorescent lighting, and walls covered in band stickers. Half-eaten pizzas sat congealing on the foldout table. This was rock and roll, all right.

Sam, Melbourne's manager, came into the room. He looked harried but was trying to pull it together. An evening of hanging around music industry execs will rattle even the heartiest of men. "Good job, guys. And Chelsea. That was a killer set. If you can bring it like that on tour, we're gonna be all good." I clung to Sam's praise like it was a life raft, relieved that I hadn't disappointed.

Pem reached up and high-fived Sam before fixing his glare on me. "Where the hell were you?" I should have known he wasn't going to let it slide.

"Yeah, Chelsea. You gotta make it to the stage on time," Sam said.

I guessed the praise portion of the evening was over. That was short-lived. "Sorry. I thought we were supposed to socialize."

"Is that what you kids are calling it these days? She disappeared with that douche bag." Malcolm grinned and winked at me. "Guess I won't be the only 'Ho' on tour."

My face burned, but the others smirked at Malcolm's clever pun. Ho was his last name, and from what I gathered, he certainly lived up to it. With his sparkling brown eyes, warm tawny skin, and easy smile, it wasn't hard to see why girls went for him. Plus, speaking from my years of experience on the other side of the stage, rock groupies seemed to have it bad for drummers. But then I watched Malcolm reach for pizza that had been sitting out for hours and thought maybe the girls should think twice.

"What was Lucas Rivers doing at our record release?" Beckett's tone was curious, not judgmental.

Sam shrugged. "He's a Melbourne fan. AEA put him on their list." Artists and Entertainers Agency, which represented us, also represented Lucas Rivers.

Pem grimaced, shaking his head. "That guy. His movies are unwatchable." As a bona fide Lucas Rivers fan, I couldn't have disagreed more, but I wasn't dumb enough to say so.

"I read he makes twenty million a movie," Malcolm said.

I was dying for them to stop talking about this. I hadn't begun to process that less than half an hour ago, I'd been mashing lips with the hottest teen star in Hollywood. It just figured that the first time I kissed a guy in almost two years, I got in trouble for it.

After our set I'd lingered by the bar, chatting up our publicist and radio promo staff as instructed, when Lucas slid onto the stool next to me and bought me a drink. Not that I'd asked for one, and not that either of us was legal. But that didn't seem to faze anyone involved in the transaction.

Here's the first thing I noticed: when Lucas Rivers wanted your attention, he got it. Beyond his well-documented physical attributes, he had a way of locking in so that I felt like I was the only person in the club. As soon as our eyes met, everyone else slowly blurred out of my vision.

"I wasn't sure how I'd like Melbourne with a new singer, but you're perfect," Lucas said as an introduction.

I tried not to look overly grateful. "Thank you."

A lot of people thought Hollis Carter *was* Melbourne, so I knew there was a good chance that in taking her job, I was setting myself up for a blog-verse of hate. Whatever. I loved the band; plus it fulfilled my contract with Pacific Records and got me out of another mind-numbing summer in Lydon, Michigan. It was the job of a lifetime.

My life had taken such a surreal detour in the past several months that initially I didn't even question why Lucas Rivers would suddenly materialize in front of me. Or why he'd down his drink, then hold out his hand and lead me to the front of the club. I thought maybe he wanted to go outside so we wouldn't have to shout over the music, but he guided me into the dingy vestibule in front of the bathrooms.

"So did you get your complimentary copy of *Barn Burning*?" I sounded like the tongue-tied dork that I was.

"I already had it. My agent sent it over," Lucas said.

"And you like it?"

"Very much. I like how you bring more power to the vocals. I'm a sucker for girls with beautiful voices."

I'm pretty sure I kissed him then. It could have been the drink (though I didn't remember actually drinking any of it). Or maybe I was finally cracking from the absurd amount of stress I'd been under. But seriously, who wouldn't want to kiss Lucas Rivers?

The next thing I knew, we were in a bathroom stall, all over each other. It was probably good that Pem summoned me back to earth before I did anything really stupid. Just because I'd watched Lucas's movies a million times didn't mean I actually knew the guy.

Now Sam finished running down the logistics for the start of our tour. I snapped to attention when I realized that all eyes were on me. "What?" I asked. "I'll be fine." I mean, they acted like I hadn't delivered on everything they'd asked of me.

Sam looked down at the ground, tense. "I know you'll be busy finishing up school, but you have to keep your voice in shape. Five shows a week is no joke. And living on a bus, eating crap food every night, takes a toll. Drink a lot of water, get good sleep. And it wouldn't hurt to get some exercise."

Great. Yet another not-so-subtle comment about my weight. I was hardly plus-sized; I was curvy in all the right places and, fine, a couple of the wrong ones. But Lucas Rivers hadn't seemed to mind. Next to the manorexic members of Melbourne, though, I'm sure I seemed out of place. Not like perfectly waify Hollis Carter. "I'll make sure to fit some in," I lied. I didn't play sports and hated any kind of mindless physical exertion. My exercise routine could easily have been mistaken for dancing around my room in front of a pretend audience.

"Your parents want to know if they can come up," Sam said.

I took a quick scan of my bandmates' faces. They didn't seem to be in the mood for company, let alone my parents. "I'll go out," I said, standing.

"One more thing," Pem said. "I'm actually glad the douche bag incident happened, because it reminded me to raise this point: there will be absolutely no hooking up between members of the band and crew." We all stared at Pem. "Am I speaking Arabic or something?"

"It's just, if you were going for subtlety, I think you missed the mark," Beckett said. He flicked a guitar pick he'd been holding across the room and it hit the wall with a satisfying *thwack!*

I cleared my throat. "Was that for my benefit?" I mean, they were gorgeous and everything, but still, wasn't he being a little presumptuous?

"Does cuddling count?" Malcolm asked. "'Cause I like to cuddle. Ask Beckett." Beckett searched for another guitar pick to flick.

Pem ignored them both. "I'm mostly talking to you, but I want to make the boundaries clear for everyone." His gaze was disconcerting.

Maybe he was worried that *he* might lose control and jump my bones, because the other two had shown me about as much welcome as they would a Hot Pocket. Maybe not quite that much welcome. Besides, I wasn't here to be anyone's girlfriend.

"Well, I'm obviously sad we won't be sharing any special moments, but I understand," I said. "Can I go now?"

"Yeah," Sam said. "See you in Pittsburgh on the twenty-first."

The house lights were on, exposing the club's grubbiness. It was empty except for a few stragglers, including Brian and Linda Ford, my parents. My stout, gray-haired, dress-shirt-wearing father couldn't have looked more out of place, but that didn't stop him from searching to see if there was anyone left to talk to. I was emotionally fried but tried to muster some enthusiasm when I saw their shining faces.

"Honey, you were sensational!" my mother squealed, giving me a hug. When I pulled back, she reached over to brush hair out of my eyes. Her heavy gold bangle clanked against my forehead. My mom's efforts to be maternal were always fraught with peril.

"Thanks. Can we go order room service?" We had an obnoxiously early flight back home. "The guys are exhausted but send hugs and kisses and said they can't wait to see you in Detroit."

My mother looked concerned. "Are you sure? We should at least say goodbye."

My parents often flat-out refused to take the hint. I started toward the exit but couldn't help glancing around on the off chance Lucas Rivers had decided to wait. He hadn't, of course. As I passed the bathroom, I said a silent goodbye to that special stall. I avoided annoying my bandmates as a general rule, but I have to say, five minutes in bathroom heaven with Lucas Rivers might have been worth it.

2

Monday morning back at my house in Lydon, I came downstairs to see my best friend, Mandy, suffering through one of my mother's stream-of-consciousness monologues. "You won't believe it when you see her with the band. And the guys, oh my goodness. You'll just die when you meet them."

"I can't wait," Mandy said. Most people seemed to like my parents; Mandy was just good at pretending she did. She looked so reassuringly the same: sandy blond hair tied up in a knot, Joy Division T-shirt and cutoffs. I'd put on jeans, red Chuck Taylors, and a black T-shirt, hoping that I'd seem the same too.

My mother hurried to answer our phone. It'd been ringing nonstop since we got home, but none of the calls were for me. "Hello, Amy . . . Just fabulous . . . Yes, they finally announced the tour. . . . Well, at any rate, she's going to have the summer of her life. . . ."

I gritted my teeth. "My parents are awesome at keeping secrets."

"Don't look at me. I kept my mouth shut," Mandy said.

I smiled, but really, who was she going to tell? She had the same number of friends that I had: one.

We left and got into Mandy's charmingly rust-eaten Honda Civic. "So. Spill it." She alternated glancing in the rearview with looking at me expectantly as she pulled onto the street.

"Let me get past this final. Then I'd be happy to bore you to death at lunch." Despite having the plane ride home, including a two-hour layover and last night to review, I couldn't seem to switch gears. For the next week I had to forget everything but school. One thing at a time. Determined, I pulled out my precalculus notes.

"That is so lame! You barely emailed me while you were there," Mandy said.

"All right. Here's one thing: I kissed Lucas Rivers."

"What? You're kidding me! Are you kidding me?" Mandy screeched to a stop in the Starbucks parking lot.

"I can definitely see why you'd go there, but no."

"Oh my God. How? Is he friends with the band? Caryn Sullivan will lose her shit. No wait, she'd never believe it—"

I got out to make our coffee run. Mrs. Carlson's final was going to be ugly enough. Only a fool would attempt it without caffeine.

I wasn't sure how my joining Melbourne had stayed a secret for the past six months with my parents bragging to anyone who'd listen. The best I could figure was that their friends didn't care about bands or music and so didn't bother to repeat any of it. Also, nobody at Lydon High had been the least bit curious when I disappeared for winter break. I'd spent it in Los Angeles recording my parts for *Barn Burning*. Turns out keeping personal information under wraps is super easy when no one cares.

Even now that Melbourne had announced me as lead singer at the Roxy when we did the record release, I doubted I was on anyone's radar. Part of the reason was that Lydon was severely lacking in the indie hipster department. The other major reason was that I'd cemented my loser status last year when I went on the reality show *American Pop Star*. Every week, the judges had picked apart my look, calling it "overdone emo" or "angry goth." Forget that those two scenes weren't even remotely friendly, or that producers had dictated everyone's wardrobe and makeup from the start. I learned a ton (some things I wish I could unlearn) and I definitely got a thicker skin, but when I was voted off, I wasn't overly broken up about it.

Half a season of reality TV was enough to send me running back to my silent, anonymous life, but first I'd have to live down the scorn. It was dorky to try out for a TV talent show, and it was even dorkier to lose. Even past winners who had gone on to fame and fortune were never really considered cool. So yeah, my first attempt to escape Lydon was an epic fail. On the upside, being mocked was nothing new to me.

When I got back in the car, I told Mandy the entire nonstory about Lucas Rivers. "I'm sure I'll be telling my grandkids about it one day, but I doubt Lucas even remembers that it happened."

"I'm sure I'll be telling *my* grandkids about it one day too," she said.

We parked and walked into the large, seventies-era building that was Lydon High. I'd always thought it looked like a prison. As we walked down the hall my bag slid off my shoulder, jerking my arm and causing me to spill hot coffee all over myself. Smooth. I handed my cup to Mandy while I dug in my bag for napkins.

"Here you go." I looked up. Mike Malloy stood in front of his locker holding out paper towels. He was the star basketball player/class stud, and I'd hardly spoken a word to him since he'd ruined my life freshman year.

I yanked the paper towels out of his hand as I passed by.

Next to me, Mandy hissed, "He knows! People know!"

"Oh well," I said. "Too late for Lydon to start trying to be decent now."

I finished the test with enough time to double-check my answers. My coffee had long since gone cold, but I drank it anyway. Acing finals was the first part of my plan, and I already felt more relaxed now that it was under way. This was also the easiest part, the only one that was mostly within my control. When Mrs. Carlson called time, I handed in my booklet and waited for Mandy.

"That was brutal," she muttered. "How did you do?"

"I think okay," I said. We walked to her locker. I stashed my stuff in there as I usually did, since my locker was in the creepy basement.

"Translation: another A for Chelsea." Mandy gave me a grudging smile. "Did you nerd out and study in Los Angeles?"

"A little," I lied. "I'm starving. Where should we eat?"

"You choose. You're the one who's leaving."

I'd been so obsessed with getting out of here that I hadn't really thought about what I'd miss. "Raspberries?"

Mandy groaned. "Seriously? I'm trying to put off the inevitable." We'd worked at Raspberries, Lydon's only health food café, last summer. The owner, a crazy, capitalist hippie named Dane, invented new sandwiches daily and bugged out if we forgot one of the nine ingredients on a particular sandwich. We both had PTSD from all his yelling, and as an annoying side effect of working there, I now found sandwiches without sprouts to be inedible. Unfortunately Lydon didn't have many jobs to offer, so Mandy would be back at Raspberries for another summer.

I'd imagined telling Dane what he could do with his crappy job at least a million times, but when the time had come to actually do it, I'd settled for sending a text. Unprofessional, but Dane deserved it.

We drove into town and tried to slip into the café unnoticed. "Please let this be one of his colonic days," Mandy muttered as we walked in and seated ourselves.

"I'll have a Jane's Special," Mandy whispered to the waiter after we sat down. He gave her a weird look.

"Make it two," I said. Mandy shushed me. The waiter went back to the kitchen. "Will you relax? Dane doesn't have dog ears."

"Easy for you to say."

I worried that Mandy was having a harder time with my leaving than she let on. "So when are you going to visit me?" I asked.

"Anytime, as long as you pay for my ticket and save one of the guys for me," Mandy said.

I rolled my eyes.

"That good, huh?" Mandy sipped her water and studied me with a furrowed brow. Seriously, who else would feel bad for a girl who was about to go live on a bus with three hot guys who also happened to be talented and famous?

"They didn't stone me or anything, but it's not like we stayed up late and did each other's hair."

"Did they stay in the *Pretty Woman* hotel too?"

I snorted. Mandy was talking about the Beverly Wilshire hotel, made famous by my mother's favorite movie. "Yeah right. That was on my parents' dime. The band stayed in some crappy apartment in Burbank."

"Things must be going well at Ford's Fast Five," she said, referring to my parents' sporting goods store. It had the usual stuff for seasonal and team sports, but they'd expanded a couple of years ago to carry things like high-end sneakers and designer jeans. "So the guys didn't come around at all?"

Bonding with the band, also known as phase two of my plan, felt like it might never happen. I'd hoped things would fall into place in December when I recorded, but aside from Pem swinging by and barking orders at me, it was pretty much just me and the sound engineer. And last week (the third time I worked with them) was so insane, I was impressed that they remembered my name. "If by coming around you mean ignoring me until I screw something up, then yes."

Mandy sighed. "I read that all arranged marriages take time. It'll be better when you don't have constant chaperones. But the actual shows were good?"

I nodded. "Everyone said we killed it."

Pacific Records and our agent at AEA put together some

closed, music industry showcases for us. They said it was to show people how well I fit into Melbourne, but I overheard Pem say it was because I had no experience in front of a live audience. I guess by his definition, three hundred studio audience members didn't count as live.

"What the hell, man?" Dane's voice rang out from the kitchen. "We're out of pickled radish. Eighty-six the Jane's Special, man! Come on!" Dane thought that adding *man* to every sentence made the difference between conversation and verbal abuse. He came into the dining area and spotted us right away. "Your discount doesn't apply unless you're actually working. Former employees get no consideration whatsoever," he said.

Mandy pushed her chair back. "Chelsea doesn't need your 'consideration.' She'll be making a hell of a lot more than minimum wage plus one sandwich per shift! And you're about to wish you were much nicer to her."

She always had my back. I didn't want her to be stuck in this crunchy hellhole while I had the "summer of my life."

Dane smirked. "You probably want to think about being much nicer to me."

I stood up and pulled Mandy toward the door. No sandwich was worth this. "She quits! So you can keep your ridiculous, overwrought sandwiches and your insulting discount! She has a phenomenal job on tour with me!" I said it on impulse, as an f-you to everyone in Lydon who'd made our past few years hell. One look at the shock and gratitude on Mandy's face and I knew I couldn't take it back.

3

We made it almost all the way back to school before Mandy broke the silence. She took a deep breath. "You don't have to—"

"Yes I do. It might take a minute, but I'll figure it out." Her giving me an out made me feel even more obligated.

A small, hopeful smile flashed across her face. I barely felt welcome on this tour; I could just imagine their reaction to me bringing an entourage. At least she'd keep me sane. I wondered if anyone in Melbourne's camp cared enough about my mental health to buy that as a justification.

"Let's go eat petrified cafeteria food by ourselves in a corner. For a change." I grinned at Mandy, trying to make her laugh.

She sighed. "What do you have next?"

"*Français.*"

We set our trays on a table by glass doors that led to the bright, grassy field outside. Lydon was most beautiful in the summer. The sky was wide, cloudless, sparkling. Deep green leaves hung heavy and languid from elm trees. Even the cafeteria was tolerable right now. Thanks to the intensity of finals, it was deserted, with only a handful of tables taken by last-minute crammers.

I ate wilted lettuce with French dressing in an attempt to get my game face on. I wasn't that stressed; it was an essay test, and Madame Kramer was lenient as long as the grammar was correct and you threw in some obscure vocabulary words.

Mandy kicked me under the table. I bit my yelp of pain short when I saw why. Mike Malloy was coming toward us, a tentative look on his face instead of his usual, haughty "eat shit" expression.

Mike and I had started fooling around at the beginning of freshman year. It went without saying that I'd had to keep it to myself; he was cool, I wasn't, but I wasn't a loser either. Not yet, anyway. When we were alone, he was sweet and attentive. My favorite was when he asked me to sing for him, because back then, nobody knew I sang. It was another special secret between us.

A few months into it, we decided to have sex. I thought I was in love and kept telling myself he'd be ready to tell his friends about us soon. Afterward, I was sick with guilt and anxiety. Probably as a result, my period was late and I was positive I was pregnant. I was such a hot mess I couldn't even bring myself to buy a pregnancy test.

When I told Mike, he froze up and only asked me to "give it another week." He didn't want to go buy a pregnancy test either. Then he started avoiding me. When my period finally came and I told him, he lost it and accused me of trying to trap him into being my boyfriend. The thing was, I already thought of him as my boyfriend.

I tried to apologize so many times that I'm sure it looked like I was stalking him. To explain why I was suddenly all over him, he told anyone who would listen that he got drunk and hooked up with me at a party and then I went psycho and pretended I was pregnant. That effectively scared off all the boys; and when the boys won't go near you, the girls keep their distance too. Mandy was literally the only person who'd risked staying my friend.

Over time, the snickers and whispers that followed me wherever I went died down, but no one ever forgot.

Now I did what I always do when confronted with Mike Malloy: I ignored him. However, as he decided to loom over us, I eventually gave up. "What?" I asked, keeping my eyes on Mandy.

"Nothin'. Heard your news." Of course Mike would be the first person to glom onto the Melbourne announcement. "You know I like that one song, 'Parietals.'"

Unbelievable. The boy was shameless. I glared at him.

Mike seemed confused by my hostility. "Anyway, wanted to see if you were coming to Caryn's party when school lets out."

"Did I finally make it off the inactive list?"

Mike just blinked at me, so I broke it down for him. "When have I ever been invited to that?" Caryn lived around the block from me, but I hadn't been welcome at her house since middle school.

"She's cool," Mike assured me.

Mandy gave him a flat stare. She was like my own personal pit bull.

"Doubtful," I said. "I leave right after finals." With any luck, I'd never see Mike again. No sense in torching a past that had already been burned to the ground.

He shrugged but looked mollified. "See you around."

I was pretty much past Mike screwing me over, but my need to get out of Lydon still kicked into overdrive when I had to deal with him. The other residual effect was that no one besides Mandy had spoken more than two sentences to me since freshman year.

Somehow, in the middle of exam week, I worked up the courage to call Sam. He might have thought I was a good singer and liked me on a personal level, but until the band stopped thinking of me as a "hired gun," we both knew who his real clients were.

A couple of months after I left *American Pop Star*, a Pacific Records executive had called my parents and explained that the network had reported that I had an unusually high Q factor for where I'd been voted off. (That's some marketing term that I never quite understood, and ninth runner-up, to answer my least favorite question.) They wanted to talk to me about a project that needed a female lead singer.

When I'd auditioned for the show, I hadn't realized that Pacific Records got three-year options on every contestant who made it to the top twenty-five. Usually it wasn't an issue, because what were they going to do with a bunch of talent show rejects? Most of us just faded into the reject sunset.

Hollis Carter had quit Melbourne and enrolled at Vassar. She was burned out and wanted a normal life. The only problem was that Melbourne owed Pacific one more record. They could have paid back their advance. They'd made plenty of money, and every one of them came from rich East Coast families. (They liked to downplay their trust funds, but since they were all prep school buddies, it was sometimes glaringly obvious.)

Pem insisted that they deliver the record. I wasn't clear on why he was so hell-bent, but Malcolm was up for the party and Beckett was all for it. Pacific wouldn't approve their first choice for a singer, because she'd had a deal at another label. Melbourne eventually gave in and accepted Pacific's recommendation. And that was my auspicious intro to the band.

Sam picked up on the first ring. "Hey, how's it going? You crushing those finals or what?"

"Chemistry was a little traumatic," I said, before it occurred to me that he probably didn't actually care.

"You getting enough rest? Eating well?" Sam was slightly out of breath, and I could hear traffic in the background.

I thought about the Reuben sandwich I'd had from Sonny's Bagels for lunch. It had given me acid reflux—seriously distracting during my AP chem final. At least it was kind of on topic. "Yeah, eating lots of fruits and veggies." Starting now.

"Good, good. I'm in New York with the guys. They're fired up about the tour."

The exclusion that I always felt reared its ugly head again, knowing that everyone except me was prepping for tour together. I had to get over it. Since I had so many practical goals hinging on this tour, I was trying to keep my emotional expectations low.

"Cool. Tell everyone I said hi."

"I will. So . . . what's up? You got questions?"

"Kind of. More like a favor-slash-question," I hedged. I'd made it a point to be agreeable, so asking for anything felt risky, though logically I knew it was too late for them to change their minds about me. At least for this record cycle.

"Shoot."

"Could I bring a friend on tour?"

"Girl or boy?"

I thought that was a weird first question, but I went with it. "Girl."

"We were saying it might be hard on you to be the only girl. I was going to hire a girl to do merch. Will your friend work?" Sam asked.

"Yeah, of course!"

Sam asked a couple of questions about Mandy's work experience and told me to email him her contact info, and then it was a done deal. I could not believe it had been that easy.

As soon as we hung up, I called Mandy. She shrieked so loudly that I had to hold the phone away from my ear. "Are you messing with me?" She sounded like she might be crying, which made me a little teary too. I was so happy I could do this for her.

"Your parents will let you, won't they?" It had occurred to me that my parents might have been a little unusual in letting their teenage daughter roam around the country with a bunch of strange boys.

"They better! Once they realize they won't have to feed me for the entire summer, I'm sure they will. How much will I get paid?"

"Uh, I don't know." I'd been so fixated on just getting Sam to let Mandy come on tour, I hadn't even thought to ask. "You want me to call Sam back?" I wanted her to say no, but I supposed wanting to know how much she'd make was reasonable.

"If you can. That'd give me more ammunition."

The Olsons were conservative, but they knew who their daughter was. Her near-obsessive concert-going had never been about anything but the music. Hopefully they'd see this as a constructive way for her to spend a summer.

Sam picked up on the first ring again. He wasn't annoyed at all; he was actually apologetic about not mentioning it before. "She'll make two percent of the net. If we go by our last tour, we usually sell about twenty bucks a head."

I felt too stupid to ask what that would mean for Mandy's take-home pay, but it sounded good enough. I didn't want to seem like an ingrate.

"Huh. I figure you'll be playing, like, thousand-seat clubs, right?" Mandy said when I called her back.

Actually, I had no idea. I knew that we'd be playing decent-sized places. In Detroit, we were playing the Fillmore, which I knew only because I'd been to a bunch of shows there. A thousand seats seemed like a good guess.

"So if you do twenty a head, and let's say net is half, that's ten thousand—I could be making two hundred dollars a night! How many shows a week, again?" Mandy sounded incredulous. The girl might have struggled with precalculus, but she was no slouch with money.

I felt a little disbelieving myself. That wasn't much less than I'd be making. I was getting paid less than the rest of the band, since they'd written every single Melbourne song in existence and were the ones people were coming to see. Sam said that we'd revisit my deal for the next record, if there was one. That was all still up in the air, which was why I was on a mission to make my bandmates love me. I could only hope they were as desperate for this to work as I was.

4

A week later, Mandy and I were waiting for our suitcases at Pittsburgh International Airport. My stomach was in knots, but luckily Sam interrupted my panic attack, tapping my shoulder and giving an awkward little wave. "You made it. Was the flight okay?"

"It was great. No problems." I mean, it was on time and didn't break down, so I had no complaints. "This is Mandy."

They shook hands while I reached to silence my phone's buzzing. It was a text from my mom: *Can't wait to hear about rehearsal!*

Sigh. Her guilty conscience was working overtime. Summer was Ford's Fast Five's busiest season, so my parents would miss most of the tour. Of course I didn't tell them, but I was looking forward to having this experience without them hovering. Besides, I had Mandy.

"Thank you for this opportunity!" Mandy was saying to

Sam. "You won't regret it. Oops, that one's mine!" She hurried to the baggage carousel. "I'm waiting for two more," she said when she rejoined us.

Sam glanced at me, and I knew I'd probably screwed up by not telling Mandy about the limited storage space on the bus. Honestly, it hadn't occurred to me that selling merch might require a full wardrobe. She only ever wore T-shirts and jeans at home, so I had no idea what could be in those suitcases.

Once Mandy had all her bags, Sam shepherded us out of the airport and into an SUV that idled by the sidewalk. "This is Nadine. She's a runner for the venue. If you need anything while you're there, you can ask her."

Nadine smiled at us in her rearview mirror.

"Are we going right to the venue?" I asked. Downtime normally made me feel antsy, but right now I was extra anxious to get to work, where my role was clearly defined. Otherwise, it was too easy to feel like a trespasser.

"We don't rehearse until three. I thought we'd get lunch, check in to the hotel." Sam looked down at his phone, tapping away.

"Is everyone else here already?"

"Yup." Of course. I tried to squelch the fluttery feeling in my chest. I might not have been their first choice, but the record label wanted me here, I reminded myself.

We pulled up to the Hyatt, a brick building with red awnings on the lower windows. Mandy grabbed my arm. "This is so exciting! Maybe Nadine can take us out after rehearsal. Pittsburgh isn't as ugly as I thought."

Being from the outskirts of Detroit, I never badmouthed

other cities. "We don't have to be all prima donna about it. I'm sure there are buses."

Mandy turned to look at me, serious as a heart attack. She placed both hands on my shoulders. "You're allowed to ask Nadine for a ride. This tour would not be happening without you."

I nodded, hoping for her sake that she knew the difference between me asking and her asking.

Our room wasn't ready, so Sam sent us into the restaurant. We waited at a table set for twelve. "Who else is coming?" Mandy whispered.

I shrugged. I combed my hands through my hair, wishing I'd had time to put on lip gloss or at least check a mirror. But I didn't want to look like I was trying to impress anybody.

The band arrived ahead of Sam. While they made their way to our table, my heart stopped beating for a couple of seconds, as it always did when I first saw them. Live. In person.

We murmured hellos and introductions. They were all wearing a variation of the same uniform: jeans, sneakers, T-shirt. Only Pem deviated slightly. Over his T-shirt, he wore a baseball jacket with cream-colored leather sleeves and metal studs covering the chest and back. That thing had to be heavy.

Under the table, Mandy squeezed my thigh so hard that I was sure I made some really bitchy face. Yup, they were still gorgeous. That much hadn't changed.

The restaurant wasn't packed, and people started to look over. While Mandy and I had gotten no attention from the waitstaff during the entire fifteen minutes we'd been sitting there, they now started to approach. At least it saved me from having to make forced conversation with the guys. I still felt awkward around them, and Mandy hadn't closed her mouth since they showed up.

Beckett took the seat next to me and tossed his phone onto the table beside his plate. Pem and Malcolm sat down on the other side of him. "We'll wait for the rest of our party," Pem said. The waitstaff scattered like bugs.

It was hard to believe Pem was only twenty. He had that innate confidence that bordered on arrogance. His full name was Pemberton Fuller III. My parents had been blown away when he confirmed that it was his grandfather's name on the door of some old Wall Street law firm. I wondered what Granddaddy thought about Pem's rock god status, not to mention his spiky blond hair and tattoos.

More guys came in and joined the table, a parade of long hair, flat-brimmed hats, and piercings. Nobody looked like this in Lydon. These guys looked like exotic and possibly dangerous creatures. One of them, the only clean-cut member of the group, summoned a waiter. "Could I have a menu, please?"

Pem gave him a dark look. "We're waiting for everyone. This is the official launch of the Business of Music Tour."

How did I not know that the tour had a name? Seemed like kind of a bland one, if you asked me. Which, of course, nobody had.

The waiter brought the menu, and Mr. Clean-Cut held him there with a light hand on his arm. "I know how you like your luncheons, Pem, but the truck's here. I have to make sure they don't fuck everything up." He turned his gaze on me. "Chelsea, it's great to meet you. I'm Rob, tour manager." Since we were too far apart to shake hands, we waved.

As Rob ordered, Beckett leaned toward me. "He's Malcolm's

cousin, which is why he got the job. First two tours were a little rough, but by now he knows his stuff."

I nodded, hating that I felt so appreciative at being let in on the smallest bit of inside information.

When Sam finally joined us, I relaxed a little. He was the only person here whose job description included being nice to me. Or at least civil. More menus were passed around, and we went through the rest of the introductions. The band and crew had already been together for a few tours, so the introductions were for Mandy and me.

Remembering names on the first try wasn't easy, but I was determined to get on good terms with everyone on the Business of Music Tour.

We had:

Reserved Rob: tour manager. He did look a lot like
Malcolm now that I took a better look. Kind of like how
Malcolm would look if he ever had to shave his head and
join the Army.
Air-Drum Aaron: drum tech. Tall, with broad shoulders
and lank blond hair. Constantly drumming on things.
Weight Watcher Winston: guitar and bass tech. I wasn't in a
position to throw stones, but he was on the heavier side.
Krazy-Eyed Kam: monitor guy. His gaze never focused,
instead darting around the room to take in everything.
Jocular Jared: sound guy. Seemed like a really happy person
with an easy, ever-present smile.
Opulent Oscar: lighting guy. Not many guys can pull off
earrings and a chain without looking like a wannabe thug.

We got to Mandy. "I'm Mandy. I'm going to be your merch girl."

Malcolm guffawed. "Merch Mandy!" A couple of the guys cracked up. I looked up, startled, like he'd read my mind and heard all my nicknames. Seriously, I had to stop being such a spaz.

"You're an idiot," Rob told Malcolm matter-of-factly.

"Get it? Merch Mandy? Like Merch Man except Merch Man*dy*?" Malcolm slumped in his seat, fully amused with himself.

Mandy's body language relaxed as soon as she was sure the laughing wasn't about her specifically. "I love it! Totally. Call me Merch Mandy. As in, I'm gonna merch the hell out of the Business of Music Tour."

Malcolm jabbed a finger in her direction. "Acceptable. She's in."

Okay, that was more than any of them had ever said about me. I tried not to fume while we ordered.

When our lunches arrived, the boys started shoveling food into their mouths. A low hum enveloped the table as the conversation splintered into smaller chats. "So. Overwhelmed yet? Ready to catch the first flight back to Michigan?" Poor Beckett was probably trying to make conversation, but he caught me at what I'd admit was an unbecoming moment.

"Wouldn't you just love that?" I muttered. "Then you could all be right about me." As soon as I said it, I wished I hadn't. If my Never Let 'Em See Me Sweat game plan fell apart this early, I was in a mess of trouble.

Beckett held up his hands in surrender. "I'm going to take that as a yes."

I gave a tight nod before looking up to see that he was grinning at me. I was taken aback; Beckett was the least expressive member of Melbourne. He was calm, steady, and reasonable, but the flip side was that he came off a little cold at times. Too bad. He should grin more often, because when he did, it was really something. I couldn't help smiling back.

Sam clinked his water glass with a spoon, right as Rob and some of the crew guys stood up to leave. "Hang on, hang on, I want to make a toast," Sam said.

Rob checked his watch (not even a retro, ironic one) and heaved a dramatic sigh.

"Just wanted to wish everyone a kick-ass tour," Sam said.

Calls of "Hear, hear" resounded around the table.

"Even though tour doesn't officially start until the day after tomorrow, I don't know if we'll get the chance to do this again. We're kind of a blended family here, and it might be tempting to give in to old feelings of loyalty or whatever. We all miss Hollis, but we should be—"

"Sam gets a little effusive. He's very emotional when we start tours. Just be glad he's not drunk," Beckett whispered so only I could hear.

I bit my lip to keep from laughing. Beckett's joking around took the sting out of what was devolving into a Hollis Carter praise-fest. I mean, she left them stranded. Should they really have been this weepy? "I think his point is that we're glad the bitch is gone, right?"

Beckett snorted.

Pem stared into his water glass, his mouth set into a thin line and his jaw tight. I guess I wasn't the only one who was uptight about tour starting.

5

Mandy practically bounced the whole way over to Stage AE, high on all that handsome testosterone and exhilarated by her successful initiation. Personally, I was wilting from the heat and humidity and cranky from feeling upstaged by Mandy. The forecast called for thunderstorms. I hoped they wouldn't screw up our first show. And that they weren't a terrible omen.

We approached the back entrance to the venue, an industrial-looking building with a modern front and a wrought-iron fence around the perimeter. A few ratty guys were smoking inside the parking lot gate and barely flicked their eyes to us as we walked into the building and into complete chaos. There were crates of all sizes strewn about, random boxes stuffed with cords, black plastic cases in all different shapes, monitors, amplifiers, lighting rigs, waste bins, clothing racks—everything needed to make a show happen.

I approached a bald guy with a beer belly. "Hi. Could you please direct me to the stage?"

He gave an exasperated sigh. "You supposed to be up there? I don't see no credentials." He reached for a clipboard and flipped through printed sheets. "You are in"—he consulted the clipboard again—"Kill for Sport?"

Ew, was that an actual band name? "Uh, no. I'm in Melbourne."

"Yeah, I see them on here now." He gave me another once-over. "Don't mess with me. You're a groupie, right?"

"She's the new lead singer," Mandy interjected.

"I'd be happy to show you my license, passport, whatever—" I heard cackling and whipped around to see Malcolm and Rob crouched behind a pillar. What the hell? "Can you guys tell him who I am?"

"And so it begins," Rob said, still cracking up.

"What are you talking about?" I whirled back to Beer Belly and was startled to see him grinning.

"Oh, man. So funny! 'Tell them who I am!' Damn, girl, you wasted no time gettin' your diva on!" Malcolm high-fived Rob and left before I could respond.

"I wasn't saying it like that," I muttered. Jerks.

"Chill out. Gotta prank the newbie." Rob slung a friendly arm around my shoulders before turning to Mandy. "Merch Mandy. Report to the production office, down that hall. Prepare for a crash course in merch management."

Rob led me through a labyrinth of carpeted hallways to one of the stage wings. I barely had time to register the details (dark, small, cluttered) before I found myself on a fully lit stage. I sucked in a breath. I so wasn't ready for this.

Malcolm settled in behind his drums, which were high up on a riser. He adjusted his drum kit, pulling his stool in closer, hitting the toms and cymbals. He stomped down on the bass drum pedal over and over again—*boom, boom, boom.* "Aaron!" he yelled.

Air-Drum Aaron hurried out to confer. Malcolm erupted in a fit of swearing.

Pem and Beckett huddled over a piece of paper, bass and guitar strapped over their respective shoulders. My hands went prickly and numb. I felt the same way I had when one of the producers of *American Pop Star* told me how many people would be watching our one live broadcast. At least this time no one would be sitting around trying to think up the meanest thing they could say. I mean, ideally. I shook my hands out and silently recited my mantra, which was the set list Pem had emailed to everyone last week. I'd memorized it in a fit of nerves.

"The rain thing sucks. I really wanted to play outside," Pem said.

I tried not to hyperventilate while he and Beckett discussed logistics. Finally Pem turned to me. "The arrangements are the same as what we did for the showcases, but we're changing the set list. We'll run through it in a minute."

Of course. I plopped down onto the stage and wished for a paper bag to breathe into. "Is that a problem?" Beckett asked. "We got new data about our single and need to move stuff around."

"So you're not just being random and cruel? Can I see it?"

"When we're done," Pem said.

I dangled my legs over the edge of the stage. One of the

judges on *American Pop Star* told us to envision singing to a packed house before each show. "Seeing is believing," she'd said, "even if you're only seeing it in your mind." I used this tip all the time.

I pictured myself singing and dancing, connecting with the crowd that would be here in two nights. I closed my eyes and imagined them singing with me. I slowed my breath and tried to feel everything—the noise, heat, the words coming out of my mouth.

My visualization was rudely interrupted. "You should warm up. We're going to do this for real." Pem looked like he wished he didn't have to spell these things out for me. I scrambled to my feet before he could start micromanaging my vocal exercises.

I found an empty dressing room, locked the door, and started singing scales. The acoustics were actually awesome. Then I tried a couple of bars of "Parietals." My voice strained on the higher notes. I tried again but didn't sound any better. I'd wanted them to cut it from the show, but it was their first big hit. Everyone agreed that they'd grown as a band and moved beyond songs about hooking up in boarding school dorm rooms, but we still had to play it.

There was a frantic knock on the door. "They want to start," Rob said when I opened it.

Everyone was ready to go. They watched me walk to the front of the stage. I adjusted the mike stand, my back turned to them. Suddenly, I felt hands on my shoulders, pinching and releasing. It was like being attacked by a lobster. "Same thing as the showcases. You can do it." Pem punctuated his pep talk with a slap on my back. I smiled and hoped they couldn't tell that I was barely holding it together.

Behind me, Malcolm banged his sticks, starting up the first song. Thankfully it wasn't "Parietals."

The next morning, I got to the venue at eight for a wardrobe fitting feeling like I could have used another ten hours of sleep. Mandy was still out cold when I left.

Rob had killed her high spirits with his extreme paranoia and anal-retentiveness. "He said, 'Malcolm is the money guy and will rip you a new one if you're so much as one T-shirt off.'" Mandy mimicked Rob's clipped, rapid speech. "'You got hired because you're in the family. You'd never steal money out of Chelsea's pocket, am I right? We never let people who are not family touch our money.' I mean, for God's sake, it's basic math."

Melbourne wasn't the type of band to do costume changes, but we each had a few outfits on rotation. The guys had jeans with either T-shirts or button-downs. Stylish but not fussy. I had a couple of dresses with fitted tops and swingy skirts, a bunch of things I could mix and match, like shorts, tuxedo-striped leggings, and some shirts, and one very questionable studded denim vest.

The woman fitting me now said, "You should wear this today. With shorts. You have great legs and amazing boobs. Sometimes, when a girl with your shape does the T-shirt and jeans look, she looks like a basketball wearing a tent." I watched myself redden in the mirror. "This is much better. Don't you guys think?" She spun me around to face Beckett and Pem. I wanted the ground to open up and swallow me whole.

Pem glanced over. "Yeah, cool. Get the boobs out. Half our fans think we sold out already anyway."

34

Beckett shrugged and went back to putting on his belt. "Hollis never had to get all done like that."

"Hollis had that dreamy, ethereal thing going for her. Chelsea's a brick house."

"Thanks!" I snapped. I hopped off the tiny box I'd been standing on. "You know what? I think I will wear this." I stomped into the hallway.

"He meant that as a compliment," Beckett called after me.

I'd probably live to regret, it but right then I didn't care. I may have had no idea what I was doing, but at least I'd look like a badass.

Sam had hired a woman to do my makeup and hair for press day. I watched her closely and asked lots of questions. "So if I wanted to put false eyelashes on by myself . . ."

"Oh, honey," she said. "This is strictly for the professionals. Don't try it on your own."

That was unfortunate. My eyes looked bluer and more luminous than normal. I tried to stop staring at my reflection like a total narcissist. But I liked what I saw. Physical transformation felt like an important part of preparing, like putting on armor. "Can we do a smoky eye? And maybe straighten my hair?"

After another hour, I was finally ready to go.

We took our places onstage. The guys looked at me. I waited. I didn't expect a compliment necessarily, but maybe some glimmer of appreciation. "That stuff's going to melt off as soon as you break a sweat," Pem said. "It's going to look like a septic tank exploded on your face. This is a rock stage, not a catwalk." I sighed.

Being behind the curtain felt cozy, like it was us against

everyone out there. Before the illusion could be broken, Malcolm banged his sticks together. Pem joined in with the thumping bass line, and then Beckett's guitar cut in with a jarring screech. The lightweight white curtain dropped to the ground and we moved downstage.

The houselights were low, but I could make out about forty people in the audience. They weren't all journalists; I recognized people who worked for the club and our agent, Mark, who'd flown in. Mandy stood by Rob and Sam. I focused on her as I began to sing. She pumped her hands in the air, waving double devil's horns. I sputtered. Singing with a giant grin on your face is impossible, so I had to look away. But not before I noticed a camera in my face. Fantastic. I had to get my head in the game.

I skipped to the other side of the stage, mostly to get Mandy out of my sight line because she was now giggling uncontrollably. Pain in my ass.

Since I'd already survived the showcases, I wasn't thrown by the blank or even bored look on some faces. But this was the biggest venue I'd performed in, so I was freaked out that most of them clustered toward the back. They felt far away, impossible to touch. I decided to pretend they weren't there. Nothing sucks more than trying to reach out to someone who doesn't want to be reached.

I visualized the curtain going back up, being recocooned, reisolated behind it. I instantly relaxed and felt my bandmates respond to the shift in my attitude. We settled into the song, a connection being woven among the four of us.

This was one of the most amazing discoveries about being in a band: you developed a common language, a flow. We'd worked out the arrangements well ahead of time, but within the structure there was room to play, to be spontaneous. No matter how many times we played a song, it was never exactly the same. I mostly stuck close to the arrangements, but I loved watching my bandmates improvise with almost telepathic communication.

By the end of our mini set, I felt invincible. The tiny crowd had responded enough that I knew they weren't totally dead inside. We had talked about our collective commitment to leaving it all on the stage each and every time we played, and I thought we'd delivered.

Interviews started right after. Now that I wasn't onstage, I felt like a clown in my makeup and outfit. As Pem predicted, my makeup had slid halfway down my face. I stopped into the bathroom to mop up, so I was late to the office, where Michaela, our publicist, was already giving talking points. "Remember, if someone brings Hollis up, go with 'We miss her, but we're excited about the new direction we're able to take with Chelsea.' That's it. Period. Chelsea, don't answer any questions unless they start with your name. Boys, be ready to chime in and save her." Michaela held a hand to her forehead and cast a nervous look at Sam. "Where's the bathroom?" Without waiting for an answer, she ran out to the hallway, moving amazingly fast for a woman in four-inch heels.

"She really thinks I'm going to nail this," I said sarcastically.

"She's pregnant," Sam explained.

The boys murmured things like "That's great" or "Awesome," whereas I blurted out, "Really?" They turned to look at me. "She's tiny. You can't even tell," I said.

Malcolm yawned, stretching his fists toward the ceiling. "Girls are weird."

The first journalist, Lewis, came in and took a seat across from the L-shaped leather sectional where the four of us sat. He turned on a pocket recorder and opened a notebook before reaching out to shake our hands. "Hey. I interviewed you guys a couple of years ago." They all nodded but didn't give any indication they remembered. "So. Let's start with the album. How was it recording without Hollis?" And we were off.

At some point, Michaela slipped back into the room. She looked pale and shiny but had put on fresh lipstick.

I tried to pay attention as the guys answered question after question that attempted to get at the Hollis issue. Malcolm did a lot of the talking, since he seemed to be the master of answering without actually saying anything substantive.

In the middle of one of Lewis's rambling questions, Beckett pulled a bottle of water from the fridge and handed it to Michaela. She frowned but took a long sip. "I think the exciting thing for us is that because Chelsea has such a powerful voice, it opens up the songs that we've done a million times in a whole new way," Beckett said.

"Do you agree, Chelsea? Do you think you're helping to reinvent the Melbourne sound?"

I focused on Lewis. "It's not my intention to reinvent anything. I'm a Melbourne fan myself, and I loved how they sounded with Hollis. But I can't replicate it, and I think that would be boring anyway." I hoped it didn't show that I'd practiced that answer a thousand times.

Michaela called from the side of the room, "Half hour is up, Lewis. Last question."

Lewis turned to the boys. "What do you want to tell former fans who've written you off because they think Chelsea isn't someone who shares your musical heritage?"

Ugh. The musical heritage BS again. I could explain until I was blue in the face that I had no control over the song selection when I was on *American Pop Star,* but everyone insisted on believing that I lived and breathed Top Forty. I was so over defending myself.

Pem spoke up first. "Our fans care about music. When they come see us or hear our record, I have no doubt that they'll get it."

Michaela clicked over in her heels. "Thanks so much, Lewis. Hope you got what you needed." We all stood as she ushered him out the door and came back with the next reporter.

No one else seemed worried that two more hours of this might not be the best way to prepare for our first show tomorrow. They'd all done this many times before and probably weren't fazed. But I could still hardly believe it was really happening.

6

Friday was our first real show. No industry, no reporters, just fans. First we had to do a sound check, a meet and greet, and say hi to the opening band, Gray Matter. I leaped out of bed at seven a.m. without an alarm. The lump in the next bed mumbled, "You're going to regret this."

But an hour later I'd wrangled Mandy into riding a red trolley car up Mount Washington. "I have to say, this isn't as lame as it sounds," she said. The view of the cityscape and rivers was spectacular and helped me put my worries into perspective. I'd done everything I could to prepare; now it was time to let go and do it.

At the top, we poked around the little museum and went to lunch. Our food had just arrived when Mandy's phone rang. She hadn't even said hello before I heard Rob's frantic voice on the other side. "Okay. We'll get right over," Mandy said. She frowned at her phone. "They're going nuts about something."

Every muscle in my body tightened. So much for touristy distraction.

We ate and rushed back to the venue. The dressing room and backstage areas were empty. We finally found Rob rolling an amp off the stage. "What's going on?" I asked.

"Forecast is clear and Pem wants to move the show outside."

"You're kidding." While I'd been soaking up the sun just moments before, it never occurred to me that this could be a ramification of the nice weather. I felt myself sliding off the edge. "But all that setup and rehearsal. Now we're just going to wing it?"

"We have just enough time to make sure everything works. Might not be the tightest show ever."

Even playing inside as we'd rehearsed five or six times, I'd be battling a monster case of nerves. But being outside, on a different stage, with a different audience setup? I might as well have a nervous breakdown right now.

Mandy circled to stand in front of me. "Deep breath. You've got this."

"Merch Mandy! Help us move stuff!" Rob hollered.

"Remember, you're amazing." She hugged me and ran.

When I got outside, techs and stagehands buzzed around, building what seemed like a small city. I joined the guys onstage, fighting dizziness with every step.

Malcolm saw my face first. "Whoa."

"Yeah. What brought this on?" I tried to keep the quaver out of my voice.

"It's not a big deal," Pem said. One stagehand looked like he wanted to jump on Pem and beat him senseless. "The weather cleared and the alternative station wanted to do a ticket promotion. So now instead of two thousand people, we'll get about five thousand."

I nodded, aware that this was supposed to be a good thing.

Beckett pulled me aside. "Okay. Calm down. You're going to have to get used to playing in unfamiliar venues anyway. Might as well start now."

"But I've been visualizing playing inside for three days." I was too out of my mind to be embarrassed. Still, I was surprised to find Beckett smiling kindly.

"You still have a couple of hours. Pem's going to do all the talking. Just focus on the people walking around. If they're walking, they can't be paying too much attention to us."

"If you say so." I had serious doubts about Beckett's advice, but he'd obviously performed a lot more than I had.

The next few hours were a blur. We sound-checked while the techs redid the lighting. When we finished, Gray Matter set up. They were a few years older than the guys in Melbourne but just starting to break out. We gave hugs, and they thanked us for having them on tour.

Rob hustled us into a large room with a few chairs scattered around, then went right back out, shutting the door. Malcolm texted like he was possessed.

I had no idea what to expect from my first meet and greet. I'd probably answer questions about how I came to be part of Melbourne, maybe pose for a few pictures.

"Are Amber and Lila coming?" Pem asked. Malcolm nodded, distracted. "Do we have room? How many spots did you give them?"

Rob came back in and moved the chairs.

"Them plus five," Malcolm said.

Pem shook his head. "Dude, that's like half our list. What about Sienna and them?"

"Hey, has anyone bothered to read that handy-dandy tour booklet I put together for you guys?" Rob glowered at us.

"It was very pretty, Rob," Pem said.

"I read it," I said. It said something about not making day-of-show guest list requests.

"I don't have anyone coming, so they can use mine," Beckett said.

"Sienna's bringing friends too." Malcolm put his phone away. "What about you?" he asked.

"I was supposed to have these friends of my parents', but they're out of town." By the time I realized how sad that sounded, it was already out of my mouth. The three of them stared at me.

The door opened and Rob led a mob into the room. Some went straight to the guys and started talking; others stayed by the entrance, causing a logjam. Since nobody came to me, I got to observe. I told myself this was a good thing, but after a conspicuously long time doing nothing, I felt like a wallflower instead of the lead singer. I drifted and hoped no one would notice that I wasn't talking to anyone.

Each guy seemed to have a type. Malcolm's fans were mostly girls. They were done up, giggly, and flat-out gorgeous. My guess was that the few boys who gravitated to him were drummers. Pem drew the die-hard music lovers in the group—overly serious and not touching him every five seconds. Not to say he didn't have his share of fangirls. Beckett's people were a mix but seemed the most normal, like they didn't have an agenda other than seeing the show and having a good time. If I was still on the other side, I'd fall somewhere between the Pem and Beckett posses. I'd pick Pem's brain about process and inspiration but talk to Beckett about music and being in a band. In some ways it was a shame that I hadn't met them when I was still just a fan. Now when I asked them questions I felt like it only made me seem more green.

Pretty soon phones came out. A girl backed up and stepped on my toes. "Oops. Sorry," I said.

"That's okay! Hey, do you mind taking a picture?"

"Sure." She and her friends squeezed close to Beckett. Oh. She handed me her phone. "One, two, three." I resisted the impulse to stick my finger in the picture and handed the phone back.

A guy and two girls huddled by the wall, darting worshipful glances at Pem. "Do you guys want to meet Pem?" I asked.

"Well, yeah. But he looks really busy," the guy said.

"Don't worry. Pem's a people person," I said. He probably wouldn't bite my head off in front of fans.

"Serious? Thanks!"

I walked over with my little trio and tapped Pem on the shoulder. "These guys want to meet you."

Pem glanced at them, then back at the guy who seemed to be dominating the conversation. "Hey, have you met Chelsea? Our singer?"

Unfortunately, Intense Guy was far less interested in me than he'd been in Pem. "So. What bands were you in before Melbourne?"

"None. I was on *American Pop Star,* though."

"Oh. Cool, I guess?"

And that was the end of that conversation.

The changeover between Gray Matter and us happened mind-bendingly fast. Before I registered what was happening I was onstage clutching the mike, as if that would keep me from bolting. The curtain dropped and I went on autopilot. It was still light enough that I could make out every person in the audience.

They were so very close. Barricades created a moat between us and them where security stood, but fans hung over them with cameras and phones. It stressed me out so much that I backpedaled and bumped right into Beckett. He shot me a sharp look that clearly meant "Calm down" but stayed by my side to make it less obvious that I'd almost plowed him over.

I would have stayed there, frozen in place, but Pem scowled at me and I knew I had to work more of the stage. I felt disoriented. The sound, which had been so clear inside, seemed to get carried away on a breeze. We had a break after the second song. "Hey, Pittsburgh!" Pem shouted. The crowd roared back. I walked to the drum riser for water and to collect myself while Pem asked everyone if they'd enjoyed Gray Matter.

Malcolm was so relaxed he looked almost bored. He reached for a water bottle and dropped his sticks on the ground. "Fuck," he said, loud enough to make people in front laugh.

Aaron darted out to tighten a cymbal. As he scooted by he said, "Give 'em hell, Chelsea!"

I tried to channel Malcolm, to just not care so much. I jumped up and down as the next song started. I sang the verse, stalking to the front of the stage, and held my mike out for the crowd to sing the chorus, which they actually did. It was like one of those trust exercises, like I'd fallen backward off a chair and they were actually there to catch me.

I knew then that I'd never get enough. The crowd feedback was beyond exhilarating. I spent the next hour running, dancing, headbanging, jumping off the low monitors, using the crowd's energy as fuel. Whatever the crowd gave me, I gave back to them, double. Halfway through the show, we'd worked ourselves up until I wasn't touching the ground.

Pem went to his mike. "So that's Chelsea." The crowd erupted. I waved before returning my mike stand to the front of the stage. "We're so glad you guys came out tonight. Change is hard, no doubt. But we want everyone to have a fuckin' great time!"

Beckett played the intro to "Smash Cut," a slower song off the new album that we sang together. Beckett had a fantastic rock voice; depending on the moment, it could be clear and powerful or gravelly and soulful. I remember first hearing his vocal tracks in the studio and being surprised that Melbourne didn't feature his singing more.

Video screens behind us showed a montage of a couple falling in love.

I gripped the mike, closed my eyes, rocked slowly back and forth, and started singing alone before Beckett sang his verse. At the risk of sounding like a total nerd, when our voices combined on the second chorus, I felt completely transported. Everything slipped away while our voices played off each other.

Pem wrote this song, which was how I knew he had a tender side. Whenever he harangued me about anything, I sang it in my head.

By the end, our video couple had broken up. A yearlong relationship compressed into a three-minute movie. The audience was silent. When I swept my arm toward Beckett, they exploded into whistles and applause.

The next song, "Curvature," brought the tempo back up. I tried to muscle my way back in, to lift my energy to where it was before the ballad. My feet and stomach felt weighted down with lead while my head and chest felt buzzy and light. I pushed on, determined to end on a high note. I was in the home stretch.

While I admired Beckett's guitar-playing, I suddenly realized he was singing the chorus. This was not supposed to be a duet. I had freaking missed my cue. I let Beckett sing through while I stood paralyzed, mind racing, feeling like a rank amateur. He and Pem stared daggers at me, but they couldn't be angrier with me than I was at myself. I jumped in, taking over when the chorus repeated. I felt like I was going to pass out.

Luckily we only had one song and the encore left. When we finished the set, Pem thanked everyone again and I sprinted backstage to the nearest bathroom. I spent the next ten minutes hurling into the toilet. There was a rapid knock on the door before it swung open. "Do we need to skip the encore?" Rob asked.

I shook my head. "I can do it."

"You sure? People are starting to leave."

My stomach felt empty. I straightened and looked in the mirror. My skin had a waxy shine and my eyes were glassy. I grabbed some mouthwash and rinsed while giving him a dirty look. "I said I can do it." I ran my fingers through my hair and walked back into the wing without crashing into anything.

The guys' expressions were mostly sympathetic. I willed myself to get it together. "She's good." Rob clapped me on the back and we went out. The crowd roared again. Beckett started the song quickly, probably afraid that I'd barf onstage if we didn't hurry.

Unfortunately, the encore was three of Melbourne's biggest hits, high-energy both in performance and crowd reaction, including my favorite, "Parietals." As soon as I waved goodbye, I raced back to the bathroom.

After dry-heaving for what felt like an hour, I was certain I'd never eat again.

A few minutes after my retching stopped, the door opened. I wanted Mandy but got Beckett instead. He handed me a towel and leaned back against the door. "It's totally normal, just so you know," he said.

"Awesome. Can't wait to do this again." I was mortified that he was seeing me like this. He was trying to be nice, but I just wanted him to go away.

"I mean, you're not used to the adrenaline of this type of show and don't know how to pace yourself. You'll get the hang of it." He smiled.

"I better." I twisted my hair up into a knot. Getting all that hot hair off my neck felt so much better. I blew out a long, shaky breath and clung to the sink.

"We're ordering food. You want anything?"

"Yeah. Double cheeseburger and a shot of tequila." I glared at him in the mirror.

Beckett laughed. "Just thought I'd check. Bus call isn't until two."

I was looking forward to my first night on the bus.

Exhaustion was setting in. "Where can I take a shower? I'm dying for one."

"Back in the dressing room. You better hurry, there's already a line."

I narrowed my eyes. "You look clean."

"I was first. Have to be quick around here." Beckett smiled in a way that could best be described as smug. It wasn't his most attractive look.

So the day had started out rich with possibility but ended with me fighting for bathroom privileges. Sounded about right.

7

Fans lined the back fence and cheered when they saw me. I waved and went onto the bus. When the doors closed behind me, they booed. Sheesh. It wasn't so long ago that I'd been one of them, waiting outside the fence.

The bus was empty, which gave me a chance to poke around. The first section after the driver's cabin was a living room/kitchenette with a flat-screen TV mounted over one of two couches that faced each other, two mini-fridges, a sink, and a couple of cabinets. A small booth took up the other side of the aisle just before sliding doors that led to the next compartment.

Suitcases cluttered the middle of the aisle. I found mine and took out only what I'd need for twenty-four hours, including toiletries, pj's, and a change of clothes.

My shower wasn't for another half hour. Jared had so generously informed me that I could go after him and Malcolm.

I guess chivalry really was dead. At least on the Business of Music Tour.

So I pulled my hood over my sweaty rat's nest of a hairdo and went back out. Maybe now that these fans had seen me perform, they'd actually talk to me. It was a theory. "How's it going? Did you guys have fun?"

They murmured, "Great show," and other vague compliments, then stuck CDs and pieces of paper through the slats. Some wanted my signature more than they wanted to talk; others congratulated me on a smooth integration into the band. If I had to win fans one at a time, I was willing to do it. Occasionally one of the guys would pass by, which was obvious from the spike in cheers.

When I went back to the dressing room, someone was in the shower. I banged on the door. "Jared?" I yelled.

"No!" Winston shouted. "You were signing. Kam's after me. You can go after him."

Nice of Jared to look out for me. I left my stuff by the door. Rob and Mandy looked like they were in "do not disturb" mode, counting cash and going over receipts in the production office, so I moved on.

The bar was still open, and Malcolm and Beckett, both fresh as daisies, held court with a bunch of girls. Could they be more predictable? I was not hygienically prepared for that scene and wasn't sure I'd be welcome anyway.

I looked at photos on the wall of all the bands that had played here. There was even a picture of Melbourne from an early tour. I studied Hollis. Objectively she looked regal, her WASPiness radiating through glam rock clothes. She didn't seem inauthentic, just cool. I smoothed down my hoodie.

The bathroom was finally free, but it was also trashed. Soaking-wet towels were piled up against one wall. The floor looked like it had been finger-painted with dirt. Bits of stubble coated the sink. Good thing I'd already thrown up absolutely everything in my system. I needed to buy shower shoes, stat.

I took a deep breath and was about to cross the threshold when Mandy careened around the corner. "Can I shower next?"

"After me. I puked my brains out and do not feel human."

"Please, Chelsea? Some bitch threw her beer on me because I didn't have any small T-shirts left." She was hunched over, exhausted. Her shirt was crusty and molded to her body.

I'd thrown up, but at least my job had some glory. What the hell, I'd waited this long. "Go ahead."

"You're the best! I'd hug you but you're gross."

"Yeah. Don't expect to get too clean in there."

I was still waiting for Mandy when Rob came by. "Almost bus call. Don't get left behind."

Did that happen? Was it two a.m. already? I banged on the door. "Hurry up! I need to get in there!"

Mandy came out fifteen minutes later. "Were you knocking?"

"Did you happen to notice that it's practically bus call?"

Mandy looked sheepish but mostly thrilled to be clean. I wanted to throttle her.

I walked onto a thumping bus, where my bandmates were hosting a full-blown party. Just what I was in the mood for. Pem and Beckett played video games while girls sat around mixing drinks. I staggered in wearing my rancid clothes. I'm sure I didn't look thrilled, and I bet I didn't smell very sociable either.

"Is there a laundry hamper or something?" I asked.

They didn't take their eyes off the screen. Pem made a face like I was nuts, and Beckett said, "Um, not unless you brought one."

I grabbed my pj's from under Beckett's butt and headed for the sliding doors.

"You don't want to go back there," one of the girls said.

I stopped and turned.

"Yeah, sorry. We're leaving soon," another one said.

"Not that we want to," the first one said.

"Those are the rules," Pem said. "Everyone off by bus call." He finally looked at me. "You look and smell just . . . offensive. Why didn't you take a shower?"

I visualized flipping him off and sat at the table. Neither he nor Beckett seemed overly motivated to mingle, yet there was an easy familiarity between them and the girls, almost like they were cousins. The girls were nice enough and seemed interested in my (short) history with the band. When I explained about *American Pop Star,* one of them wrinkled her nose. "Really? How did I miss that?"

"'Cause. We try to pretend it never happened," Pem said. He was really starting to respect me.

"Don't listen to her," another girl whispered. "She's drunk. Anyway, you're much sweeter than Hollis. She acted like her shit didn't stink."

I was thankful when the bus driver climbed on board and gave the two-minute warning, like we were in preschool.

The entire crew, including Mandy, materialized at once.

Rob banged on the sliding doors. Moments later, two girls stumbled out fully dressed, but matted hair and smeared makeup gave them away. Mandy and I exchanged looks.

All the guys got cheek kisses as the girls filed off and made promises to text. Finally, only the people who were supposed to be on board were left. Malcolm emerged from the sleeping area looking very pleased with himself.

"Do you have to wait until the bitter end?" Pem asked.

Malcolm shrugged. "They wanted to spoon. Who am I to say no?"

"You're a real gentleman," Oscar said. The crew laughed. Malcolm was a crack-up even if he was kind of crazy.

"Listen up!" The bus driver wore a threatening "interrupt me and die" expression. I hoped I didn't look as cowed as I felt. "Who here has never been on a tour bus?"

"Like, I've been on one, but never overnight," Mandy said, totally leaving me hanging with my hand raised like an idiot.

"Your answer would be no, then," Rob said. "Raise your hand."

Mandy huffed but put her hand up.

"Number one rule: Do not take a dump on this bus. Ever. You wait till we get to the venue. If there's an emergency, let me know and I will find a place to stop. Got it?" He stared hard at Mandy and me. We nodded. I, for one, was ecstatic that this rule was in place.

"Number two: Don't drink the water. Use bottled water to brush your teeth. There's a shower on the bus. Don't use it."

Oh my God. I was going to have to sleep in my own stench and filth. It was all I could do to not break down.

"Rules three and four: Do your own dishes. Make your

own beds. Five: I do not like extraneous people on my bus. Except the ones I already know. If you have to bring somebody on who for some reason cannot be off by bus call, run it by Rob first." We nodded in unison.

"You okay?" Beckett carried his toothbrush, his iPad, and a bottle of water as he passed by me. I tried not to get too close.

"Yeah. I just didn't expect the driver to be such a hard-ass."

"Dave? Total softie. He's been our driver forever. He just likes to run things tight." Evidently.

I dialed my parents before remembering it was after two in the morning. I still hadn't completely come down from the show, and they'd said to call anytime. While it rang, I noticed Malcolm studying me.

"I got the pool for this tour," Malcolm said.

Winston chuckled. "Already?"

Malcolm continued. "Who do we think will get laid first: Pem or Chelsea?" I pushed the hang-up button in a hurry and Pem threw something at Malcolm while everyone else cracked up. "Should we do twenty or fifty? Fuck it. Fifty. We're all men. And women. Get your bets in to Rob. He'll manage the pot."

"I'm honored, but why?" Really I was more curious about why Pem, because it seemed like he knew his way around the ladies.

"'Cause. I'd bet the farm right now that you're calling the parents. Only a complete naive would call home after their first show. That's not punk rock."

My phone buzzed with a text from my mom. *Everything okay?*

I turned the phone facedown in my lap and covered it with

55

my hand. Malcolm smirked, snapped a picture of me with his phone, and then started tapping. "Make sure you caption that 'The Naive,'" Beckett said. Malcolm laughed.

"Don't post that! I'm disgusting," I exclaimed.

"You said it, not me," Malcolm said.

"Let me guess. You're also the social media guy."

"It's called being multitalented." Malcolm and Beckett high-fived.

I ignored them and texted my parents back: *Forgot how late it was. Call u tomorrow.*

Mandy nudged me. "Come on, let's see where we're sleeping."

The sleeping compartment had twelve bunks—two sets of three on each side of the aisle. Almost all of them were taken, since we had a total of eleven people and everyone but Mandy and me seemed to have claimed one. The first two top bunks were open, so we picked those.

"Are we supposed to levitate?" I asked. There was no ladder or step stool. I put my foot on the rail of the middle bunk and hoisted myself up.

The narrow twin bed was already made. I plugged my phone charger into the wall outlet and drew the curtain closed. There wasn't enough room to sit upright, so I probably sounded like I was wrestling an alligator as I struggled into my pj's. Once I was in my lounge shorts and T-shirt, I climbed back down with my toothbrush.

I turned toward the front lounge to get a bottle of water and smacked into Rob. "You can use the back lounge to change. Just lock the door," he said. The back lounge was basically the same as the front lounge minus the kitchen area. Some of the guys were already watching a Japanese horror movie.

The engine whirred to life and I swayed with the turns of the bus as Dave backed out of the lot. I'd barely seen Pittsburgh and couldn't believe our time there had gone so quickly. Obviously the shows were my priority, but who knew when I'd come back?

Holding the bunk rails for support, I headed to the front, where I managed to brush my teeth and wash my face without making a huge mess. Then I settled into my bunk and tried to sleep. The bus rumbled at full speed, so I assumed we were on a highway. I tried to let the engine lull me to sleep, but it was too foreign to be relaxing.

My curtain slid open, a surprisingly noisy maneuver. I stuck my head over the side. "What?"

"You're sleeping already?" Mandy asked.

"I'm not going to be very agreeable if I don't get eight hours."

"Are you comfy?"

"It's kind of like camping in a box. And I'm sticky. It's pleasant."

She snapped my curtain shut again. Someone shushed us from a bunk.

I thrashed myself awake having a nightmare, almost fell out of my bunk, then sat up and smashed my head on the ceiling. I let out a squeal. Holding my head, I reached for my phone and groaned. Four a.m. I'd been asleep less than two hours.

I pulled my curtain open and climbed down. I tiptoed

up the aisle but not carefully enough because I tripped over something and banged my head on the door. Tears stung my eyes. The cabin was completely dark, so I couldn't see what it was, but I made it to the lounge without maiming myself again and before anyone woke up and busted me.

As the door whooshed open, Beckett leaned out from the jump seat—the one next to the driver's. "Hey. Can't sleep?" I was glad it was him. I took the seat behind the wall that shielded Dave from band shenanigans. "Dave's telling me about the country tour he just did. Lots of whiskey." Dave nodded. "Have you officially met Chelsea yet?" Beckett asked.

I stood up. "I'd shake your hand, but I don't want to distract you."

But he turned in his seat—took his eyes off the road and everything—and clasped my hand in both of his. "Welcome to life on the road."

My eyes shot to the highway in front of us and I yanked my hand back. I looked at Beckett to see if he had any reaction to our driver not actually driving. He yawned.

Dave laughed. "I'm playing with you. These things are so heavy they just roll straight unless I turn. Relax. You've entrusted me with your life and I take that very seriously."

I gave him a dubious look and sat back down.

Beckett and I spent the next two hours listening to Dave's funny stories about past tours. His regular speaking voice was deep and soothing, fitting for his size.

The sky was still black, so we could see only as far as the headlights allowed. Few cars passed us, and businesses on the roadside were closed. I felt like we were sneaking through the night.

Beckett turned to me during one of Dave's lengthier pauses. "You should sleep. It's all about pacing yourself."

"You don't seem to be following your own advice," I said. Dave chuckled.

"I never sleep much. Besides, I had to catch up with Dave."

"I'm okay. I'm having fun."

Dave looked at Beckett. "Uh-oh."

I stood up so I could see both of them. "What? What do you mean, uh-oh?"

"He means if you're having fun now, you're going to love it by the end."

Dave smiled at me. "And then good luck gettin' rid of you."

8

I could hardly keep my eyes open as I stood in the production office of the 9:30 Club and made three packets of instant oatmeal. I'd picked up a variety pack along with some flip-flops for the shower on my grocery store run. The runner even took us past the White House so I could check that off my bucket list.

All the oatmeal tasted the same: mushy. At least now I had food for the bus. I told Rob where to find me, took the longest shower in human history, and then crashed. The club had bunk beds for bands, which was lucky for me. Clearly I'd never appreciated stationary beds enough before.

There was a sharp knock followed by the door swinging open and crashing into the wall. I sat up, dazed. "Time for sound check?"

Beckett chuckled. "No. Still have a couple hours. We're going to some record shops. Want to come?"

And that's how I found myself walking with Beckett down 18th Street. We'd left Malcolm, Pem, and Aaron sifting through punk records down the block.

Becket held the door for me at a small storefront on the ground floor of a brick building. The clerk did a double take and looked around the store like he wished someone else was there to verify what he was seeing, but it was empty.

I went to the bins and started idly flipping through records. Becket had made a beeline for the folk section, where he picked up each record and scrutinized it. Before long, he had a nice little stack to add to the bags he'd already filled at the other stores.

"What are you looking for?" Beckett's voice at my ear made me jump and whirl around. "Sorry."

"Just browsing." The edge of the bin pressed into my back as I tried to maximize space between me and Beckett in the tight aisle.

"You haven't bought anything." He noted my empty hands.

"I don't have a record player."

"What?" Beckett studied me with a half smile like I might be kidding. I shook my head. "You call yourself a musician? You need to get one as soon as you get home, like stat. Before you hug your dog or eat your grandma's home cooking or whatever. In fact, order one now and have it waiting for you." He dropped a hand onto my shoulder and forced me to look him in the eye. I knew that when I nodded, I was making what he considered the most sacred of promises.

He reached over to the row next to me, pulled out a record, and held it up. "You need this." It was an Elvis Costello album called *This Year's Model*. I'd obviously heard his songs, but he wasn't one of my go-tos. "And this. And this."

Beckett's delight as he discovered or rediscovered albums was completely endearing. I couldn't help smiling as he piled record after record into my arms. He made a final selection, *Songs of Leonard Cohen*. "That's a decent start."

"Wouldn't it make more sense to buy these digitally so I can listen to them now?"

He stared at me in horror, like I'd just dropped the f-bomb in a church. "I'm going to pretend you didn't say that. I can put some stuff on your iPod as a temporary fix, but trust me, it is not the same thing."

We went to the register. I was giddy about using my shiny new credit card for the first time but didn't want to seem any less cool than I already did.

The clerk kept darting glances at Beckett, clearly working up the nerve to ask him something. He rang me up, then handed me a plastic bag containing my very first album purchases. I have to say, it was pretty thrilling to buy music and be able to hold it in my hands.

"So I have some posters in back," the clerk said to Beckett. "Your label sent them. Would you be willing to sign them?"

"Sure, no problem," Beckett said.

The clerk disappeared to get the posters. He brought them out and laid them in front of us. Beckett glanced down, pen in hand. "Sorry, man, I can't sign these." I looked and saw that they were from Melbourne's last tour. "Hollis isn't our singer anymore. She is." Beckett jutted his chin in my direction.

They both looked at me. "Oh no, it's okay. They're kind of vintage in a way, right? I don't mind," I said.

"Yeah, well, you should," Beckett said.

"He's right. I didn't think about it." Embarrassed, the clerk packed up the offending posters and shoved them under the counter.

Beckett took a business card off the counter and slipped it into his pocket. "We'll send you some from this tour. Thanks for understanding."

I smiled and did my best not to melt into a puddle. For the first time I felt like an actual member of Melbourne.

We hurried back to the club for sound check and then stopped by catering. The crew and venue employees were already eating at large round tables in the center of the room. We grabbed plates and inspected all the food warmers lined up on banquet tables against the wall.

Rather than risk a full meal, I filled a plate with fruit and cold cuts. No need to tempt fate. "Someone's learning," Pem said.

"Don't have to tell me twice," I replied.

Malcolm spoke midchew. "Hey, Rob needs you. Your mom called about getting someone into the meet and greet."

"Seriously? She's out of control." I realized I'd forgotten to call my parents back. Going over my head was so like her. I hadn't taken a bite but scraped my plate into the trash.

"It's not a problem," Rob said when I got to him. "You have room on the band list."

"That's great, but if she calls you again, ignore it."

"I can't disrespect your mom."

I was getting the sense that Rob was kind of a Boy Scout. Honestly, he didn't look like he minded taking my mother's call, but I'd given her his number strictly for emergencies. If you gave that woman any foothold whatsoever, it wouldn't be long before she ran your life.

The meet and greet was much the same as last night except this time I was surrounded by my parents' middle-aged friends and their squawking kids. When they were no longer entertained by my vomiting story, I had to interrupt my bandmates to make them sign numerous articles of clothing and show posters the kids had probably torn off a wall somewhere. I felt guilty that my parents' friends had hijacked actual fans' time with the band.

When we got to the stage wings, I noticed that the white curtain—the one that hid us from the audience until into the first song—wasn't up.

I turned to Pem. "Where's the curtain?"

He exhaled sharply. "What?"

"She's talking about the kabuki drop," Beckett said.

Pem gave me one of his impatient looks that were becoming oh so familiar to me. "That was just for the press set. And we did it the first night for a little drama. Since it was there."

"The kabuki drop was a reference to our last tour when we played arenas. It would be overkill in the venue sizes we're doing on this run," Beckett whispered. Fantastic. More evidence of how Melbourne was suffering the loss of Hollis, plus I'd used those last few moments of being hidden to get psyched up. Now what was I going to do?

We took the stage while I scrambled to find another way into the performance. I hated curveballs. Malcolm started the first song. I didn't miss my cue, but I was mesmerized by the sea of people swaying to the beat, and not in a good way.

The 9:30 Club was general admission only, which made the audience look like one giant, amoebic mass. I still spotted my parents' friends because there weren't many little kids. That brought on a fresh wave of annoyance at my mother, which I used to drive my performance. I was scared to go for the same intensity as last night, but I didn't want my delivery to feel flat or safe either. It turned out being a little aggravated at your mother could be energizing.

When it was time for our encore, I thought I caught a grudging look of respect on Pem's face. I hadn't spazzed out and didn't have to run offstage and puke my brains out. I did throw up, but at least I made it through the encore this time. Maybe that counted as progress.

I wasn't the first in the shower, but I didn't move from the bathroom door until it was my turn. I made it in third or fourth. Not nearly as revolting as being last.

I'd left my clean clothes in the room where I'd napped, so of course when I walked out of the bathroom in my towel, Beckett was standing there. Everything was covered, but he pointedly kept his eyes on my face, which almost made me squirmier.

"If you want food, we're going now. Bus call's early tonight."

I got into my jeans and tank top, dried my hair into what I hoped was a casual, messy do, and put on some lip gloss.

We made it back just before bus call. Beckett and I stopped and signed for people waiting. He asked if everyone had had a good time and laughed easily with some of them. By the end, he had a pile of gifts twice as big as mine. "What do you do with all that stuff?" I asked.

"Keep it. Except for the food. It's like trick-or-treating. Has to be factory-sealed and nonperishable."

I made a mental note to throw away the homemade cookies I got yesterday. I think they were for Pem anyway. "But you keep everything else? The photos? The clothes? The . . . ceramics?"

Beckett smiled. "Especially the ceramics. Just sentimental, I guess."

Mandy was already in her pj's, but she and Rob huddled over a computer in the back lounge, going over the next day's schedule for Nashville. "No, they can't do that then. Gray Matter has a sound check. Take that out." Rob pointed at the screen while Mandy typed. "Great. Print it." He nodded at me, then disappeared into the front.

Mandy was clearly fried. "That'll teach me to try and have fun during the day."

"What'd you do?" I asked. She was already gone by the time we'd left for record shopping.

"Took a Segway tour with Oscar and Winston. We saw the Lincoln Memorial, the World War Two Memorial, and the Washington Monument."

"Sounds like a sixth-grade field trip."

"Totally. I even rode the Metro."

Beckett opened the door with my iPod in his hand. "Here you go," he said. I reached for it, but he pulled it back out of my grasp. "Remember what I said?" I laughed and nodded. "This does not replace listening to your records."

He slid toward me on the table. He'd added all the albums I'd bought that day along with a bunch of other ones.

Mandy was staring at me. "I need to, um, ask Rob a question. Be back . . . later."

"It was so nice of you to do this," I said as the doors closed behind her.

"My pleasure. I know no one's said it yet, but you're doing a good job. And you're only going to get better," Beckett said.

My shoulders dropped as tension left my body. I didn't care if he was throwing me a bone; I'd been desperate for any kind of feedback. "Thank you."

"I don't understand 'Parietals,' though. It's not outside your range. I've heard you hit higher notes when you're just messing around."

"Yeah? Maybe it's a fluke." I thought it best to leave it there.

"Are you feeling at home on the bus? With the crew and everything?"

"Definitely. Everyone's really cool." Beckett tilted his head, so I added, "Dave's so interesting. What great stories."

He smirked. "Who knows what he tells other bands about us?" What was there to tell? Aside from Malcolm, everyone seemed pretty PG. But maybe that hadn't always been the case. "So do you have a boyfriend?" Beckett asked.

I blinked. Where did that come from? And then I remembered. "I'm not saying. How big's the pool, anyway?"

He grinned. "Big."

"Bet on Pem," I said.

"Really?" Beckett persisted. "Talented, pretty girl like you? No boyfriend?"

"Believe it," I said. "I learned my lesson the hard way. I once liked a guy and it ended in disaster." I smiled and Beckett laughed. Too bad I wasn't kidding.

9

"Keep it down!" someone hissed from one of the bunks.

I bent down to see what it was I'd just tripped over in the aisle. Again. It was a pair of large sneakers. Why were boys such slobs? Rob insisted that keeping the bus temperature at minus-ten degrees prevented germs from spreading. Even with a hoodie and Uggs, my thighs broke out in goose bumps.

Through the tinted windows, the morning looked bright and clear. "I want to cover more ground while there's no traffic. You don't have to stop, do you?" Dave asked.

"No way, man. I'm a pro." I was glad I hadn't had to make any embarrassing requests yet.

I filled a bowl with bottled water and popped it in the microwave. Seemed like I'd be eating a lot of oatmeal this summer. I rifled through the cabinet but didn't see my oatmeal anywhere. The shelves were stuffed with packets of turkey jerky, cups of instant ramen noodles, and tubes of what looked to be Asian gummy candies.

The lower cabinets housed chips, crackers, and cereal. I pulled out a box of Lucky Charms. I probably hadn't eaten them since I was twelve, but whatever, I was hungry. *Malcolm* was scrawled across it in black Sharpie. He wouldn't miss one bowl, I reasoned, though knowing him he probably weighed the box after each meal. I pulled out a carton of milk, which Malcolm had also labeled. Apparently when you live on a bus with ten other people, you write your name on everything.

The bowl went down so quickly that I poured another. I got rid of the evidence, washing my bowl and spoon and hiding the empty milk carton under other recycling.

After watching *Real Housewives* for two hours, I was still the only one awake. I was officially bored enough to call my parents.

"Honey! How are the shows going?" my mother asked. "I've been so busy at the store, but Sharon Stanslow said that her kids adored the show. She said to thank you again for introducing them to all the guys at the meet and greet."

"About that. Don't call Rob for those things. Call me."

"Well, honey, you're so busy—"

"Rob's even busier, I promise."

I felt my mother's sigh through the phone. "Fine. We don't have friends in Nashville or Charlotte." She knew my tour itinerary better than I did.

"How is that possible?" I put a hand to the back of my head. The bump from cracking it on my bunk ceiling this morning had swollen up into a hard little egg.

"Girl, did you eat my Lucky Charms?" Malcolm had stumbled out into the lounge, rubbing his eyes, wearing pajama pants and no shirt. He glared at me with wild disbelief.

Crap. I'd left the box out. "Gotta go, Mom." I hung up and tried not to stare at Malcolm's abs. "Someone ate my oatmeal."

"I don't give a flying fuck. I wrote my name on that shit." He slammed the cabinet shut.

I couldn't tell if he was serious. "Sorry. I'll replace your milk—"

"You drank it all?" I nodded. "Unreal. Do you know nothing about bus etiquette?"

"I thought we might be sharers, but it's cool. I can see that we're not."

"Don't eat stuff that doesn't have your name on it! And don't open your curtain when you get up at some ungodly hour!"

I nodded, even though I wanted to ask how I was supposed to get out of my bunk without sliding the curtain. As I watched him shovel dry Lucky Charms into his mouth looking pouty and disgruntled, I actually did feel kind of bad.

Beckett came in wearing sweats and a T-shirt. He looked adorably rumpled, his green eyes bleary and unfocused. Even thought he was fully clothed, it was weirdly intimate to see him just waking up.

He grunted at me. "Where's that oatmeal?" he asked Malcolm. Was nobody on this bus a morning person?

"I ate it all," Malcolm said

"You are such a hypocrite!" I cried.

"It didn't have your name on it!" Malcolm shouted.

"If it doesn't have a name, it's fair game," Beckett said.

"I get it! Okay?" These two knew how to belabor a point. Beckett peeled a couple of hard-boiled eggs and plopped them into a cup of ramen noodles. "That's your breakfast?" I asked incredulously.

"I like to start the day off with some protein. What?" he asked, catching my horrified look. "This isn't that far off from a traditional Chinese breakfast."

Malcolm nodded. "Throw some dried fish and some pork in there and I might even eat it." I must have shuddered, because they both shot me chiding looks. "Wake up, Dorothy. You're not in Kansas anymore."

I didn't bother to argue. Who knew my unsophistication would show up even over breakfast choices? "Can't wait to try," I said. Beckett held out his Styrofoam cup, offering. I shook my head. "I'll wait for the real thing." Baby steps.

"Now, what have we learned today?" Malcolm asked, looking a bit less grouchy now that he'd eaten.

"The bus hasn't even parked yet. Kind of early for lessons," Beckett said.

"She's starting out behind the eight ball," Malcolm said. "We all know how not to piss each other off."

"Yeah, sometimes that knowledge is wasted, but fair point. What have you got?" Beckett asked. They looked at me expectantly.

"One, learn how to apparate so I don't have to open the bunk curtain. Two, don't trip even if people leave their size-twenty-five shoes in the middle of the aisle. And three, don't eat things that don't have my name on them," I recited.

Beckett gave me a thumbs-up. "Except, did you just make up a word?"

"Apparate. It's from Harry Potter, which means it's an official part of the English language," I said. "Look it up."

"Good God," Malcolm muttered.

10

When we arrived in Nashville, Rob asked Mandy to help with some administrative jobs, and no one else wanted to sightsee. Eventually Beckett caved and agreed to go with me. "Let's go to 12 South," he said. "It's a little taste of Brooklyn below the Mason-Dixon Line."

People stared at us as we walked down the few blocks that made up the neighborhood. At first I thought they recognized Beckett, but then I realized it was how he was dressed— flat-billed Yankees cap, low-slung jeans, and crazy-bright sneakers. He was also really tall. Next to him I felt like a walking Gap sales rack.

We stopped into a coffeehouse that looked like a converted bungalow and got drinks to go. Two things stood out about the people: abundant facial hair and thick, nerdy glasses. Where I was from, not many people rocked this look, which also featured some kind of plaid shirt and expensive denim. I referred to it as "hickster chic." We poked around a vintage clothing shop and smelled really expensive candles at a store that sold both housewares and jeans. A couple there told the shopkeeper that they'd done an apartment swap for the summer with their place in Brooklyn. Beckett gave me a conspiratorial grin. "See?"

He stopped in front of a hair salon. "Can we go in here? I need some stuff."

The reception staff promptly fawned all over him. One of the girls said she was going to the show tonight and was so excited to tell her girlfriends that Beckett Moore had stopped into the salon. He assured everyone he'd be hanging out after the show. I'm not going to lie: it was nauseating.

He then proceeded to pick out an unreal number of hair products. I'm not talking just shampoo and conditioner. There was gel, wax, grooming cream—stuff I'd never purchased and had no idea how to use.

Beckett signed a few autographs and posed for pictures, and we left. The girls stood in the doorway, beaming and tapping on their phones as we made our way down the sidewalk. "So are we not going to talk about what just happened?" I asked.

His brow furrowed. "Fans? That stuff happens. It's going to happen to you soon enough."

"Not that. I'm talking about the absurd amount of product you just bought."

Beckett smiled, looking embarrassed. "It's a long tour. And Pem steals my stuff." He rambled off some other defensive-sounding reasons and I started laughing. "All right, just wait until we go someplace with weird water. Don't come begging," he said.

"You just don't strike me as the fussy type."

"Yeah, well, it sounds bad when you say it like that. But this doesn't happen by accident." He took off his hat and ran his hands through his perfectly piecey dark hair.

"I know. I saw you this morning."

Beckett gave me a playful shove, which made me laugh harder.

We crossed the street and went into Burger Up. It was all glass, steel-gray beams, and wood. We were on the early side for lunch, but all the tables were taken. Rather than wait, we took seats across from each other at the communal table. At least having other people at the table kept it from feeling like a date.

I opened the menu. Beckett didn't even look at his. "The lamb burger is the best thing."

"Really? Can't say I've ever tried one."

"Probably not too many places serve them where you come from."

I sighed. "Detroit isn't exactly the sticks. Anthony Bourdain did a show there."

"Sorry." He tried (and failed) to suppress a laugh. "Didn't mean to offend. New Yorkers can be, well, New York–centric. So do you get to Detroit a lot, then? You're about an hour outside?"

Closer to an hour and a half. And if I managed to get into the city a few times a year, that was a major achievement. "I go in enough. It's easier now that I have friends who have cars." Well, *a* friend who has a car.

"I need to do that soon. If I ever leave New York, I'll be stranded. Unless I move to Paris or something."

"Do what, now?" I gave him a perplexed look.

He ducked his head, looking at the table. "Get my license."

My jaw dropped. "You mean there are teenagers who don't get their licenses the second they turn sixteen?" Since I'd never had an active social life, I never bothered to ask or save up for a car, but I still took the test. If I needed to get somewhere, at least I could borrow my parents' car. I couldn't imagine being dependent on them one second longer than necessary.

"In Manhattan, you don't need a license. Between taxis and subways, you can get anywhere."

"Don't you ever want to, I don't know, leave Manhattan?"

Beckett gave a crooked smile. "Sure. Sometimes we go to Brooklyn."

"And here I thought I was the sheltered one."

Beckett laughed but not in a mocking way.

By the time our food arrived, the vibe was definitely getting more first-date-like. Not that I had anything to really compare it to. We talked about our families, high school—getting-to-know-you-type stuff.

Not surprisingly, we had almost nothing in common. I was an only child, whereas he was the youngest of three. I went to a typical suburban high school; he'd gone to an elite boarding school. My parents were born and raised in the Detroit area; his dad was a native New Yorker, and his mom was British. I'd worked at a health food café run by an angry hippie; Beckett had been a famous rock star since he was sixteen. And he'd rowed crew competitively, which explained those insanely cut arms.

When we finished comparing notes, I felt small, inadequate,

like I'd never catch up. But then he asked the million-dollar question. "How'd you get into music?"

Turns out we'd both been forced to take piano at a young age. He attended a famous conservatory on weekends and that's where he discovered guitar. "I stayed with piano and even learned to love it, but they still haven't been able to pry the guitar out of my hands." I smiled, loving the image of a ten-year-old Beckett sleeping with his guitar. "Do you still play?" he asked.

"Of course. Music was my only hobby, and there's not much going on in the suburbs."

"I thought everyone got drunk and hooked up."

"Yeah. Exactly."

He laughed. "What about singing? When did that start?"

"There was no real start. It's just always been part of the way I enjoy music."

"You never sang with a band or in chorus?" I shook my head, leaning in for a sip of lemonade. "Huh. I'm surprised, but I'm also not surprised. Your voice has that wild, untrained quality that a lot of great rock singers have. You also don't oversing, which sometimes people with a lot of training do. It's like they have all this skill, why not use it? It's too busy for a stripped-down band like Melbourne. But you harmonize like you grew up singing in a gospel choir."

I was ridiculously pleased that he'd said that. The first real experience I'd had singing with other people was on *Pop Star*, and that was only when we did those chaotic full-group numbers.

"Have you ever written songs?" Beckett asked.

"No," I said.

"Never even tried? Lyrics? Nothing?"

I shook my head. "Did Hollis?" I asked before I could stop myself.

"She wrote all our lyrics until this last record. Pem and I wrote those together." Beckett's statement hung in the air as I processed that it wasn't just Hollis's singing I was competing with. "You make much more sense in a rock band than you did on the reality show. I can totally see why you didn't win," Beckett said, almost like he was thinking out loud.

"Wait a minute. Are you saying you didn't vote for me?"

"I mean, you were clearly the best singer in your season, but you don't have the temperament of a real singer," he said, ignoring me. "Which I personally think is a good thing. Singers can be needy and annoying."

This time I didn't ask about Hollis, even though I was dying to know if he meant her too. I'd worked hard at owning the stage when I performed and liked the way it felt to be seen up there. But mostly I didn't like to analyze it too much. When it came to music, it was better not to think.

"Why even go on a singing competition show?"

"I just needed to try something new. And it got me out of Lydon." And it got me here, didn't it? I kept that to myself because I knew my bandmates didn't like connecting those dots.

We'd finished our phenomenal burgers and were now picking at our fries. "Dessert?" I asked.

Beckett shook his head. "Not here. Popsicles." I must have looked skeptical. "Trust me." He signaled for the check.

An older couple sat down beside us. "Enjoy your meal, kids?"

"Very much, thanks," Beckett replied.

The man looked at the woman with a knowing smile. "When I was a youth, I went to the pizza parlor on dates. What do you two lovebirds have planned for the rest of the day?" he asked.

"We're going for Popsicles," I blurted out, as if to cut Beckett off from assuring this stranger that we were not, in fact, lovebirds.

"Then we have a show at the Ryman tonight," Beckett said.

"Well, son, don't hesitate to spend your father's money, okay? Show this young lady a nice time." He gave a condescending smile, misunderstanding Beckett's meaning. His repeated insinuation that Beckett and I were on a date made me feel like I had red ants crawling down my neck.

"We both have jobs," I said. Beckett shot me a look, but I didn't care.

"Is that right? You invest in the stock market? Develop a little real estate?" He grinned as the waiter slid our check between us.

"Jim, leave them alone. They're enjoying themselves!" his wife chided.

"We're musicians," Beckett said, when it was clear that Jim wasn't going to stop talking to us.

Jim slapped his knee and threw his head back with a laugh. "That's a good one. One of you better figure out how to make a real living someday."

I threw down some money, including a ridiculously large tip, and stood up. "Actually, he's a rock star. He's just too polite to say it. He's been on magazine covers, played concerts all over the world, and probably has already made more money than you." Even as I was speaking, I knew it was possible I'd gone to the crazy place.

I forced myself to stroll out so it would look like a tell-off rather than a tantrum. Beckett followed right behind me. "What the heck was that?"

"I've always worked—even when I was underage, I helped at my parents' store," I said.

"Well, he would have been right ninety percent of the time." Beckett started down the block. "Anyway, who cares what Jim thinks? Where are those nice Midwestern manners when you need them? You never make a peep when Malcolm and Pem get on you, but you go off on some random old guy?"

"He was being obnoxious." And also embarrassing the hell out of me. Squirming over the date reference was immature, but I'd never been on a real date, so playing it cool wasn't part of my repertoire.

"You're going to meet tons of people doing this job. You can't have it out with everyone who says dumb things. Just ignore them and move on."

I didn't feel like explaining that that was exactly what I had been doing for the past two years. Ignoring absolutely everyone and everything. Convincing myself that slights didn't matter. So instead I said, "You're right."

He gave me a sidelong glance. "But it is nice to see you have some fire. I was beginning to worry. Can't be a good front person without it."

We stopped at a shop with a line out the door. I peeked in the picture window. It was barely big enough to hold a couple of floor freezers that doubled as counters and a few square benches. The humidity outside made Popsicles seem like a genius concept. What felt like eons later, we finally got through the door and into the air-conditioning.

Flavors of the day were scrawled on a chalkboard. "I recommend avocado," Beckett said. I wrinkled my nose. I had my money ready, but Beckett swatted my hand. "I'm buying."

I ordered a blueberry-lime one and squeezed my way outside. When Beckett came out, he handed me two Popsicles. One had a distinctly green tint to it. I gave it a suspicious look.

"Just try."

I bit into it, half expecting to spit it out right away. But instead the creamy goodness slid right down my throat. I took another bite.

We walked across the street to a small park and found a shady spot. I offered Beckett a bite of my blueberry-lime Popsicle. He wrapped his fingers around mine and leaned in for a bite. "Yum."

Kids played on swings and a climbing structure. They seemed not to notice the oppressive sun beating down on them. "You feel like playing a show tonight?" I asked.

"I guess." He leaned back on his elbows. "Or we could hide out here."

"I think someone might notice if we didn't show up," I said.

Beckett yawned. "Pem can sing, and Winston can always jump in on guitar. We can say we fell into a Popsicle coma."

I imagined whiling away the day with Beckett, but he stood up and held out his hand. I let him pull me up to standing. He ordered a car on his phone, and minutes later we were on our way back to reality.

11

Fans were already lined up, so we asked the car to drop us in the alley leading to the backstage entrance. We walked into sound check right on time. Going through a couple of songs allowed the techs to check our mikes, in-ear monitors, and instruments. There were issues with the drum microphones, so Malcolm had to keep playing after the rest of us finished. "Fuck this," he said. "Aaron, can you deal?"

Pem and Beckett looked at each other. "We have time before the meet and greet," Pem said.

"Aaron can figure it out. I don't need to be here."

Another look passed between Beckett and Pem. "Everyone else is good?" Beckett asked into his mike. From the soundboard, Jared gave a thumbs-up.

"Why are you rushing it?" Pem asked Beckett.

"You know it's useless once he gets like this. At least maybe he'll get his head right before the show," Beckett said.

I was observant enough to know that Malcolm wasn't quite the stickler that the other two were, but I'd thought that was probably a good thing. His easygoing ways seemed necessary to balance the other two. Pem jumped off the stage to talk to Jared. Malcolm slipped backstage, looking vaguely annoyed. Aaron took Malcolm's place at the drum kit and got to work.

Mandy lay down across a couple of folding chairs in the dressing room while I got ready. "Your day sounds about a thousand times better than mine." She flung an arm dramatically across her eyes.

"What happened? Inventory problems?"

"I wish. Rob made me issue all the per diems, book Dave's hotels for the next five cities, reserve your flights to LA."

"If you're good, maybe he'll make you assistant tour manager."

"I guess. But if he keeps me this busy, how am I supposed to see the country and find boys to flirt with?" she asked.

"Where there's a will, there's a way," I said.

"Easy for you to say. You've decided celibacy is a good thing. It's unnatural. Speaking of which, how was being alone with Beckett? He's so hot."

"Yeah. Too bad he's off-limits." I wasn't sure if I said it because I really felt that or because it seemed like the thing to say.

"Really? Otherwise you'd go for him?" Mandy sat up, excited by the turn this conversation had taken.

"I didn't say that. I barely know him. Plus, he's got no shortage of female attention." I told her about the girls in the hair salon.

83

She came up to the mirror to fix her ponytail and reapply lip gloss. "Did you ask if he had a girlfriend at home?"

"No. I have boundaries."

"Boring," she droned before leaving the room.

I took advantage of the rare moment alone to emotionally prepare for the show. Some bands had preshow rituals, but Melbourne didn't seem to be into that stuff and I wasn't about to suggest it. So it was up to me to figure one out for myself. "You're going to have an amazing show. These fans have no idea what's about to hit them." I talked a big game, but if anyone had overheard me, I'd shrivel with embarrassment.

Even though the Ryman hadn't been used as a church in decades, it still felt like one. The audience sat in actual pews. Stained-glass windows, soaring ceilings, and graduated seating that continued onto the high balcony gave a special, hallowed feeling to performing there.

But not all of us were feeling reverent. A couple of songs into the set, Malcolm summoned Rob over, then pointed into the audience. They were clarifying gestures; then Rob disappeared. I didn't know what that was about, but the show was so fun, I quickly forgot about it. Tonight's crowd was really responsive and we sounded amazing. I must have covered five miles running back and forth across the stage, but I hardly felt it. When we broke for the encore, it seemed like no time had passed. Right before we began, Rob reappeared and waded into the audience where Malcolm had been pointing to talk to some girl.

The show had gone off without a hitch, and I was practically delirious with excitement. On the reality show, I'd always rehearsed hard to get songs right and give a good performance, but we'd only had a week in between shows. I'd been working on these songs with Melbourne in some way for about nine months. To have the payoff of all those long months of practice coming together in a musically perfect show, with an amped-up crowd in a beautiful and significant venue, was unbelievably satisfying. It felt like putting in the last piece of a jigsaw puzzle, or the first time you ride a bike without training wheels, only better. I didn't need anyone to tell me I was good tonight; I had that feeling I'd only achieved once or twice on *Pop Star*—that feeling of holding the audience so tightly that I could take them wherever I wanted them to go.

On impulse, I took a running start and leaped over the barricade into the audience, sprawled out, limbs fully extended. Oddly, the fear didn't hit until after they'd caught me. They flipped me over so that I sang to the ceiling and passed me around on hands stretched up high. With the constant threat of being dropped on my head and people's hands jabbing me in impolite places, crowd surfing definitely wasn't as relaxing as the name suggested. Still, the high was incomparable.

What felt like seconds later, Rob pulled me back over the barricade and gave me a boost onto the stage, where I finished out the encore.

When we got off, Winston high-fived me. "That was awesome! Didn't know you had that in you."

I was just about to bask in the glow of his compliment when Pem stormed over. "What the fuck was that?"

"What do you mean?" I was still smiling—that's how confused I was. Beckett hurried toward us.

"First of all, you looked like a flying squirrel. Second of all, we are not that band. We don't resort to poser antics. That shit has jumped the shark." Pem was on a roll and my humiliation spiraled. Beckett hearing the whole thing and probably agreeing made it a million times worse.

"Sorry. No one told me." That sounded weak, but it was all I had.

"The crowd didn't hate it," Beckett said. That was a ringing endorsement.

Pem glowered at him. "Don't. We've worked too hard." He shot me one last withering glare and stalked away.

Beckett shrugged. "With Pem, less is more."

"Yeah, I got that." I don't know what I expected him to say. I wanted him to whisk me back to my happy place of witty banter and Popsicles in the sunshine.

The girl Malcolm had summoned and one of her giddy friends were already backstage. He was too busy flirting to participate in my drama.

Pem had stopped to hug a cute Asian girl. She had long dark hair and thick bangs that highlighted warm brown eyes. "You made it," he said. Good. Maybe her presence would improve his personality.

"Of course," she replied. "Wouldn't miss it."

Beckett went over to them while I tried to slink by unnoticed. All I wanted was to hide out in the hotel. I didn't break my stride, which was a feat, because I'm pretty sure I stopped breathing when Beckett swept the girl into his arms and kissed her like he was returning from a war.

12

With the dressing room suddenly seeming like a crappy place to be, I took a shower and went to look for Mandy at the merch table. Judging from my popularity at the meet and greets thus far, I was pretty sure I could hang out there without causing a stampede.

Some fans came over and asked me how I liked touring and said that they really liked what I brought to the band. Before long there was a line in front of me. I signed CDs until my Sharpie ran out of ink, then stayed on to chat with people who wanted to say hi. Some of them even asked about *American Pop Star*, and not in a disdainful or ironic way. Maybe I was making inroads.

I helped Mandy pack up once the lobby emptied out. "What are you doing here?" Rob asked when he came to check on Mandy.

"She's been great for business. Maybe the guys will come out here sometime," Mandy said.

"Nope. That would be disastrous," Rob explained.

I turned to Mandy. "Will you come get food with me?"

"There's pizza in catering," Rob said.

"Would've been more of a newsflash if you'd said, 'There's no pizza in catering.'" Mandy shot Rob a disgusted look and we left.

We walked to Music Row because we wanted to see a famous Nashville spot. It was loud, raucous, and very touristy—perfect for us. Getting something to eat turned out to be a challenge; every restaurant was packed. We wandered up and down the few blocks, taking in the lights and music blasting from clubs and bars and reading all of the store signs. Boot shops may have actually outnumbered music venues.

The Shelby Street Bridge, lit up with spotlights, twinkled off the river below. A handful of people were out enjoying the walk. I filled Mandy in on Beckett and the girl.

"You had to know there was someone in one of these cities," she said. "How could there not be?"

She was right, of course. I hadn't considered that she might just be a one-stop girlfriend, like Malcolm always seemed to have. Thinking Beckett was a dog actually cheered me up.

We stood at the apex of the bridge, overlooking downtown and the stadium where the Tennessee Titans played. I took a picture for my father. It was dark, with only pinpricks of light, so he'd have to use his imagination.

Back at the Ryman, fans still lined the parking lot. Mandy accompanied me while I signed more things. The girls from the hair salon were waiting. "Is Beckett coming out?" one of them asked.

I shook my head. "Something came up. I'm sure he'd love to be here, though." They looked crestfallen and kind of irritated, almost like Beckett stood them up for a date. I sympathized. Mandy and I stayed out until Rob told us that the last runner was leaving.

At the hotel we took obscenely long showers, then watched a sappy romantic comedy. Lying clean in a real bed and not having to set the alarm felt so heavenly.

A day off with Mandy couldn't have come at a better time. I could be myself and not have to watch what was coming out of my mouth all day. We managed to avoid everyone from the Melbourne camp and had the best time, letting loose and gossiping about the band and crew.

When we reported to the bus, I was surprised to find Beckett's girlfriend sitting in the front lounge in her pj's, nestled next to him. She jumped up as soon as we got on. "Hi! I'm Lauren. I didn't get a chance to meet you after the show last night, but you were amazing."

I had trouble finding words. Apparently she was already known to Dave and welcome on the bus. "Thanks. This is Mandy. She does merch."

Dave maneuvered out of the lot.

Malcolm came out of the sleeping compartment. "Hey, girl," he said to Lauren. "Nice to have a sister alongside."

"I'm Japanese." She laughed but bumped fists with him regardless.

"You think these fools can tell the difference?" He grabbed

a bag of chips and sat down, shoveling handfuls into his mouth. Mandy cleared her throat. "So, Lauren. Where are you from?"

"Charlotte," Lauren replied with a friendly smile. Her teeth were perfectly white and even.

"Oh, next stop. Does that mean you're only with us for the night?" Mandy asked.

Lauren glanced shyly at Beckett. "No, I think I'll hang out for a couple more cities." Beckett grabbed her hand and played with it, lacing his fingers through hers.

I stood up. "They're watching a movie in back," Malcolm said through a mouthful of chips. Like there were so many activities available on the bus.

Mandy continued to interrogate Lauren. "Now, how did you two meet?"

"Cool." I pushed the door button and escaped just in time to miss the adorable story of how Beckett and Lauren met and fell in love. At least now I knew why Beckett wasn't included in Malcolm's pool.

I spent about twenty minutes trying to sit through the horror movie du jour, but I wasn't fooling anyone. "We should probably switch up the genres once in a while," Winston said. This met with apathetic grunts. I smiled at him anyway; it was nice of him to try.

"It's either this or porn," Kam said.

Winston slapped him on the back of the head. "Man, no one wants to watch porn with you." He looked apologetic. "Sometimes we watch Food Network."

I had no one to blame for my suddenly foul mood, so I did the mature thing and climbed up to my bunk to stew for the rest of the night.

13

I'd gotten used to having the front lounge to myself in the mornings, but when the doors slid open, there sat Lauren, sipping my ginger tea. I knew it was mine, because the box sat on the counter. I really needed to start writing my name on my food.

"Morning! Sorry, is this yours?" She looked all beautiful even with her hair up in a knot and not a lick of makeup on. She didn't even have dried-out bus face like I got every night. There were so many reasons not to love Lauren.

"Help yourself," I said.

"Did you sleep okay?" she asked.

"Like a rock. You?" This was a total lie. I'd heard her and Beckett whispering and laughing, and God knows what else, all night long. It had been unbearable.

Lauren nodded. "Great. Didn't even hear Jared snoring."

I'd wondered who the snorer was. "How do you know it's him?"

"Last tour. He was the first one asleep one night and then no one else could fall asleep. They made him buy Breathe Right strips after that."

"Guess that didn't work."

"Nope." Lauren giggled. I turned away, rummaging through the cabinets but not really looking for anything. "Hey, Beckett said we had to buy this for you." She jumped off the couch and reached into a lower cabinet. When she backed up, she was holding an economy-sized variety pack of instant oatmeal. It even had my name written on it.

"That's so sweet." I was surprised Beckett had given me a single thought during his romantic reunion with Lauren.

Pem came out, dressed and surprisingly alert. "Can I have some oatmeal?"

I slid the box to him. He microwaved a chicken breast, made a packet of plain oatmeal, and combined them. I gagged as he sat across from me.

"We need to talk." He took a bite of his revolting breakfast.

"Can it wait until you're done? I don't think I can sit here while you eat that. Sorry if it's some ethnic meal that I'm too unworldly to know about."

Pem looked at his bowl and shrugged. "Just protein with carbs. Not that different from rice or pasta with chicken."

"I'm going to have to disagree. And who eats chicken for breakfast?" I asked.

Lauren laughed. "Boys are disgusting."

"Whatever." Pem swiveled around to face Lauren. "Your friends coming down tonight?"

"Definitely! Should I tell anyone in particular that you're asking?" Lauren had a sly, amused look on her face. Everything she said sounded flirty.

"Nope. Not like that. What have you been up to?" Pem asked.

"You know: school, graduating. I got a job waiting tables until school starts."

"Where did you decide on?"

Lauren suddenly got very interested in her tea mug. "Yale."

Pem grinned. "Congratulations! To be closer to Beckett?" He didn't seem to care that he was making her blush like mad.

"I'm going to get an amazing education. Isn't that reason enough?" Lauren jutted her chin out.

"No argument here." Pem shrugged. Apparently he wasn't too impressed, but I was.

He finished eating, then brought his dishes to the sink. Actually, for a boy, he wasn't that disgusting. He sat down again, looking at me expectantly, like he wanted me to start the conversation.

I took a deep breath. "So. How do you think tour's going?" The only thought going through my head was *Please don't fire me, please don't fire me.* Despite having a mostly great show at the Ryman (ill-advised stage dive aside), I wasn't fooling myself into thinking this was going to be a congratulatory talk.

He looked at the table, batting my empty oatmeal packet between his hands. "Fine. Really well. I mean, you're still getting your sea legs, but it's coming along." Sometimes when talking to Pem, I felt like I was talking to a random crotchety old man. "I'm more talking about after the shows. We noticed that you like going out and meeting the fans." I nodded, uncertain if I should be preparing an excuse. "That's cool, but we need to be careful not to create an imbalance."

"I figured since I'm new, I should get out there more."

"Sure. But it creates an expectation for the rest of the band to be out there too." He looked at me to see if I was getting it.

"Beckett doesn't seem to mind," I said.

"He's just being supportive," Pem said.

I couldn't figure out why that was a bad thing, but I didn't say anything. Lauren, who'd been pretending to play on her phone, glanced over and shifted in her seat. The fact that she could overhear every word was humiliating. "I didn't realize," I said. "I thought it was part of what we do."

"And it is. Sometimes," Pem said. "Also, the reality show is coming up too often in comments online. You need to dial that down."

"How?"

He sighed. "Be evasive, act like you don't want to discuss it."

"I don't sit around talking—"

"Then it should be no problem."

"But I'm giving honest answers to questions." We stared at each other but both knew that I'd be the first to back down. "You think they'll just forget?"

"No. But it'll be less of an issue if you don't keep elaborating."

"So basically the rules for talking to fans are the same as the rules for talking to journalists."

"Pretty much." He watched me for a reaction. I deliberately didn't give one even though I thought he was being paranoid. "Cool?"

I gave a tight nod.

"How's your music education going?" Pem asked.

"What do you mean?"

"I know Beckett gave you some stuff to listen to."

"It wasn't for that." At least, I didn't think it was. It irked me to think that maybe Beckett's gesture wasn't totally altruistic.

"Even if it wasn't, I hope it's sinking in. I have some other listening assignments. Give me your iPod."

"It's in my bunk, but you can grab it."

Pem stood up and left the lounge.

After a few uncomfortable minutes, Lauren slid into Pem's empty seat. She took my hand. "Don't let him get to you. He's always seriously cranky."

I stared at her hand, wrapped around mine. An assertion of friendship that had neither been earned nor invited. I extracted my hand as unbitchily as possible. "I've picked up on that."

"When Hollis quit the band, it rocked his world." Lauren looked into my eyes. I saw her warmth and sincerity. She was going to make it impossible for me to hate her.

"I don't know much about it." I was fed the same line as everyone else—that Hollis was burned out and wanted to go to college and have a normal life. It sounded reasonable and no one was saying anything different, so I never asked questions.

Lauren gave me a conspiratorial look. "I've only overheard things in passing, but I know it was ugly." I was bugged that she knew more about the band than I did.

"How long have you been going out with Beckett?" I asked.

She sat back and looked down at her lap, plucking at the hem of her T-shirt. "We aren't really going out. Whenever I hear he's in this neck of the woods, I text him and we make a plan to meet up."

I tried to ignore the inappropriate feelings of relief flooding my body. "That sounds . . ."

"Incredibly noncommittal. I know. I've been fine with that for the past couple of years, but it feels like we're at a make-or-break point. I love seeing him. FaceTime and texting just aren't doing it anymore. I mean, that dies off after we haven't seen each other for a few months anyway."

I tried to remember a time when Beckett seemed in a hurry to make a call or overly absorbed in his phone. I couldn't think of one. "Maybe he feels the same way."

Lauren's hopeful look made me sad. "Do you have a boyfriend?" she asked.

This question again. "No," I said.

She bit her lip but then broke into a bright smile. "I bet you're meeting tons of people. There's bound to be someone cool soon."

"Or not. Either way, I'm good," I said.

Lauren obviously wanted to get something off her chest, so I stared out the window while she thought about it. "I hate to ask," she finally said, "and I know it's only been a couple of days, but have you seen or heard of anyone else? With Beckett, I mean?"

"Uh, no. But my relationship with all the guys is still mostly professional. I've been kind of busy trying to learn everything."

Lauren clapped a hand to her forehead. "Of course! You must think I'm so self-absorbed. I should have realized you had your own stuff going on. I'm so sorry."

She looked so chagrined that I tried to soften my statement. "No worries. I just haven't been the most observant lately."

"Well, from what I saw you're going to own this band soon. People won't even remember Melbourne with Hollis." She smiled, but her eyes were glistening.

"Try not to stress about Beckett. You're here for the next few days, right?" I asked. She nodded. "Then just try to enjoy it."

She came around the table and hugged me. After a brief pause, I hugged her back. "Thanks," she said. "I've been so anxious about coming on tour and dealing with this. You and Mandy are so easy to talk to."

I smiled. "Anytime."

We played the Fillmore that night, a cool club that had been redesigned to look industrial. During the show you'd never have guessed that anything had been bothering Lauren. She was the carefree girlfriend of a rock star, queen bee reigning over the five girlfriends she'd gotten into the show. Beckett seemed almost as into Lauren as she was into him. They were constantly touching and laughing, but at times it felt to me like he was holding something back. Maybe that was just wishful thinking.

14

*F*ortunately (or not, depending on how you looked at it) Sam came to check on us in Atlanta. Pem seemed especially relieved to see him. Sam was the voice of reason, and even though the tour wasn't even a week old, some things needed course-correcting. He planned to stay on the bus through Miami then fly ahead of us to LA, where we'd shoot our next video.

Before we sound-checked at the Tabernacle, we sat down with Sam in the production office.

"I've been hearing really positive things about the shows. Promoters are happy, you're selling a crap ton of merch, and venues that weren't sold out before continue to show strong ticket sales as the show date approaches. That's all word of mouth. That's not something a marketing plan can do for you. So congrats!" Sam looked at each of us as he spoke. The boys remained poker-faced, but I offered a smile. That did seem like pretty exciting news. "Anyone else want to say anything?"

"That's all good, but it's not the same buzz builder as a sold-out tour," Pem said, reprising his role as Mr. Positivity.

"It's the same money, though," Malcolm said.

"You're both right," Sam said. "But the best thing we can do is to keep putting on kick-ass shows." He looked around. "Cool. I wanted to meet before sound check to remind you that it's not just sound check for you guys. People who work the building need to make sure their stuff is right too." We all nodded, but Malcolm's mouth tensed, anticipating what was coming. "And sometimes promoters bring their coworkers down to show them what they bought. If you guys are being sloppy, that gets around. So we need to tighten that up."

Malcolm heaved a theatrical sigh. Someone had tattled. But he didn't try to justify his actions, and Sam didn't ask for any verbal commitment that we'd follow his directions.

"How are the meet and greets going?" Sam asked. "Fans seem happy?"

"Yeah. I've been liking how casual they are," Beckett said.

"I don't know why we can't do it the old way. It was more efficient," Pem said.

I had no idea what the old way looked like, so I had no comment. Malcolm was still mad about being called out, so he didn't add anything either.

"We're doing it this way for now because it's like acknowledging that the band is in a slight reorg phase. We want fans to know we're not trying to slip one by them with Chelsea. They need reassurance that you guys are the same, but you're not pretending you're the exact same band."

"We're already playing smaller venues so the shows can be more intimate. Doesn't that count?" Pem asked.

Sam put on what I thought of as his exaggeratedly patient voice. "You're asking fans to almost start over with you. The singer is the thing, you know? They love you guys, of course. You're the engine that makes the whole thing go. You write the songs and you play the hell out of them. But it's the singer that most people identify first when they hear a song."

I swallowed, trying to get the sudden dry, cottony feeling out of my mouth. When Sam described my job that way, I felt a lot of pressure. I had new appreciation for the chance my bandmates had taken on me.

"So we have to be willing to start over with them too," Beckett said.

"Exactly," Sam said. "That fan relationship is key. It cannot be messed with."

"Does that mean we have to go out and sign every night like Chelsea does?" Pem asked.

"I don't do it every night" was my big contribution to the discussion. "You guys take it for granted that you even have fans. I can't do that."

Sam leaned forward, resting his elbows on his knees. "Look. It's your band. You're adults. Run things however you want. But you want to keep being successful, and I'm telling you how we can make that happen."

"How's the single doing?" Beckett asked.

"It's climbing," Sam said. "We keep getting more adds. The rock station here is promoting the show, so they put you on heavy rotation."

"If it's still building, why are we rushing the second single?" Pem asked.

"We're not. We just want to have the video ready to go,

and that's the only time you can get a few days away from the tour."

"I can't believe we have to spend the Fourth of July in LA," Malcolm said. "That place has no gravity, no appreciation for historical significance."

"Complain, complain, complain," Beckett said. Malcolm laughed.

"Actually, we got an offer to play a private party in Vegas on the Fourth," Sam said.

"Vegas? Sign me up," Malcolm said.

"LA has no sense of history, but Vegas would meet with the Founding Fathers' approval?" Pem asked.

Sam ignored them both. "It's good money, but you'll have to use backline gear. We're not flying in crew and equipment for a private."

"We can handle that," Beckett said.

"Chelsea. What've you been wearing onstage?" Sam asked.

I looked down at my plaid leggings, boots, and neon-yellow T-shirt tunic with the short sleeves rolled up. "This."

"Yeah. That's not good. It's time for you to have a look," he said.

"What's wrong with this?" I thought I looked like a rock girl should.

"It's not sexy," Sam said.

"*They* don't have to look sexy," I said, tilting my head toward the guys.

That met with a chorus of protests. "I resent that," Malcolm said.

I rolled my eyes. "You know what I mean."

"What they have to do is look uniform," Sam said.

"Except for Malcolm," I replied.

"You're the front woman. They're not." Sam looked at me until he was sure I understood.

I groaned inwardly. "That stuff just doesn't feel like me."

After going over a few more things about shows and scheduling, we wrapped up the meeting and went to sound check with our new marching orders to take it seriously fresh in our minds.

Pem studied a poster advertising an upcoming show and frowned. "Ryder Hart's playing here next week." He glared at me like it was my fault. Ryder was the winner of my season of *American Pop Star*.

Feeling emboldened by our meeting (Sam hadn't told me to quit my signing frenzy, after all), I asked, "How can you possibly hate all pop music?"

"It's not music," he said. "It's drivel. Mass-produced, spoon-fed drivel."

Okay then. "There's not one single pop song that you like? In the history of pop songs?"

He rolled his eyes. "Of course I like some stuff. I'm talking about the culture of Auto-Tune. The whole army of 'I can't sing, but I look good' that assaults our airwaves."

"Actually, Ryder can sing." Why I felt the need to be stubborn about this at this particular moment, I had no idea.

"He can sing, but so what? He doesn't write any of his own songs. If you sing but don't write, then you're not the artist; you're just the docent." Pem stared at the poster like he wanted to rip it down. I made a mental note to look up the word *docent* later.

I wasn't sure if this was supposed to be (yet another) dig

at me, but I now felt like a complete loser for never having written a song. "Well. Hopefully he can do something to save himself from becoming washed up and irrelevant before he turns twenty."

Walking out into the main room, I was struck by how gorgeous the Tabernacle was. Like the Ryman, it was a converted church with the same high ceilings, stained-glass windows, and raised balconies, but the colorfully painted ceiling and wall panels made it less subdued. It was like being inside a fancy box of candy.

By far the best part of that night's show was watching Sam rock out at the soundboard. Of course he knew all the songs by heart, and a few drinks in he was an air-drumming, air-guitar-playing fool. His enthusiasm put even the most die-hard fans' to shame, and it was fun to play off his energy.

I didn't expect to love the South, but the little I'd seen of it was totally charming. I enjoyed the pace, the accents, and especially the food, and I wanted to leave feeling like I had an invitation to come back. As we in Melbourne liked to say, I left it all on the stage.

15

From Atlanta we headed to Florida, which really doesn't count as the south anymore. Especially when your first stop is Orlando.

The venue was great but it was a little bit like performing a rock show in a theme park. "I feel like I didn't get to experience the real Orlando," I said to Rob after the show.

"What are you talking about?" he asked. "This *is* the real Orlando."

When we arrived in Miami the next morning, Lauren accosted me before I could make it to my hotel room. She wore leggings and swam in one of Beckett's hoodies. "Did he tell you that I'm flying home today?"

I shook my head. "You're not even staying for the day off?"

"No. He didn't say anything? It seems like you're the only one he talks to around here. You and Dave."

"And I told you I'm not getting in the middle," Dave said as he passed us on his way into the hotel.

"I thought you only planned to stay for a few days anyway," I said.

"But I wanted him to ask me to stay longer."

"And he didn't?"

"Oh my God!" Lauren dropped her head back and looked to the sky for help.

"Sorry. I'm a little out of it." It was, after all, butt-early in the morning. "Maybe he thinks you're bored."

"Are you kidding? I love being on tour. I have fun hanging out with you, and I really want to go to LA." Lauren went on with a lengthy list of reasons she wanted to stay, but none of them was to be with Beckett. Call me crazy, but maybe he picked up on that. It made me feel protective of him and resentful of her.

I felt cornered and annoyed and like I was over this conversation. "I don't know. You should probably just ask him."

"Okay, since you've never had a boyfriend before, I'm not going to totally laugh in your face—"

"Who told you I've never had a boyfriend?"

"It's no big deal, but let me just spare you the pain of learning this the hard way. You don't just come out and ask a boy why he's not begging to be around you more. Act like you don't care and like you have tons of stuff going on."

That advice sounded suspect, but what did I know? Lauren bit her lip and stuffed her hands into the pockets of Beckett's sweatshirt. I felt bad for her, even though she was driving me up a wall. "Beckett probably likes you *because* you have a life," I said.

She glanced at me with a weak smile. "You really are sweet." She said *sweet* in the way people use it when they really mean *dim-witted.* "Yeah, maybe. I guess. But compared to their life? I mean, yours too—my life is as boring and vanilla as they come."

"You get to go to Yale."

"You get to be a rock star."

At the moment all that meant to me was that I got to be sleep-deprived, claustrophobic, and malnourished.

I'd collapsed onto the bed, when Mandy came in looking annoyingly well rested. "What do you want to do today? Beach?" she asked. Since we were from the middle of the country, frolicking in an actual ocean was a rare treat for us. So rather than argue for twenty minutes and lose anyway, I put on my bikini and threw on a pair of cut-off shorts and a T-shirt. Mandy wore a cute caftan and a floppy canvas hat.

Pem and Malcolm were in the lobby when we got downstairs. "Where are you guys going?" Malcolm asked.

"To the beach!" Mandy said.

"What about you? Undercover stakeout?" I asked. Malcolm looked the way he always did, but Pem wore khakis and a checkered button-down with long sleeves covering his tattoos even though it had to be ninety-five degrees. His hair was flattened and parted. Nobody would ever recognize him.

"We're going to see my grandmother in Palm Beach," Pem said.

"Yeah. Third has to kiss the ring. And for some reason he thought bringing his minority friend along would be a good idea," Malcolm said.

"What's third?" I asked.

"His nickname. For Pemberton Fuller *the Third*. The entire family calls him that."

"Well . . . that's . . ." I tried to think of something to say.

"The word you're looking for is *dismissive*," Malcolm said.

Pem stared at Malcolm. "Don't ask me why, but my grandmother actually likes him."

"It's 'cause my parents are doctors. Old ladies love anyone associated with doctors. Plus my mom does all her friends' neck lifts," Malcolm said. "You guys should ride with us. Pem's grandma has a beach."

"That's not a good idea," Pem interrupted. "She's really ornery and doesn't like unexpected guests. But there's public access to the same beach just down the block."

Mandy and I looked at each other and shrugged. We didn't know where to go, and any beach was going to be amazing as far as we were concerned. And I certainly didn't need to meet anyone cranky enough to be identified by Pem as ornery.

We piled into a cab and rolled out of the city, leaving behind the concentration of white high-rises. I was fascinated with reading street signs. So many of the street names had the word *sea* in them, like Sea Foam or Seaspray. I felt like I was on a tropical vacation.

"Listen to that bass line," Pem said, indicating the taxi radio.

Malcolm was quiet for a few seconds. "Sick, dude. You wrote something like that on 'Game Over.' "

"Kind of. This is way better." Pem turned to look at me. "Have you listened to those albums I loaded on your iPod?"

I nodded. He'd given me Patti Smith's *Horses,* the Beatles'

Sgt. Pepper's Lonely Hearts Club Band, and the Beach Boys' *Pet Sounds.* "I have listened to the Beatles before, you know. I didn't just time-travel to this century."

"Yeah, but have you *listened* to them listened to them?"

I decided to quit while I was ahead. Pem liked to work everything out long-division-style, and I just didn't have it in me. "I liked them all except *Horses.*"

He stared at me for a long minute. "Listen to it ten times all the way through." He turned back around. He was lucky he was brilliant, because he was definitely a little short on charm.

The drive to Palm Beach took over an hour, and after listening to Pem and Malcolm's banter for half the ride, I think Mandy and I wished we'd stayed closer to our hotel.

"Where's Beckett?" I asked.

"He took Lauren to the airport. That guy is such a sucker. Who goes to the airport on their day off?" Malcolm asked.

"That doesn't make him a sucker. He's a good guy," I said. Pem snorted.

Our single "Hard Words" came on the radio. The driver started humming it, oblivious to the fact that most of the band members were in his taxi. We all stayed quiet. The feeling I had of essentially spying on someone enjoying music that I had a part in creating was so surreal, I felt like I should ask him to stop before we both died of embarrassment. But following Pem and Malcolm's lead, I didn't say a word.

We crossed over the bridge into Palm Beach, a wealthy neighborhood with beautiful buildings and houses awash in pastels. The town center was one fancy designer shop after another, like a mini satellite version of Beverly Hills.

The cab drove past gently rolling golf courses and a few

sprawling, upscale resorts, then turned onto a road with some of the biggest houses I'd ever seen. I think they were what you'd call estates. Lydon had rich neighborhoods, but they were nothing like this.

"Dude, can't you stash these two in the pool house or something? It's like a mile from the main house," Malcolm said to Pem.

Pem looked seriously stressed out at the prospect. Clearly his grandmother scared the bejesus out of him.

"Don't sweat it. We'll go to the beach and then find our own way back to the hotel," I said.

"Maybe we'll walk down and hang out a little later," Pem said. I wasn't going to hold my breath.

The beach was comfortably crowded. Families played in the shallow waves while bigger kids either bodysurfed or boogie-boarded. Older couples walked briskly up and down the shoreline. I made a mental note to live near a beach one day if I could afford it. Soaking in the bright sunshine, watching the swells build up so high, then that breath-holding moment right before they crashed down, I felt weeks of tension slip away.

"You look skinny," Mandy said.

I shrugged. I'd noticed my clothes fitting differently, which I attributed to jumping around onstage for two hours every night and not being able to eat for hours leading up to the shows. No one besides my best friend would ever refer to me as skinny, but I was glad I still had my curves. I liked that I filled out my bikini.

Mandy had bought trashy magazines from the hotel shop.

She held up a photo of Lucas Rivers leaving a restaurant in LA with a buddy. He wore dark glasses, a baseball cap, and a giant smile, like he'd just heard the best joke in the world. I still couldn't believe I'd kissed him. It had been less than a month but seemed like a lifetime ago. I could barely remember what it felt like. It was like trying to hang on to the details from a really great dream.

Mandy sighed. "I wish I got to see more of the shows. Rob wants me at the merch booth the entire night."

"Have you met any cute boys, at least?" A group of guys playing football had come into my field of vision.

She made a face. "Yeah. Tons. But I don't want some random who only cares about going backstage and getting free stuff."

"Yuck. Is that really what they're all like?"

"I have no idea. But I don't have enough time to find out. Also I'm probably paranoid after what happened to you."

Thankfully, the dramas of Lydon High seemed far away. I couldn't even replicate that feeling I had each time I stepped through the doors of my school of wanting to shrink into the shadows. Not that I wanted to. Still, I felt bad about Mandy internalizing so much of my problems. "You should take a leap of faith," I said. "Not every boy out there is a sociopath."

"Maybe," she said, sighing. "Life would be so much easier if I could hook up with someone on tour."

"Who would you pick?" I rolled over and peered at her over the top of my sunglasses.

"Probably Malcolm."

"Why? Because you want an STD?"

She swatted me with a magazine. "Because there'd be no

pressure. And at least I know it would be fun." She grinned suggestively and I laughed. "And then there's that."

Malcolm was walking toward us, wearing long board shorts and no shirt. We both watched him as he approached. Staring at him out in the open seemed less egregious than ogling him on the bus. "I completely see your point," I said.

"You've been landlocked your entire lives," Malcolm said as he spotted us. "It's time to get in the water."

"You know, Michigan does have beaches," I said. "The Great Lakes are actually huge."

"Gimme a break. Those things are like big puddles. Do you get waves like this?"

I couldn't argue there. "What happened to Third?"

"He's sitting through some boring meeting with Grandma's estate lawyer, talking about changes to his trust fund. Come on. I'll race you."

Mandy and I stood up. I didn't wait for anyone to say go. I just took off running down to the water.

"You cheat!" Malcolm shouted. I could hear him right behind me.

I hit the water first, an icy-cold shock to the system. But after I submerged myself and bobbed around for a minute, the water temperature began to feel as warm as end-of-summer lake water.

The three of us had so much fun, diving under waves, getting in splash fights. I didn't want the day to end. Almost an hour passed before people recognized Malcolm. To be fair, there wasn't a whole lot of long hair and tattoos going on in Palm Beach. Hell, there weren't a lot of Asians. So naturally, curious stares turned into recognition.

He was a lot more gracious about talking with fans away from the shows. Maybe he couldn't bear to give up any of his precious groupie time. And that was interacting with fans. Of a sort.

Malcolm ended up tossing the football with those boys I'd seen earlier. He was naturally athletic and also hyperactive, so he looked pretty good. I leaned over to Mandy. "Since you can't hook up with Malcolm, maybe you should ask him to be your wingman."

Mandy's eyes lit up. "That's a great idea! Especially since you suck at it."

I had to give the girl credit. She got up and worked her way into the game. She caught everything and even threw decently. Before the fun was over, we had plans.

Mandy brought over one of the football players, who was apparently supposed to be my date for the night. His name was Corey, and he seemed fine but didn't quite do it for me. His swim trunks had whales on them. The things I did for friendship. Mandy mouthed, "Thank you," behind his back.

"We want to go to a club!" Mandy smiled at her date, Nathan, a tall, lanky guy with dark eyes, dark hair, and a charming smile.

"We know a good one in Miami on a hotel rooftop. It's pretty easy to sneak into because the pool's up there and they have to let hotel guests up," Corey said.

In the cab ride on the way back to our hotel, Malcolm praised Mandy on her fast work.

"You're coming, right?" she asked.

"Hell no. What do I want to do that for?" Malcolm said.

* * *

After an hour at the club, Malcolm looked like he wanted to gnaw off his own arm, despite the fact that every single girl there was supermodel beautiful and wearing next to nothing. Corey—my date—wouldn't leave him alone.

He bombarded Malcolm with questions about bands, drumming, and being rich and famous. "Did you seriously date Paisley Parker? She's hot but seems whacked." "Who do you think is the best drummer of all time?" "What's the dumbest thing you ever blew money on?"

Corey was undeterred by Malcolm's monotone answers or the fact that Malcolm was slumped so far down on the couch that he was practically lying down, taking and posting selfies. The whole dynamic would have been entertaining if it wasn't so exhausting.

Mandy and Nathan were off getting friendly on the dance floor. They hadn't reached "get a room" status, but it was obvious they'd rather not be interrupted.

Pool lights shimmered under the water, making it gleam aqua blue against the darkness. Dance music with a Latin twist heated up the crowd and the club.

Suddenly Malcolm righted himself and looked alert for the first time all night. "Be right back." He got up and disappeared somewhere behind me.

I braced myself as Corey took a long swig of iced tea. "So do you think you can get us backstage passes for tomorrow?"

Yuck. "How about the meet and greet?" I suggested.

"Thanks, but we want to hang out and, like, kick it in the dressing room."

"Ookaaayy. What do you think happens in the dressing room?" I was genuinely curious. Because what I'd seen

113

involved fighting over clothes and food, not unlike an eighth-grade slumber party.

"Come on. That's where the real dope shit happens, right?"

I was so done with this guy. "Maybe for some bands . . ."

"Whatever. I'll ask Malcolm when he gets back." And apparently he was done with me too.

A couple of hours later, Mandy and I sat in the back of Nathan's car with Malcolm passed out over our laps.

"I don't understand what happened," I said.

"He spent the whole night at the bar."

"But if you saw him, why didn't you say something?" I'd just assumed he'd ditched us. Honestly, I wouldn't have blamed him.

Mandy sighed. "The bartender was young and hot, and she recognized him. I thought he was just flirting. I had no idea she was serving him."

I groaned. I just wanted to go to bed.

"I'll run our stuff up to the room so we have less to carry. Give me two minutes." Mandy gave Nathan an unnecessarily long kiss. I cleared my throat.

When she returned, I pushed while she tried to pull Malcolm to a sitting position. Instead he slid off the seat onto the floor.

"I feel like I'm trying to roll him for loose change," I said. "He's solid muscle. He must weigh seven hundred pounds."

"He's not that heavy," Nathan said, laughing. "I'll help."

"Where are we even moving him to? Do you know who he's rooming with?" I asked Mandy.

114

She shook her head. "Let's bring him to our room."

Nathan slid his arm under Malcolm and hoisted him up, slinging one of Malcolm's arms over his shoulder.

"Could we make it look like he's mostly walking on his own?" I had no idea who was in the lobby, and Sam would feel obligated to get on our cases if he saw this online.

Nathan nodded. "Yeah, I understand."

Mandy and I walked directly in front, to lead him but also to shield Malcolm from view. We got into an empty elevator and breathed a group sigh of relief.

We got to our room and looked at each other. "Key card?" I asked.

"Nope. You?"

"Seriously? You just went to the room!"

"I know! And I put everything inside!" Comprehension dawned. "Whoops." Hormones made people stupid.

Nathan was starting to buckle under Malcolm's dead weight. "Sorry. He is heavier than he looks."

I clenched my teeth and glared at Mandy. "I'll get a key."

Mandy slipped under Malcolm's other arm while I sprinted back to the elevator.

"Hi," I said to the guy at the front desk. "I'm locked out of my room. Twenty-four oh five?"

He looked at me with zero interest. "Can I see your ID?"

"I don't have it on me. Can you call Rob Chang's room?"

He typed a few things and then held the phone to his ear while staring over my head. "No answer," he said after a minute. Mandy had locked my phone in the room along with all our other stuff, so I didn't have anyone's cell numbers handy.

"What about Beckett Moore?" I asked.

The guy gave me a knowing look and didn't bother searching the computer. "We don't have a guest by that name."

I sighed and looked over my shoulder, wishing that someone in the band or crew would pass by. No such luck. "Look, maybe you recognize me? I'm the new lead singer for Melbourne?"

Front desk guy shook his head. "I don't know much about them."

"Well, you know they're staying here—we, we're staying here. And I need to talk to someone in the band or crew."

"Sorry, miss, I can't give out guest information."

"Can you look me up? I have a profile page on Melbourne's website. Will that be good enough to ID me?" Is there anything more pompous than asking a stranger to Google you?

He looked skeptical but started typing. He squinted at the computer screen, then at me. "This doesn't really look like you."

"It's called Photoshop. But trust me, it's me. And I really have to get into my room. We have a big show at the Fillmore tomorrow. If I get you two great seats and passes to the meet and greet, will you let me in?"

He looked around. The other front desk person was busy with another guest. "Make it four. And can I sell them online?"

That was ballsy, but I was desperate. "I don't care what you do."

"I'll let you in and then you produce your ID right away. If you can't, we come back downstairs and you leave the hotel."

"Deal."

The rest of that transaction was drama-free, thank God. Unless you count walking out of the elevator to see Malcolm sitting slumped against the wall and Mandy and Nathan making out, pressed up to our door. Awkward. I took front desk guy's name and promised to leave his passes downstairs in the morning.

"Good call keeping him upright," I said. "In case he pukes." I really knew how to enhance the romance in any situation.

Mandy pried her lips off of Nathan's. "That's what we were thinking. Okay, let's get him inside."

Since we weren't big partyers, Mandy and I had no idea what we were doing. Nathan talked us out of putting Malcolm into the bathtub and turning the shower on. "They only do that in movies, for, like, crack addicts," Nathan said. "Let him sleep it off, but not on his back. He'll know what to do when he wakes up. That didn't look like his first time working a bar."

We put Malcolm in my bed, and then I went to the bathroom to give Mandy and Nathan time to say a private goodbye. When I came back out, they still had their arms around each other. "Tell Corey we'll see you guys tomorrow night," Mandy said. She smiled as the door closed behind him.

"Well, that almost went as planned," I said.

"Chelsea, you're the best—best wingman, best everything. Malcolm has nothing on you." She came over and enveloped me in a hug, which almost made me not want to kill her. "I can't believe he was so bored he practically drank himself to death."

We looked at him. He was starting to snore. At least we knew he was still breathing.

16

*B*ands always described themselves as dysfunctional families, and after yesterday I understood why.

"Can you go wake Malcolm up? He's sleeping on the bus, but I'm afraid. He smells disgusting." Mandy pantomimed retching. We were in the production office, where she was trying to cobble together the passes we needed to accommodate everyone who'd participated in Malcolm's Ballin' Night Out. Pem had lots of family coming, so he'd taken all of the band passes.

"Why do *I* have to? Where's Rob?" With things like this it seemed only fair that actual family should draw the short straw.

Mandy dropped her face into her hands. "Dealing with show security. The venue wants us to pay for more because it's a heavy-drinking crowd. Since Miami's a vacation spot, everyone's ready to cut loose."

Wonderful. I wouldn't put it past Malcolm to go big two nights in a row.

The bus was unnervingly quiet. I walked into the sleeping cabin and stuck my hand into Malcolm's bunk approximately where I thought his ankle should be. I grabbed it and shook. There was a high-pitched squeal, followed by the curtain snapping open. I peered down at a girl with long, disheveled blond hair and red lips. She was really pretty, even with the murderous gleam in her eye. "Get dressed. Time for sound check!" I yelled past her.

I waited in the lounge, sensing that leaving them alone again was a bad idea. The girl stumbled out first, rumpled but dressed. "I'm Joelle," she said.

"Fantastic. Malcolm!"

"Jesus Christ. What?" He came out stark-naked.

My hands flew up to cover my eyes. "What is wrong with you?"

I heard kissing noises, murmuring, and then what I hoped was Joelle getting off the bus. "You can open your eyes now," Malcolm said.

I lowered my hands. He'd only put on underwear, but it was a start. He stood there grinning at me like a complete jackass.

"Weren't you on death's door a couple of hours ago?" I asked.

"It's amazing what Gatorade and Red Bull can do." He pulled a T-shirt over his head.

"Wow, maybe think about adding a shower to that mix." Alcohol seeped from his pores. I fanned the smell away.

The bus door opened and Beckett walked in. He stopped

short when he saw Malcolm standing in front of me getting his clothes on. "Am I interrupting?"

"Yeah, right." I didn't bother to hide my laughter.

Malcolm shook his head. "You could do a lot worse." He turned to Beckett. "Bartender from last night."

"Awesome idea to have sex with the girl who almost killed you," I said.

"Have you never seen a drunk person before?" Malcolm asked.

"Not as drunk as you."

"That was nothing."

"Everyone's looking for you guys," Beckett said as he walked back out. "You're late."

Outside the bus, I caught up to him. I hadn't seen him in a couple of days and he looked a little down. "Everything okay?" I asked. "Lauren stuff?"

He exhaled loudly. "That was rough, but nothing I haven't dealt with before."

I wondered what that meant.

Inside the venue, Mandy, Rob, and a couple of stagehands flew by with boxes, scrambling to set up the merch booth. Rob glared at me. "Everything is off schedule. That guest list bullshit ate her entire day."

"Okay," I said, confused. I wondered if he was going to get mad at Pem and Malcolm too.

"I told you, it's not her fault," Mandy said as she rushed past us.

Beckett looked at me. "I'm starting to be glad that I was MIA all day."

We walked toward the stage. "Wasn't Lauren's flight yesterday?"

"She was so angry, it kind of freaked me out. I just needed to be alone. She's been sad before, and I know she wants more of a commitment, but I always thought we were ultimately on the same page."

"You see each other when you swing through the Southeast and then forget about each other the rest of the time? Definitely a love story for the ages." I wanted him to be smarter and better than that.

"It doesn't sound like much, but it was great until it wasn't."

"Who are they?" I pointed to a preppy gang in the middle of the floor. It looked like Ralph Lauren dropped a bomb on the place.

Beckett glanced down. "Pem's cousins. He has like a million. I can never remember all their names. Some of them even went to Lowell with us."

"They flew in for the show?"

Beckett waved his hand. "They all have homes down here. Right near the grandmother."

Malcolm strolled onstage followed by a very harried-looking Pem. "This show's going to suck, just so you know," Beckett whispered. I gave him a quizzical look. "I'm just saying, Malcolm's wrecked, and Pem has family here. He's practically guaranteed to be off his game when his family's around. It's like he's embarrassed to be great at something they don't approve of."

"Why do they come if they're so against it?"

"Because. They're WASPs. They don't tell him to his face

that he should quit. They invite him to tennis and shake their heads in regret when he says he has to protect his wrist for playing. And they always ask him how 'work' is, like they want to pretend he has an office job."

The Fuller cousins listened politely, then applauded at the end of sound check. I did a little curtsy and then went to get ready for the meet and greet. As soon as we were offstage, Gray Matter swooped in to set up. I nodded hello but still didn't know them at all. Beckett made it a point to watch their set every show. Those poor guys were troupers. They never complained about being second-class citizens. They didn't get consistent sound checks and weren't even staying in the same hotel as us. Their budget only allowed for a single room in a dingy, highway-side motel.

I could almost understand that some bands might never accept me because I'd never had to rough it on a van tour. There was a whole band dues-paying thing that I hadn't gone through. And Melbourne, despite the fact that they were all trust fund kids, did do it the scrappy way. Their cred was so important to them; they never wanted other bands to be able to say that they didn't earn it. I decided to show some support and watch Gray Matter's set with Beckett. But first we had the meet and greet.

"We came down early to hang out, but Mandy's working, so she sent us in here," Nathan said, coming over to me. Awesome.

Across the crowded room, rogue front-desk guy caught my eye and raised his glass. His date looked like a stripper. Hopefully she, at least, was a Melbourne fan. I didn't see anyone with them, so I assumed he'd managed to sell the other two tickets.

By the doorway, Rob clapped for attention. "Okay, everyone! Let's wish these guys a great show and leave them to it!"

I didn't end up watching Gray Matter with Beckett, because I spent almost up until showtime babysitting Nathan and Corey. I tried to get Rob to escort them to the front of house. "Everyone's responsible for their own groupies," he snapped. I was about to tell him that they were Mandy's groupies, but I didn't want to get her in trouble.

Onstage, I had no feel for the audience, and my singing was all over the place. Drunk didn't begin to describe this crowd. The extra security we'd hired had their hands full, pushing people off the barricade so that they wouldn't get crushed. More than one smashed fan had to be carried off the floor. Beckett even spoke up between songs and asked people to ease up. My parting words of the night were "Don't drink and drive!" That met with a lot of sarcastic laughter.

Fortunately, Pem's performance wasn't good either. Technically he was flawless, as usual, but he was wooden and not all there. Hopefully he wouldn't notice my flubs.

Sam called a band-only meeting on the bus before we were even free to shower. "Show blew," he said. "I'm not going to ride you too hard about it because Atlanta and Orlando were great. Pem, if you can't deal with family, I'm going to have Rob ban them. Or at least limit the number."

"You thought I was bad? What about Malcolm?" Pem asked.

"Dude, my shit was on point," Malcolm said.

Sam ignored them both. "Chelsea, drunks at shows are a fact. Get used to it."

"Don't forget Beckett. He had a bad show too," Malcolm said. Beckett shot him a nasty look. "What? I'm keeping it real. If we're going to call people on the carpet, we shouldn't be exclusive about it."

"I never thought I'd be thanking Malcolm for holding the show together, but he totally did tonight. I dig the theatrics," Sam said.

Malcolm dismissed the compliment, but I could tell he was pleased. "Maybe we should bring Joelle on tour." He winked at me and I rolled my eyes.

Beckett was already talking with people outside when I headed toward the bus, so I started at the opposite end. Pem stopped on his way to the shower and signed for about every tenth person. Malcolm didn't appear to be anywhere nearby. So much for starting over with the fans.

Beckett made his way to me. "Sorry about 'Smash Cut.'"

His guitar had sounded slightly off during that song, and it bugged me to the point that I'd walked over and whispered, "One of your strings is out of tune."

He was already messing with the tuning pegs and said, "I *know*," through gritted teeth.

I wasn't trying to hassle him, but it was like having a mosquito in my ear. I was sure the audience hadn't noticed, but it yanked me right out of the zone. I moved a little farther down the line. "That's okay. Basically everything sucked tonight. And no big. You were on it." I shrugged and Beckett laughed. "How's it going?" I said to the boy in front of me. "Thanks for coming out."

"You guys are awesome! You know 'Parietals'? Every girl at my high school wanted to hook up to that song."

"Well, aren't you just the ladies' man!" It killed me that "Parietals" was still such a crowd-pleaser. Besides being a total Hollis trademark song, it still made me think of Mike Malloy. Beckett had been right, though: it hardly mattered that I didn't sound great on it, because the fans owned that song and sang it so loudly they drowned me out. I looked at the thing the boy wanted me to sign. "You sure?" I asked.

"Totally," he said, smirking at me. It was a naked picture of himself. In person, he was puffy, with fair hair and eyebrows and a face red from drinking. The picture wasn't much better. He reminded me of a pork chop. I scrawled my signature over his privates. "You covered the best part!"

"If you say so," I said.

His friends laughed and elbowed him. "We apologize for him," one of them said. "Hey, can we get a picture with you?"

I gave them a wary once-over. They were stupid, sure, but harmless enough. I called Beckett over to take their camera and then stood in front of them. "Say 'I love Chelsea,'" Beckett said.

They all screamed it in unison. Pork Chop inspected the picture while the others grabbed for the camera. "That's totally going on my Instagram!"

Beckett cracked up, getting way too much amusement from my discomfort.

Mandy had to work as soon as we got to St. Petersburg, so I didn't hear about her night with Nathan. Beckett and I borrowed bikes from Jannus Live, where we were playing that night, and rode to Flora Wylie Park. We hadn't worn swimsuits, but I couldn't resist going into the ocean in my shorts and T-shirt. The water was even warmer than it had been in Miami.

Beckett took off his shirt and dove in after me. He still had a rower's body, with well-muscled arms and shoulders. Lauren was a very lucky girl. He was acting more lighthearted than he had in a while. "You feeling better?" I asked.

"Yeah. We just need to pull it together. Can't have another lame show."

I dove down and did a handstand. My T-shirt billowed out, making me self-conscious even though my torso was under-water. I came up for air.

"Anyway, thanks for being cool to Lauren. I know she appreciated it," Beckett said.

"What are you going to do?"

He shrugged and lay into a back float, looking up at the sky.

Our blissful day was cut short by Beckett's writing session with Pem. When we got back to the bus, Pem was already set up with his guitar and laptop in the back lounge. "Did you work out that section?" Beckett asked.

"I feel like I'm circling like a seabird, surface feeding," Pem said.

"You'll get there," Beckett said. I had no idea how he understood what Pem was talking about half the time. It was one of the more mystifying parts of the dysfunction. "I'll be back."

"That's good, Beckett. You and Chelsea go have fun. I'll be here, working hard."

"It'll just take a minute." Beckett sounded like he was talking to a toddler. We ducked out, and Beckett decided it was a good time to give me advice. "The only way to change Pem's view of you as a hired gun is to write. I'm sending you a song that we finished. Try writing the lyrics." I gave him a skeptical look. "Nothing's going to be perfect right out of the gate. Just experiment. This has a simple structure: verse, chorus, verse, chorus, bridge, chorus. I think you can handle it."

"So does this mean you like me?" I had no idea where I was going with this.

Beckett smiled. "I like you fine."

"No way. If you're trying to help me win Pem over, you like me more than fine."

He laughed and I felt happy that someone was pulling for me. I opened my email and downloaded the file. I put headphones on and clicked play. The tempo was slower, but it was still definitely a rock song. When it was over, I played it again. And again. I played it until I memorized the song. But no words came.

Jannus Live was set up like a large, open-air courtyard. A few trees grew through the floor, giving it a friendly, backyard feel. Outdoor shows naturally have a celebratory atmosphere, which I was too freaked out to appreciate that first night in Pittsburgh.

I concentrated on the band as they started playing. Without the kabuki drop, I'd come up with this as my way to get pumped up for each show. It actually worked better. I blocked out everything and zeroed in on the building tension. The way those first bars sounded tonight told me this show would be something special. When I joined in, a floodgate opened— everyone's pent-up *stuff* came crashing down, including the crowd's.

Group catharsis was in full effect as the audience roared lyrics while I sang as hard and loud as I could. When I turned around, my bandmates were already lost in the music. Pem was back to his usual brilliant self, which let the rest of us relax. I caught Beckett's eye, but it was almost like he was looking through me.

I wasn't dumb enough to think about Beckett in any serious way. Pem had made himself perfectly clear on the intra-band fraternizing policy, plus I was in no rush to get my heart stomped on. But that didn't stop me from enjoying the view a little too much.

17

The band landed in LA early the next day and drove straight
to the studio to prep for the video. No rest for the weary. The
crew, including Mandy, would take the bus and meet us at our
next show. There had been some talk of them stopping in New
Orleans to celebrate the Fourth. That sounded fun but also
like potential trouble. I knew Oscar and Winston would look
out for Mandy if the partying got out of hand.

At the studio, we went over storyboards and wardrobe options and watched the extras casting. Beckett reviewed the
treatment for our video for Michaela, who'd come in to get us
ready for the private party in Vegas. "It's a simple concept, but
that's why we chose it. We're supposed to be disenchanted,
zombielike employees of a seedy club. After we've waited on
the last ungrateful customer, checked the last ID, finished
cleaning beer and food off the floor, and closed up for the

night, we live out our dreams of being a band. And that's when we come alive."

"And it's about how music elevates us from the drudgery of life," I said.

"Exactly. It's about the love of music saving people, helping them through unpleasant things," Beckett said.

"Maybe they should get better jobs," Michaela said.

Beckett thought that as the "employees," we should retain our band personas as we left the club, "because the music transformed them."

Pem felt that we should revert back to our zombie-employee selves: "The point is not that music gives you a new life. It's that it can lift you out of a dark moment and how that means something even if it's fleeting." He turned to Sam. "And I want the imaginary audience on stilts so they're looming over the band, and I want a rain machine on the whole time."

"You're barely even going to see any exterior when they're in the club," Sam pointed out.

"Even if it's only glimpses through the door and window, it'll still enhance the mood," Pem said.

"We don't have the budget for all that," Sam said.

"That seems fatalistic. Are we really trying to tell people that all music can give them is a temporary fix?" Beckett asked. "We want to affect lives, not just moments."

"That's too grandiose," Pem said.

"And the other way sounds too bleak," Beckett shot back.

Next to me, Malcolm mumbled, "See why I don't get involved in this shit?"

Sam threw his hands up. "We need to decide. Today. When we come back in two days, we're shooting, not talking."

"And the zombies, you know they're going back to their normal lives. They may or may not get that moment back. It's realistic and open-ended," Pem said.

"I get that. I think we want to say something different, something—yeah—more grandiose. Like if you live life focusing on the highs instead of the lows, you can have the exact same life but be a different person," Beckett said.

Malcolm leaned back in his chair, looking at the ceiling. "No one's going to be writing their dissertation on our video. We're just trying to get the song out there." Both Pem and Beckett glared at him. Malcolm groaned. "I want a divorce."

"Chelsea, thoughts?" Sam asked.

"I like the open-ended thing, but I also like the positivity idea," I began.

"Okay, never mind," Pem said.

"But wait. Wait. You know how in the 'Thriller' video, Michael Jackson starts out human and ends up human but then turns back to the camera and flashes his monster eyes so you know it wasn't just a dream? Can it be something like that, where we go back to the way we were but acknowledge that something's not the same?"

Pem and Beckett looked at each other. Beckett sighed. "We need an hour."

Malcolm and I killed time in the strip mall down the road. He spent the entire time texting and tweeting, lining up "honeys" for Vegas. When we got back, Pem and Beckett were in much better moods. "We're taking Chelsea's suggestion and have them going back to being zombie people but then burn the club down," Pem said.

I squinted at him. "Wait, what? What happened to positivity?" I didn't even have a minute to celebrate my creative contribution, because in my mind that idea was in no way related to my suggestion.

"It is positive. Positive in an edgy way. The club where they work had them depressed, shackled to meaningless jobs. Now, even though they're the same people, they're sticking together to break free and move on to something better. Plus it works as a reference to the album title," Beckett said.

I'd never really thought about what *Barn Burning* meant, but Pem had explained that it was the title of a great short story by William Faulkner. Something about oppression and railing against authority.

Beckett and Pem both seemed exhilarated. I'd never gotten to witness this before—the spark they so obviously felt when they were connecting creatively. I kept staring at them, and Malcolm must have thought I was about to object, because he said, "Don't rock the boat," out of the side of his mouth.

Even though I thought their idea was weird and maybe even nonsensical, I was jealous that Pem and Beckett complemented each other so well in the creative process. They were lucky to have each other.

All of a sudden, the meaning of what they'd been saying hit me with complete clarity. It was one thing to practice and perfect singing someone else's words. That was a true craft. It was a whole other level of satisfaction to deliver something you created to an audience and feel how they were affected. That was art.

18

The electronics company that hired us for the private party in Vegas put us up at the Delano, which was part of Mandalay Bay. That's where it would host the very swanky launch of its newest cell phone later that night. We each had our own suite furnished with enormous gift bags. They contained all kinds of gadgets, including their best-selling video game console and their brand-new phone. My first swag. I almost felt like a real celebrity.

We didn't play until ten, so there was plenty of time to kill. Malcolm invited a bunch of girls to hang by the pool, and Beckett and Pem decided to join. Shocker. That left me to go shopping solo.

A woman at the front desk told me that the monorail that ran between some of the properties was the easiest way to get around. It was also a great way to get a quick tour of Vegas. I passed a few crazy-looking hotels—one in the shape of a pyramid, one that looked like a castle, another that was a scaled-down version of New York City. Everything was huge and colorful. I wasn't even on street level and I was still overwhelmed.

I got off at the end of the line and went to Saks Fifth Avenue, straight to the hip and expensive department, and introduced myself to a young saleswoman named Paris. "I'm performing at a private party tonight and I've been told to wear something modern and kind of sexy," I said. I was paraphrasing. Michaela's exact words were "Wear something hot so you get photographed a lot."

Paris gave me a once-over. "Performing where you eventually take your clothes off?"

"God no." I should have worded my request better. I hoped I hadn't offended her with my response. Maybe she was a salesperson by day and an exotic dancer by night. "The performance is outside, late. I'd like to wear something comfortable but attention-getting. Something that I won't feel weird hanging out in after the show."

"Uh-huh." Paris looked at me like I'd ordered a dress made out of steak knives and rabbit tails. "Comfortable? That's a priority?"

"I mean, within reason." I followed her around the floor while she plucked items off racks and threw them over her arm. She didn't ask me who I was or where I was performing, so I assumed she thought I was full of it.

Paris staggered to the dressing room under all the clothes. She arranged them in outfits and hung them on pegs, curating as she went. "Okay, I mostly went with pants for comfort. You're going to have to invest in shoes. I mean seriously invest. And not in comfortable ones either. Now, if you go with pants, you need to be all about the boobs. You said attention-getting, right?"

"Right." I tried to sound confident, and reassured myself it was just for one night of pictures.

The next thing I knew, I was trying on a billion outfits. She had me step out wearing the first few, sometimes not even taking a full second to evaluate before sending me back to change. "No. Next!"

I tried on a pair of black harem pants, which I had no idea they still made. Paris paired it with a clingy white sleeveless shirt with a plunging V-neck. She wasn't kidding when she said it was all about the boobs. I hadn't worn anything like this since our press day back in Pittsburgh. I liked the way the harem pants draped over my hips and butt—less obvious than tight pants but still did the job. There was also a skinny leather tie that I decided to ignore.

When I came out, she said, "Where's the tie?"

"Uh. I didn't see one."

Paris stormed into the dressing room and grabbed it off the lounge chair. She expertly wrapped it around my neck, letting the knot hang low. "Half Windsor. Don't do a full or it'll look stupid." She stepped back. "I need to see it with shoes. Wait here. And don't change."

I hated to say it, but Paris was right about the tie.

I sat on the lounge chair and checked my phone for Mandy's latest text.

Me: How was Nathan?
Mand: Dorky but adorbs :)

Me: ?

Mand: No. Too weird.

I didn't know what she meant by "too weird," but it seemed like a longer conversation than I had time for.

Paris reappeared with boxes. As she opened them, I was sure she'd meant to bring these to a drag queen in the next dressing room. The first box contained a pair of white peep-toe stilettos with a hidden platform and gold spikes all over them. Yikes. "Just humor me," she said.

I put them on. They weren't remotely comfortable but added a definite pop to the outfit. Surprisingly, I liked the overall effect. "Do you stand onstage? Or sit?" Paris asked.

"I stand. And jump. And sometimes even run," I said.

"That's not going to work, then."

She pulled out another pair. A black pair of high-heeled booties with a web of straps crisscrossed all over the front. They weren't as eye-catching as the other two, but they were cool. "I can live with it," she said. "They reference the tie. Only you need a better bra."

I wasn't sure if she was just trying to upsell me, but honestly I didn't care. She asked my bra size, took off again, and returned with a bunch of nude bras. She made me try each of them on under the white shirt until we found one that pushed me up and out ridiculously far. "Good," she said. "Now, you're going to think I'm crazy, and I don't know if it's within your budget, but I'd get the boots for the show and the shoes with the spikes for hanging out after."

She spent more time with me in the cosmetics department and even showed me how to do my hair. I was so grateful, I told her to text me later if she wanted to get into the party. She lit up. "You're in Melbourne? Oh my God, I'd love to! Do you think they'll give out free phones?"

"Probably," I said, even though I had no idea.

All I could think about was how I'd spent more money on clothes in one shot than I'd previously spent in an entire year.

By the time I got back, Malcolm was out cold, poolside, snoring with a bevy of beauties surrounding him. I mean, come on.

Pem and Beckett were still hanging out too. Pem had his nose in a magazine, but Beckett was being social. They'd gotten a cabana, and the staff was doing its best to keep people away, but they were definitely attracting interest.

I was stopped on my way into the cabana. "Is she good to come in?" one of the staff asked Beckett.

"I guess," Beckett sighed, before cracking up.

The staff member hesitated, but I barged in. "Thanks," I snapped.

"Did you buy us anything?" Beckett asked.

"No." I slipped out of my shorts and T-shirt.

I walked back out of the cabana and down the steps of the nearest pool. It was empty because the Lazy River and wave pool were so popular. I sat on the lower steps, getting cool, watching the blur of action around me.

Workers set up the stage in the center on a platform that covered one of the pools. The stage itself was complete, but they were in the process of putting up a screen in the back and adjusting the few spotlights in the front. It was a smaller stage than we were used to, and I wondered if I could get away with wearing the ridiculous shoes the whole time. I felt a tingle of excitement about the party.

A shadow fell over me, giving welcome relief from the late afternoon sun. I looked up as Beckett slid into the water beside me. "Did you take care of the wardrobe issue?" he asked.

I shrugged. "I think Michaela would approve."

He laughed. "Can't wait to see it."

Something about the way he said it flustered me. After a minute I said, "Lazy River?"

Beckett pulled two inner tubes out of a pile and handed me one. We waited for a break in floating traffic and then waded down the steps into the river. I lay across my inner tube with my butt in the middle. Beckett stretched across his on his stomach. I closed my eyes, letting the current take me for a ride.

Every now and then, other floaters jostled me, but I didn't open my eyes. Then freezing-cold water doused me, making me squeal and sit up on my elbows. I opened my eyes and turned to see that I'd just passed under a bridge with a waterfall. Beckett was laughing at me from the other side of the river—the one without the downpour.

He kicked over to me once I'd cleared the bridge. He grabbed one of the handles of my inner tube and hung on. "You can close your eyes again. I'll keep you away from waterfalls."

We'd all agreed to be at the party by eight. Up in my room, I put the finishing touches on my makeup and pulled my hair back as Paris had instructed. After I sprayed it down so it wouldn't move, I reached for my tie.

I tried a few different ways of tying the knot, thinking I remembered what Paris did. But she'd done it so quickly that I missed a step. I got my phone and searched "tie tying." I forgot what Paris called the specific kind of knot. Despair was setting in. I did not want to walk into that party by myself.

There was a knock at the door and I rushed to open it.

"Come on. You don't want to miss the fireworks." Beckett looked so amazingly handsome. He wore dark jeans and a black blazer over a black T-shirt.

"You dressed up," I blurted out, then noticed that he was staring at me too. The bra might have been too much. "Do I look like a cartoon?"

"Yeah. I mean, no. Yeah, I dressed up for the photos too and no, you don't look like a cartoon." He cleared his throat and looked away.

I somehow felt better knowing that I wasn't the only one who had to look different tonight. "Can you help me for a sec?"

He didn't ask questions as he followed me into the bathroom. I handed him my tie. "She said to tie it in a half nelson or something. I don't remember."

He smiled down at me, trying not to laugh. "Half Windsor?"

"Yes!" I spun around and faced the mirror. Beckett got behind me and expertly tied the tie. I hoped he couldn't feel how fast my heart was beating, or at least that he'd attribute it to something other than his arms being around me. He watched me slide the knot out a little so that it hung lower, then reached around me again to tighten it a little more. We stood for a moment before I turned to face him. "Perfect. Guess being a WASP is good for something."

He turned away. "That's quite an outfit you picked out."

I forced myself to snap out of it. "I know. So not me. Wait till you see the shoes."

I slid into the gold-spiked heels and then held up the black booties. "What am I supposed to do with these? Paris told me to wear the gold ones unless I was performing."

"Who's Paris?"

"She picked all this out."

Beckett took the boots from me and tucked them under his arm. "I think I like Paris." He held the door open, and I walked past quickly so he wouldn't see me reddening. But I had to admit, I was pleased he noticed.

19

"Anyone know who's throwing this thing?" Pem asked as we surveyed the scene in front of us. The electronics company had slapped its logo and name on everything—banners, the screen behind the stage, tablecloths, even the cocktail napkins. "I feel like a whore."

The company knew how to throw a party. There was a mermaid ice statue in the middle of an enormous sushi spread. The taco station offered made-to-order guacamole and specialty margaritas. A pig turned on a spit for some kind of barbecue sandwich.

Beckett walked to the bar setup closest to the stage and asked the bartender to stash my booties behind it. While he was there, he ordered a beer.

"Don't tell me you're feeling festive," I said. The sun had set, but it was still too light for fireworks. I loved this time of the day, when shadowed objects defined the edges of the sky.

"I'll get there." He looked at his phone for the fiftieth time. I felt bad. I knew he'd been text-fighting with Lauren over the past few days. "Can I get you something?" he asked.

"Vodka tonic?" I picked something clear in case I spilled.

He looked skeptical. "You sure?"

"Just tell them to put lots of ice in it."

Beckett turned back to the bartender, then handed me my drink. "Just don't go overboard. At least until after we play."

Malcolm and Pem came over with drinks. "Cheers," I said, holding my cup up.

"Cheers." We all clinked our plastic cups together. I smiled.

"Chelsea, you look smokin'," Malcolm said.

Beckett shot him an irritated look. It was so quick I immediately wondered if I'd imagined it.

"You guys all look great too," I said. Like Beckett, Pem and Malcolm had dressed up but still kept their rocker vibe. I'd never seen Malcolm perform with a shirt before.

Malcolm went off to figure out who he was going to pick up. I noticed a white backdrop against the hotel wall. A woman with two cameras slung around her neck adjusted large light reflectors.

"Should we get pictures out of the way?" I asked.

Beckett shrugged, downing his beer. "Come on, man," he said to Pem, then led the way.

The photographer clapped when she saw us. "Perfect! Let's do these now and then I'll be taking pictures during your show. You'll also see me wandering around getting candids with my assistant later. Wonderful! Okay. Where's the other one?"

Beckett went to reel Malcolm in while the photographer

took some pictures of me with Pem. "These are just test shots. Try to relax."

I attempted to breathe and smile naturally. When Beckett and Malcolm reappeared, relief flooded my body. "Wow, what a difference," the photographer said. "Anyone who thinks chemistry between people isn't a real thing should photograph them for a couple of days. Okay. This is for real now." She started snapping away.

"Oh my God. Is that Vanessa Thomas?" Malcolm asked.

"What? Where?" I asked, turning to look. If Vanessa Thomas, the famous swimsuit model, was here, I wanted to see her too.

"Please don't geek out on us now," Malcolm said, although he wasn't being too subtle about looking either.

"She's even hotter in person," Pem said.

"Guys, camera," the photographer said. Apparently the boys had come to life, because she muttered, "There we go. Just give me a pretty girl. I should keep one handy at all times." Part of me wanted to laugh, but the other part of me felt like chopped liver. "Okay, we're done."

Another group moved in front of the backdrop. I recognized them from a TV sitcom. They had a fresh-scrubbed-but-still-fabulous air about them.

A thin whistling sound made everyone look up. The first firework exploded, a short burst of red, white, and blue pompoms.

"Come on." Beckett led us to some lounge chairs. We tilted them back so we could look directly up at the sky. I didn't take my eyes off the fireworks for the next half hour. At one point, I felt Beckett watching me, smiling while I oohed and aahed over all the colors, especially the ones big enough to illuminate the sky.

After the finale, I stood up and went to the bar for my boots. The cute bartender came over. "Vodka tonic, right?" I hesitated but nodded. He fixed me a new drink and handed me my boots. "Have a great show."

I wished Mandy were here. This poolside party on the Strip was epic, just like she'd predicted. The mood of the party was so celebratory and decadent, I imagined it was like prom—only with more attractive people, better food, real drinks, and a million times more fun.

"Thanks for coming out to celebrate the launch of the Stratospheric, our newest mobile smartphone!" the CEO of the electronics company said into the mike. "We'll be announcing a few lucky raffle prizewinners throughout the evening. We've already given away three Stratospherics! And to help us kick things into high gear, we've invited the hottest band in America to play for you."

Cheers erupted from the guests. "Please welcome . . . Melbourne!" she yelled.

Screams and whistles rang in my ears as I adjusted the mike stand downward. "How's everyone doing?" I asked. More screams and cheers. "We're excited to play for you tonight!" Pem had agreed to let me do most of the talking because this was a "low-risk environment" for me to practice my frontwoman skills.

Malcolm counted off and we launched into our first song. We played fast and loud, and I imagined we could be heard up and down the Strip. Most guests clustered around the stage, but there were people hanging back, enjoying their conversations. I gave myself the challenge of drawing them into the show.

After our fourth song, I addressed the crowd. "Is this the sickest party you've ever been to or what?" That got loud screams. Beckett started the next song. We'd decided to only play up-tempo songs, but people in the audience yelled for "Smash Cut." I looked at Beckett.

A fan had shot concert video of this song and posted it online. It wasn't supposed to be released as a single at all (even though he wrote the lyrics, Pem said it was "too on the nose"), but now Sam and the label were talking about it as a third single due to all the views.

"Let's give the people what they want," Beckett said.

When he joined in, he sounded so, so good. I fell more in love with the way we harmonized every time we sang this song. I'd never asked him about it, but I think he did too.

We finished to wild applause. "Beckett Moore, ladies." He shot me a quick smile and winked. He'd better appreciate me; this song got him more longing stares from girls than any of our others.

Our contracted hour was up, but the crowd wanted us to keep going, and we were having a great time. We played a couple more songs before saying good night. "We've loved playing for you, but the night's not over yet! Thanks again for inviting us!"

I hopped offstage, changed my shoes again, and slipped my boots back to my bartender. "Do you mind?"

He took them and handed me a new drink. I hadn't even had time to drink the last one. "Great show. You're amazing."

"Glad you enjoyed it!" I said. He was really cute.

145

"I get off at one. If you're still here, maybe I could show you around?" He had a self-assured, almost overconfident look.

"Uh, okay. If I'm still awake." I was sure I wouldn't be; we'd scheduled an early flight back to LA.

"Great. I'm Ben. I'll find you." His warm smile made me think I should reconsider. Maybe an older guy was what I needed. Maybe I could skip right over teenage boys.

I spotted Malcolm and Pem chatting up Vanessa Thomas. She was stunning in person. I started over, hoping to find Beckett before I had to interrupt them.

Someone grabbed my arm. "Hey. I may not have your number, but I still tracked you down."

Oh my God. Lucas Rivers. He smirked at me, his blue eyes bright with flirtation. "Took you long enough," I said.

He laughed. "I'm happy to see you. That was a killer show." He gave me a subtle once-over, somewhere between admiring and leering. He wore jeans and a white button-down shirt that showed off his tanned skin.

"What are you doing here?" I asked.

"I wanted to check out the new Stratospheric, of course," Lucas said. I narrowed my eyes. "They have a product placement deal with my next movie. I came to show the love. And when I heard you were going to be here, well, that was the icing on the cake."

The photographer came by, her assistant in tow, holding a light. "Can I get some shots of you two?"

"Of course," Lucas said. He took my drink and set it down on a table out of the shot. He walked back, holding my gaze, then slid his arm around my waist.

"Fantastic!" the photographer said. I'm sure my smile was ten miles wide, and I wasn't even faking it.

"Have I mentioned how stunning you look tonight?" Lucas asked, his voice low so only I could hear.

"Actually, no," I said.

"Think fun, you guys!" the photographer called.

"Should we give her some good stuff?" Lucas asked me. I nodded, struck dumb by the improbability of it all. He reached for my tie, wound it around his hand, and pulled me in close so that the distance between us disappeared. "How's that?" he asked without taking his eyes off me.

"Phenomenal!" she said.

I could barely breathe. The photographer continued to encourage us even though we hadn't moved, and she was getting the same shot over and over. At the last minute, Lucas leaned down and kissed the tip of my nose, somehow striking the perfect balance between affectionate and sexy.

He let go of me, the sudden space between us feeling like a cold whoosh of air.

The photographer stopped snapping. "You guys make my job easy." She and her assistant went off in the direction of Malcolm, Pem, and Vanessa. I was positive she'd get some good pictures there too.

"Look for that one tomorrow," he said. Of course he could be casual—his pictures showed up in magazines all the time. "Are you in Vegas long?"

"We go back to LA tomorrow," I said.

"What a coincidence. So do I," Lucas said. "You want a ride?"

"Thanks, but we're flying. We have to go right to work on our video."

He chuckled. "Yeah, I'm flying too. I meant, do you want to come on my private jet? The studio hired it for me."

I tried to play it off like I wasn't impressed, but I wasn't sure it worked. "Maybe another time." I barely knew him. I wasn't sure flying off with him into the sunset was the smartest idea.

"At least let me take you out in LA," Lucas said. "Do you have time for dinner tomorrow?"

I tilted my head. Was this really happening? "I don't know when we'll be done shooting."

He walked over to the table to retrieve my drink. He handed it to me and took out his phone. "Can I get your number now?"

He dialed it into his phone, then tapped send and waited for my voice mail to pick up. I'd left my phone in my room. "Hi, Chelsea. It's Lucas. I really hope you'll let me take you out in LA. Give me a call. Shoot me a text. Whatever. I'll make myself available whenever you're free. Can't wait." He hung up, and naturally I was grinning like an idiot.

"Let's see how tonight goes. Then I'll let you know about dinner." I took his hand.

"Fair enough," Lucas said.

The rest of the night passed in a blur. Lucas and I sat near a fire pit, out of the way of most of the action. Out of the corner of my eye, I saw Beckett glance in my direction and then leave the party, phone still in hand. Ben finished his shift at the bar and sat down for a drink with a tall brunette. I even thought I saw Paris dancing with some girls. I definitely noticed Pem and Malcolm playing some kind of drinking game with Vanessa and a group of what had to be model friends.

But none of it mattered at the moment. Lucas wanted to know everything that had happened to me since we last saw each other. He filled me in on what he'd been doing—finishing up reshoots for his next movie, taking some time off before starting press on his current one.

Before long, it felt like we'd actually known each other, that we hadn't just shared some random makeout session in a bathroom. Lucas was attentive and charming, and just like last time I found myself caught up in his spell.

I had no idea what time it was when a couple of men came over to tell Lucas it was time to go. He introduced me to his publicist and manager. Then he leaned in, not caring that they were still standing there. "Don't forget to check your voice mail," he whispered before he kissed me.

20

The next morning, we climbed into a town car. We all wore dark glasses and didn't speak a single word to one another. Beckett sat up front with the driver and stared straight out the window.

Malcolm was my seatmate on the plane, and all he said was "Again with the douche bag?" Then he yawned and fell asleep.

When we arrived at the studio, Sam took one look at us and made us down coffee and water. We perked up a little and got to work, but it still felt pretty hellish.

"When the patrons finally leave the club, there should be a moment of recognition, like a pause or breath before we go into the song," Pem said.

"Okay, we'll all breathe before picking up our instruments," Beckett said.

"You know what I mean," Pem said.

"No, I really don't." If Beckett didn't know what Pem was saying, we were in serious trouble.

Michaela came to the set in the afternoon. She and Sam huddled over her laptop. When our director let us take a break, we went over to see what they were looking at.

"I love you guys. I ask and you deliver. Look at these." Michaela scrolled through pictures from last night.

There were hundreds. The ones with the four of us were first. We looked a little stiff, but it could be read as aloof and cool. The pictures of Pem and Malcolm with Vanessa Thomas were hilarious. They were mostly Malcolm and Vanessa doing ridiculous poses and Pem looking on and laughing.

When we got to my pictures with Lucas, I sucked in a breath. The photographer had released what seemed like every single millisecond of our exchange.

"If you played them in a sped-up slide show, you'd basically have it on video. And I did not authorize video," Michaela grumbled. "This is my favorite one." She clicked on a frame and enlarged it.

It was the moment Lucas reached for my tie. My expression was guarded, nervous, but it could be mistaken for flirty. His was all cocky and suggestive. I reminded myself that he was an actor.

"And then there's this one." Michaela clicked on another photo. It was the kiss on the nose. My eyes were closed. I looked like I was in ecstasy, but it was just because he'd moved in so suddenly.

There were groans behind me, a chorus of big brothers.

"I'm already getting calls, asking if this is a thing," Michaela said. Everyone looked at me, waiting for an answer.

"I don't know if it's a thing," I said. "I might have dinner with him while we're here."

"If you don't do it someplace private, it'll turn into a circus," Michaela said. "Not that I'm complaining."

Pem sneered. "Does that guy know how to do anything in private? I'm pretty sure I saw a video of his morning grooming routine, and it wasn't even supposed to be funny."

I walked away irritated and made up my mind right then to text Lucas. *Dinner at 8?*

My phone pinged with an immediate answer. *Thought you'd never ask. Make it 9. I'll pick u up. Txt address.*

I looked up to find Beckett watching me. I forced myself to stop smiling. "Hey. You disappeared last night. Was everything okay with Lauren?"

"I ended it."

I was surprised that he looked so bummed out about it. "Are you okay?"

"I'm fine. Thanks." His expression was neutral, hard to read. I wondered if he was lying.

Lucas didn't say where we were going, so when the shoot wrapped for the day, I stayed in my video "show" outfit. It was strapless, black with a fitted bustier top and a full, ruffled skirt. It was more date-appropriate than anything else I'd brought with me, but I practically had to sign my name in blood for the wardrobe coordinator, promising that I wouldn't ruin or lose the dress.

I went to the dressing room to wash off my makeup then reapplied a toned-down version. I left my hair pinned behind my ears with fat, demure curls that rolled over my shoulders. It made me look like a starlet from the 1920s.

My phone pinged. *Sending Ray in to get you.*

I threw my phone and lipstick in my bag and walked to the front door. A large man waited, arms crossed. "Chelsea?" he asked. I nodded. "I remember you. From the bathroom at the Roxy." Terrific. He held the door open for me and I walked through, trying to hold my head high.

Ray opened the back door of the black SUV that idled in front. I slid in next to Lucas. "Ray remembers me," I said. "From the bathroom." I made a face.

"Hey, Ray. You gotta keep that stuff to yourself, man," Lucas called to the front seat.

"Always do," Ray replied.

I could not have been more uncomfortable. We pulled into traffic. "Hi." Lucas leaned in to kiss me. "You look gorgeous."

"Thanks. You look nice too." I mean, talk about stating the obvious. Even after last night, Lucas Rivers giving me a casual kiss hello wreaked havoc on my conversation skills. I looked out my window. "Where are we going?"

"My friend's turning twenty-one and she's having a party out in Malibu." He took my hand and brushed his thumb across my palm.

Malibu! I'd always wanted to go. (On *Pop Star* we spent a week rehearsing with our coaches in what was supposedly a luxurious Malibu beach house, but it was really in Santa Monica.) I tried to enjoy being whisked through the streets of LA and holding Lucas's hand, but instead I fiddled with the automatic door lock. The clicking noise of the locking and unlocking wasn't exactly unobtrusive. Lucas smiled. "Nervous?"

"Should I be?" I asked.

"I don't know. But if you are, it's pretty cute."

When I didn't react, he elbowed me, eliciting a reluctant and decidedly uncool grin from me. I had to stop acting like I won our date in a contest. "I just like to know where I'm going. It has nothing to do with the fact that you're . . . you."

Lucas laughed and pulled me closer. "You know me," he said.

I looked at my phone. Committing to a late night wasn't the best idea. Oh well, that's what concealer and retouching were for.

The drive out there was epically long and not particularly scenic in the dark. Sitting nestled against Lucas's side with my head resting on his shoulder as we wound up canyon roads relaxed me after what I realized had been a very long day.

We finally stopped in front of a house that was concealed by trees and hedges with a few black SUVs just like the one we were in, parked in front. Lucas, Ray, and I hurried between them to dodge the paparazzi stationed across the road. It was a tight squeeze and my dress snagged on a grille, but I freed myself before the photographers got close. They kept shouting our names. I couldn't believe they knew it was me already.

Behind the hedges, paper lanterns hanging from trees lit up the small yard. Closer to the door, two women dressed as mermaids—totally realistic with tails, shell bras, and six-pack abs—lounged by a long, narrow indoor/outdoor pool. "Is this a costume party?" I asked.

"They provide atmosphere," Lucas whispered, chuckling. "I knew this party was going to be nuts."

A glass wall separated the outdoor portion of the pool from the indoor. The living room was visible beyond the pool. People danced with their arms waving high in the air and wore costumes ranging from togas to gypsy dresses (anything "exotic" and culturally appropriative seemed acceptable). As we walked in, a couple of guys came up to us. "Hey, man. You should leave. It's half past ugly."

"Really? Shit. Should have made an appearance earlier." He nodded to me. "This is Chelsea Ford, lead singer of Melbourne." Lucas introducing me with my credentials made me uneasy, like I had to justify being there.

"Awesome."

"That's cool. You're the new one, right?"

I guessed these guys weren't big music fans. "Thanks. Pretty new, I guess." I smiled. My gaze drifted to an open room filled with soft, plush couches and chairs. Guests sat on floor pillows, partaking in the four hookahs that were stationed on a low, square coffee table.

"No you did not! You did not show up to my party three hours late!" A skinny girl with long dark hair arranged in beachy waves wearing a sari staggered over to us and draped herself on Lucas. "Hi, babe."

Lucas did his best to shift her into a self-supported standing position. "Hi there. Happy birthday!"

Recognition suddenly hit me. The birthday girl was none other than Kate Martin, Hollywood royalty and Lucas's ex. "Why did you come so late? Did you bring me a present?" Her words slurred together, and she kept stroking his neck with long manicured fingernails. I was about to excuse myself and go smoke whatever was in those hookahs when Kate noticed me. "Who are you?" she asked, except it sounded like "Whore yuuuhhh?"

Lucas grabbed my hand before I could run. "This is Chelsea."

I watched Kate take in our linked hands and add everything up in her addled—but now legal—brain. "What?"

"Yeah, I wanted to stop by and say happy birthday, but we have to go. Chelsea has an early morning."

"Is that a hole in your dress?" Kate pointed. I looked down and saw a rip in the bodice from where it must have caught on the SUV. Kate wobbled forward, stuck a finger in the hole, and tugged. A sickening tearing sound ensued. I shrieked. At first I couldn't look. "Oops," she said.

Lucas got between us. "Oops? Are you freaking kidding me?" He was loud enough that heads started to turn. I felt the rip in my dress. Now the top ruffle was also hanging off of it. I had to hold the fabric closed with my hand.

One of Lucas's friends stepped forward. "Dude, dude. Just get out while you still can. It's her birthday and she wants to be a bitch."

Ray ushered us back outside. Cameras instantly went off in our faces. I shielded my eyes with my clutch. "You brought me to your ex's birthday party?"

"We've been broken up for over a year. We're supposed to be in the friend zone." Lucas put a hand on my waist. "Trust me, I thought she was way over it, otherwise I wouldn't have gone near that place." We climbed into our SUV, flashbulbs still going off all around us. "I'm sorry. Really." Lucas leaned over and kissed my cheek.

"I don't mean to be freaking out over a dress, but I have to shoot in this tomorrow. Wardrobe is going to flay me alive."

Lucas pulled out his phone and started texting. "Ray, let's stop by my place."

At least there was less traffic this late at night. We pulled up in front of Chateau Marmont. "You live here?" I asked.

"Just while my house is being redone," Lucas said.

"I really should get back to my hotel." I was already cringing about Pem's reaction when he found out Lucas had taken me here. He was of the opinion that the Chateau was a played-out Hollywood nightmare "where D-listers go to OD."

"Just come in for a little while," Lucas said. We hurried inside before anyone could spot us. "You can take off. I'll drive her home," Lucas said to Ray.

"I don't think that's a good idea," Ray said.

"It'll be okay." Lucas opened the door into a spacious, beautifully decorated suite. He went into the bedroom and came out with a sweatshirt and a pair of shorts. "You can put these on."

I was about to ask him if he seriously thought I was going to fall for that when there was a knock at the door. Lucas opened it and let in a tall, very thin, impeccably dressed African American woman. She was young, probably in her twenties, but her humorless expression made her seem older.

"This is my assistant, Lisette." He turned to her. "We have a dress situation."

"Can I see it?" she asked. I gestured down at myself. "You need to take it off so I can look at the tags."

I looked at Lucas and he held his hands up as if to say "Don't look at me." I took the clothes he'd given me and brought them into the bathroom. I didn't even have time to put them on before Lisette handed the dress back. "I got what I needed."

When I went back to the living room, she was talking on one phone, texting on another. "Hey, Maria, I have a dress that was being used for the Melbourne video shoot." She went on to describe the dress. "Call me ASAP. It's, uh, size eight." She glanced at me as she said the size. I knew what she was thinking. She typed on her phone then made another call. She left a few more messages.

"If this dress exists, it'll be delivered to the studio first thing." Before I could thank her, she said, "It looks like it was let out in certain places, so they'll need time to fit it." She took my number and left.

I turned to Lucas. "She's . . . efficient."

He laughed. "I should take you back." He came over to hug me.

"I'm going to get fired for screwing up the video," I murmured into his shoulder.

"They'd be crazy to lose you. You kick Hollis Carter's ass."

We kissed for a really long time. Unfortunately, I was hyperconscious of the fact that I was in a hotel room with a movie star. It detracted from the moment more than would have been ideal.

The valet attendant ran to get Lucas's car as soon as we approached. Even at this hour, photographers crowded the entrance, so we ducked back into the lobby. An obnoxious, neon-yellow hybrid coupe pulled in front of the building. Paparazzi rushed down the block. The valet opened the door and Lucas said, "Let's go."

We climbed in and shut the doors as fast as we could. Given the color of Lucas's car, we couldn't have made it easier for the paparazzi to follow if we'd mounted the Bat-Signal on top of it.

Lucas screeched out onto the street in a scary, reckless way. I held on to the door handle and the side of my seat. "I do this all the time," he said, like that was comforting. "My mom hates it."

He made a quick cut to change lanes. While it was sweet that he wanted to see me home, I was too busy fearing for my life to get all sappy about it. I closed my eyes, hoping the ride would be over soon.

We made a few sharp turns and then skidded to a stop. He turned to me. "Normally I like longer goodbyes, but . . ."

I gave him a peck on the lips, then jumped out. I hurried through the lobby toward the elevator bank, unable to shake the feeling of being chased.

Out of the corner of my eye, I noticed Beckett sitting in the hotel restaurant. He was deep in conversation with a girl. They sat on the same side of a banquette, and he had an arm around her, his hand casually stroking her hair. Who was she, and why hadn't he ever mentioned her?

I was so busy analyzing the situation that I was still standing there, gaping, when Beckett glanced over. He freed his hand from the girl's hair, but before he could wave I turned and walked away. Clearly he had plenty of shoulders to cry on.

21

The rest of the video shoot was an ordeal. Even though the dress did exist, was delivered on time, and was paid for by Lucas, Lisette had been right; it needed altering and that shut production down for two hours.

To say that Sam and the guys were furious would be a mild understatement. By the time shooting started, no one would talk to me. I felt like crying, but that would only have angered them more. We were all tense because we had to fly out the next day no matter what.

The dress was only the beginning; none of the other problems were my fault, but the shortened time frame definitely tightened the noose. Most of the delays had to do with Pem's and Beckett's differing creative visions. Beckett was more obstinate than usual. I couldn't figure out what was going on with him. I just wanted to get back to tour so things could be normal.

We worked late into the night, so I couldn't have called Lucas even if I'd wanted to. He didn't call me either, so I figured he was sufficiently turned off by my dress meltdown. I sent him a text thanking him and offered to reimburse him.

By the time we wrapped, we had the video but were all tired and miserable. Upon landing in Houston, we took a car service to the Bayou Music Center. I was practically holding my eyes open with my fingers. All four of us climbed on board our bus and promptly fell asleep.

I'd heard that some people went stir-crazy from the repetitiveness of touring, but not me. When it was time for sound check, I bounded onto the stage, thrilled to be back. The guys seemed to feel the same way; nothing was said about the acrimonious shoot, but I could tell we hadn't quite put it behind us.

I caught up with Mandy before the meet and greet. She'd seen party pictures from Vegas and some paparazzi shots of me and Lucas in LA. "Don't show those to anyone," I said. "Those guys already think Lucas is awful; if they find out he took me to the Chateau, they'll be brutal."

"And you care why?" Mandy gave me an incredulous look. "You went out with Lucas Freakin' Rivers. Those guys can suck it. Vanessa Thomas is a sun-damaged hag. Which one ended up with her, anyway? Beckett?" My displeasure at that idea must have been written all over my face. "Whoa. Down, girl," Mandy said. "Only because he's the most normal."

"I don't even want to know. Those guys think I'm a train wreck, Lucas thinks I'm a drama queen—I want to forget it ever happened. Tell me about your days off."

Mandy sighed, getting dreamy. "I loved New Orleans. We totally have to go back sometime."

"Were the crew guys nice?"

"Yeah, they're always cool. Even Rob's fun when he's not working."

"What was the whole 'too weird' thing with Nathan?"

She bit her lip. "Maybe I'm a complete dork and making it up, but I started worrying that I'd hurt someone else's feelings."

"Really? Tell me!" I knew she and Oscar had been getting close. "Are you following the rules?"

She nodded. "He was just being kind of protective. I'm sure he was just being a good guy." She walked me to the meet and greet before leaving to count in the merch.

The meet and greet was the same as usual, except for a handful of girls who came over to ask whether Lucas and I were dating. "We're just friends," I said, not sure if we were even that. They wanted to know what he was like, whether he was as cute in person, and if he was dating anyone. This was unfamiliar territory for me, being the girl that other girls envied. I didn't totally hate it.

We played an amazing show that night and the next night in Dallas. Our personal chemistry was still off, but oddly enough it didn't affect the shows.

I knew Malcolm would come around eventually; he had a memory like a fish. Pem seemed like he could hold a grudge forever, so I didn't want to go near that one.

That left Beckett.

We ignored each other through most of Texas. I knew he was still stewing about the video and probably about Lauren. And I was mad at him. He'd been really hard on me with the dress problem, which wasn't like him, and I was annoyed about the girl in LA. Was she the reason he ended things with Lauren?

I tried to appear indifferent, but truthfully I missed hanging out with him. I finally lost it on the ride to Austin.

Everyone else had gone to sleep, but I stayed up to get Beckett alone in the back lounge. He worked on his laptop with headphones on while I pretended to watch a movie.

I finally turned the movie off and waited for him to notice. He eventually looked up. "Going to bed?"

"I want to know what's wrong with you," I said.

"Nothing." He looked back at his computer screen.

I went over and pulled his headphones off. "Why aren't we talking?"

He sighed. "What do you want to talk about?"

"I don't know. Lauren, the video, whatever's bothering you."

"It's all that stuff," he said. "And some old band stuff that I won't bore you with."

"I don't care. Bore me. I want to know." He didn't say anything. "Who was the girl in the hotel?" I knew I sounded jealous but I didn't care.

"She's no one. We see each other sometimes when I'm in LA." He wouldn't look at me.

"Is that all you're capable of? Passing through?"

"Why do you want to know?"

"Because . . ." I searched for an answer. Nothing was coming.

"Don't worry about it. It might not be all I'm capable of, but it's all I have time for," he said. "Have you finished that song yet?"

163

I shook my head. When had I had time?

"You should spend more time worrying about what's important."

We had a day off in Austin, and I would've loved to spend it running around with Beckett or even Malcolm, but everyone was still in separate corners.

Before our call time, Mandy, Oscar, and I walked around South Congress, eating and shopping. It was a welcome break from all the drama. Oscar, a native Texan, helped me pick out a pair of cowboy boots. "I dare you to wear those onstage," he said.

"With a dress," Mandy added.

"What's wrong with that?" I asked. "That's a cool look."

"But it's not a Melbourne look," Oscar said. "It's not even really a you look."

"It's more me than some of the stuff I've been wearing," I said, specifically thinking about the Vegas outfit.

We checked into the Embassy Suites downtown, and then I spent the afternoon doing laundry near the hotel. I even did Mandy's so she could keep hanging out with Oscar. They obviously liked each other, but so far neither one of them felt like discussing it.

My phone rang as I loaded our clothes into dryers. My mom. "People keep mentioning these pictures with you and Lucas Rivers. Are you guys an item?" She couldn't keep the excitement out of her voice. In her mind, actors were a step up from rock stars.

"We've met a couple of times," I said evasively.

We hung up when it was time to fold. I hummed the song

Beckett had given me. I hadn't had a chance to sit down and work out lyrics, but the melody stuck with me. I tried to pay attention to how I felt. It wasn't meant to be a love song—there was nothing sunny or hopeful about it—yet I found myself thinking about relationships and how complex they were. I kept humming, letting my subconscious play with it while I finished my laundry.

That night at Stubb's, I finally got to watch Gray Matter. Beckett was there as usual. He was right: they were a solid band. The singer had front-man skills that made me envious. Even though their crowd was less than half the size of what it'd be for us, they played like the venue was full of fans screaming for them.

After a few songs, I leaned toward Beckett. "I see why you like them. They're good."

He looked down at my navy-blue tank dress and cowboy boots. "You better go get ready," he said.

I stomped off, even though it warmed my heart to see his teasing smirk again.

Right after "Smash Cut," Beckett, who normally barely said anything during our set, said, "Did you see Chelsea's boots? She's trying to fit in. Cute, right?"

The audience cheered; I glared at Beckett.

I stomped offstage after the encore. I was feeling the boots. All the stomping made me feel authoritative. I went into the dressing room and let the door slam behind me.

"Hey, cowgirl."

I stopped short when I saw Lucas sitting there.

22

"What are you doing here?" I stood frozen in place.

Lucas stood up and kissed my cheek. "I dig the boots." He grinned.

The dressing room door opened again. My bandmates stood in the doorway, and I swore I heard one of them groan. Assholes. I finally regained consciousness. "Just let me change and we'll get out of here."

"Make sure you wear the boots." Lucas turned toward the door. "Hey, guys," he said as he pushed past them. "Great show."

"It followed her," Malcolm said.

"You should be glad." I grabbed a different dress. "Maybe now your stupid bet will end." I ignored Beckett's stony face and Malcolm's appreciative laughter. At least their collective dislike for Lucas reunited them against me. Just like old times.

Lucas stood with Ray in the hall. "Hey, Ray," I said.

"I know exactly where I'm taking you in those boots."
Lucas took my hand.

"Are you excited to see me or the boots?"

"Ha! Both."

I stared at our intertwined fingers. I was still coming down from the show, and having him here was making me flustered. Maybe I needed calories for brain function. "I could go for some barbecue. Stubb's did the catering." In addition to being a fun place to play, Stubb's was also one of the most famous barbecue restaurants in Austin.

Lucas laughed. "You're kidding, right? This late?"

Ray escorted us into an idling SUV. I held my breath, waiting for photographers to descend. When none did, I exhaled.

The car dropped us at the door of a squat building that looked like it was dropped from the sky and had landed randomly in the middle of a residential neighborhood. The neon sign above the door, which hung between two illuminated wagon wheels, read Broken Spoke. Honky-tonk music blared from inside.

We stood in line to pay the cover, but the bouncer said, "Lucas Rivers! Come on in, man." He put out his hand, which Lucas shook.

"You sure?" Lucas asked.

"Totally. If you have time to take a picture for our wall, they'd probably appreciate that. But y'all are welcome as our special guests!"

And that's how it went all night long. Unlike every other customer, we didn't have to jump up and down for the bartenders' attention, let alone pay for the actual drinks. I wondered if others found this offensive, but they seemed just as tickled about Lucas as the employees were. Women waiting for the restroom even let me cut to the front of the line because I was "with that adorable Lucas Rivers."

I kind of loved this place. All the waitresses looked like they should be named Flo or Lurleen. We stayed toward the back of the dance hall, watching a seventy-five-year-old cowboy performing onstage. "That guy's amazing," I said.

"I heard Willie Nelson still plays here sometimes," Lucas said.

Lucas's plans didn't end at standing around and people watching. He could actually two-step and was determined to teach me. "Of course you know how to do this," I said.

"I once auditioned to play a kid who learned to dance to win the girl." Lucas positioned my hand on his shoulder.

"So now you're an expert?" I focused on mirroring his feet.

"That's the job. Don't look down. It's a six-count, you got it! I'm not surprised you have rhythm." He smiled as he steered me around the room and even spun me a couple of times. I was by no means graceful, but at least I didn't embarrass myself. Besides, the dance floor was so packed that no one could really tell if I was doing it wrong.

Lucas tilted my chin up. "Are you glad I came?"

"I think I'm still in shock." I couldn't believe he'd flown halfway across the country. For me. He certainly knew how to impress a girl.

A flash went off to my right. I turned, but Lucas tapped my back. From his spot at the bar, Ray glared in the amateur paparazzo's direction. "You were so worried about the video and the dress. I couldn't leave it like that."

"I would have called you when we got back to LA," I said.

"But this is more fun. Right?"

"Absolutely. I even have the day off tomorrow."

"I know. And I have a great idea."

Knowing that he wanted to spend more time with me made me giddy. We went outside to the porch, where Ray stood in front of us, staring down anyone who even thought of approaching.

"I met some of your fans the other day at the band meet and greet," I said.

He looked thoughtful. "I don't think of our fans as the same people."

I didn't want to tell him that my bandmates would enthusiastically agree. Those guys were such artistic snobs. Even Malcolm. Any movie they watched had to be "original," any book they read had to be "important." It was like they were anti-fun.

We talked about Lucas's upcoming movies. He had one coming out Labor Day weekend, a comedy called *Spring Forward,* and was finishing up another one in which he played an LAPD cadet who has to solve a crime that unravels the police academy. This was the first time he'd played someone out of high school. "If the movie tanks, there'll be nowhere to go. I can't go back to playing teens."

"You *are* a teen," I pointed out.

"Doesn't matter. Once you cross that bridge, that's it. Or it should be. Anyway, that's why I wanted to get away before the whole promotion machine fires up." Lucas grew distant talking about his movie. I felt for him. I knew from various articles that he supported his whole family and a small staff.

"You must be exhausted. Maybe we should call it a night," I said.

His playful smile returned. "Have you ever been to the Driskill?" he asked.

I shook my head. I'd heard of it because it was the guys' favorite hotel in Austin, but staying there wasn't within our tour budget.

"You have to come see it—it's a landmark," Lucas said.

We said goodbye to the Broken Spoke and drove to the stately hotel, which was all lit up from inside. Columns and arched windows gave it a castlelike feel. Inside, the decor managed to be both opulent and yet securely masculine. As in lots of leather and dead animal heads mounted on walls. Rich old men with cigars would be totally at home here. Which was probably why my bandmates liked it.

"Do you want to come up?" Lucas asked.

Did I? I wasn't sure. I didn't want to completely disappear on the band, but it was freeing to be away from all the tension. Lucas picked up on my hesitation. "We can order room service. Anything you want."

"Deal," I said, smiling.

When we headed toward the elevators, a family rushed over. Ray started to get in front of us, but Lucas murmured, "It's cool."

The mom wore a giant smile. "I hate to bother you on your date, but could our girls get a picture with you? They refused to go to bed until I asked."

"Sure," Lucas said. He stepped between the two daughters, who looked to be about twelve and fifteen, and put an arm around each of them. The girls had dumbfounded grins plastered on their faces as their mother snapped away. Being this close to a heartthrob was frying their brains. I could relate.

Lucas gave them a quick squeeze. "Thanks so much, guys. Great to meet you."

He was stopped twice more on our way to the elevator. "Once they see you do it once . . . ," Ray grumbled.

But Lucas didn't seem to mind. I didn't either, but when he saw me yawning he tried to hurry things along. "Sorry," he said. "You don't get as much paparazzi outside LA, but you do get a lot of fans."

"I don't mind at all. But it's past one. Maybe I should go back."

"No way. I owe you room service. You can stay over." He saw my expression. "I'll sleep in the bathtub."

I laughed. "I'm not sleeping with you."

"I like how you put that right out there. Get on the elevator." Ray dropped us off at Lucas's door and told us to come get him when I was ready to leave.

Lucas opened the door to his suite, which was big enough to host a party. There was a private outdoor patio, a dining room, a pool table and bar in the living room, and the biggest TV I'd ever seen. "Are you planning on staying awhile?" I asked.

"Only as long as you are," Lucas replied.

I looked around while Lucas found the room service menu. His suitcase lay open in the middle of the living room with stuff spilling out of it. He'd certainly brought a lot for someone who was only staying a night.

He handed me the menu and sank into an easy chair. "Order away."

As I dialed, Lucas pulled me onto his lap and rubbed my neck. It felt amazing. After I ordered a feast for one, I hung up the phone.

"Is this okay?" he asked. I leaned forward and kissed him. I was much less distracted than last time, but I still had that surreal awareness that I was kissing someone super famous.

Things were getting pretty heated when the doorbell rang. I sent a silent thank-you to the universe. It wasn't that I didn't enjoy making out with Lucas (I mean, I had a pulse), but I didn't want to rush.

The doorbell rang again. "You want to ignore it and re-order later?" Lucas mumbled against my lips.

"That's rude, moneybags." I gave him a last kiss and went to the door.

Once I was eating, Lucas channel-surfed until he landed on a movie that he starred in. I actually stopped chewing to watch him watch himself with a serious, critical expression. "I'm totally kidding!" He fell back into the chair, cracking up.

I let out a breath. "Wow. That was . . . wow."

Still laughing, he changed the channel. "You should have seen your face. That was one of the best reactions I've ever gotten."

We settled on some soapy melodrama that featured Lucas's costar in *Spring Forward*. Her name was Nina Maras, and she was adorable. In this movie, she looked like she was about thirteen. Lucas took occasional digs at her acting chops, but I figured he was just venting after having been on set with her for two months. After all, who talks trash about a little kid?

By the time I finished eating, Lucas was falling asleep. "Are you going to stay?" He rubbed his eyes.

It was almost three. Mandy probably wouldn't want me banging around the room at this hour. "I'll sleep on the couch."

"You will not. Come on. The bed's huge. You won't even see me if you don't want to."

We brushed our teeth side by side in front of the twin sinks. I had to admit we looked pretty cute. He gave me a T-shirt to sleep in, and we climbed into bed. As promised, he stayed way over to his side.

"Come here," I said, rolling my eyes.

We met in the middle and I settled my head on his shoulder. I listened to the sound of his breathing and couldn't believe that I was actually where I was. I ran my hand down his arm to make sure he was real. Within minutes, I fell asleep.

The next morning I was jolted awake by my phone blaring a horrific ringtone. I reached over to answer it.

"Morning," I croaked. I shielded my eyes until they adjusted to the sun-drenched room.

"You're not dead," Mandy said.

"No. I stayed with Lucas."

"A: That's not going to make anyone around here happy. And B: Omigod!"

"I know. To both."

"What should I tell everyone?"

I looked at Lucas, who was starting to stir. His face lit up when he saw me sitting up and watching him. He looked so cute and relaxed just waking up that I could almost think of him as a regular boy. An extremely good-looking regular boy. "Just say I'll be back by bus call."

"Seriously?" Mandy screeched. I had to hold the phone away from my ear.

"Yup. I'm getting a VIP tour of Austin." I hung up and dove onto Lucas, who grunted. "What are we doing today?"

23

Lucas and I spent the day around Lady Bird Lake. Lucas had to get in his daily six-mile run, but after that we wandered around and even rented a canoe. "Bonus workout," he said as we paddled.

He wore dark glasses and a baseball cap so no one would recognize him. Ray stayed with us but kept his distance, not wanting to arouse curiosity. Sneaking around with Lucas felt like a huge secret that I was dying to broadcast to the world, especially when he held my hand or kissed me.

We had to drive all the way to Phoenix for the next show, with a travel day in between, so bus call was early. It was getting dangerously close to that time, but I didn't want my date with Lucas to end. "Can you come to the next show?" I asked.

"You mean follow you around like a real groupie?"

"Exactly," I said. "Except if you were a real groupie, you'd come on the bus."

"Seriously?" He stopped walking and faced me. "That would be awesome. I've always wanted to spend the night on a tour bus."

I gulped. "Really?"

He nodded. "It's on my bucket list. I always wished I could play a musician in a movie."

"I'm sure it'd be fine," I said. "We have an extra bunk—"

"I want to bunk with you." He leaned over to kiss me.

"You say that now, but when you see how small those bunks are . . ."

"I'm willing to risk it. You think it'll be cool with everyone?"

"Let me text our tour manager." I reached for my phone and hoped Lucas couldn't see my face burning as I typed. The guys were going to hate this. Part of me didn't care. I put up with Malcolm's shenanigans and had my morning alone time taken away by Lauren. They could deal with Lucas for a couple of nights.

Ray set Lucas's bags by our suitcases when we got to the bus. Mandy had been sweet enough to move all my stuff out of our hotel. I introduced them to Dave and showed them around, grateful that no one else was on board yet.

Rob came on first. "Hey, man," he said. "Rob. Tour manager."

"Thanks for letting us ride along," Lucas said.

Somewhere in my brain, I registered the fact that he said "us" but didn't think anything of it.

The rest of the band and crew started to filter in. Rob must have gotten to everyone in advance, because they were all being impressively civil. Mandy had a bit of a freak-out, but who could blame her? "I love every single one of your movies," she said. "Even that one where you played a good twin and a bad twin and the bad one was so completely evil."

Lucas chuckled. "Thanks. Happy to be traveling with a fan."

"Chelsea's a fan too. Is she acting like she's not? 'Cause she's full of it. She's a huge fan."

Lucas winked at me, which totally made me swoon. Unfortunately, Pem watched this exchange looking like he was smelling something rancid the entire time.

"So explain the bunk situation to me?" Lucas asked. "Where's the extra bunk in case we get too cramped in yours?"

I pointed to our junk bunk. "We'd just have to clear this one out."

"But that's where Ray's going to sleep." Lucas looked back and forth between Rob and me. "Right?"

I sent Rob a silent plea. Our bus was already maxed out, but I realized that Lucas couldn't travel without Ray. Fortunately Rob read my mind. "Yeah. I guess if you need extra space, you'll have to crash in the back lounge. Which you'll probably want to because Chelsea's a snorer." Rob glared at me. "Chelsea. Why don't you help me clean out the junk bunk?"

Lucas went to check out the back lounge. "I know," I whispered. "It was stupid of me to not know that Ray would have to come with."

"Who the fuck is Ray?"

"His security. He goes everywhere with Lucas."

"You better get them off the bus in Phoenix. Pem, Beckett, and Malcolm are going to lose their shit when they find out about this. Everyone's going to be pissed about the overcrowding, but they hate that guy. He, like, offends their sensibilities. You should have heard them go off when you first hooked up with him at the Roxy."

"Trust me. I'm not trying to make things worse, but it's not like any of them exactly asks for my stamp of approval when they bring a girl on the bus. Does anyone give a second thought to whether I actually enjoy babysitting the parade of girls who come through here? No! So let's be real—if anyone else wanted to bring someone on for a couple of days, we'd figure it out."

Rob sighed. "That person would probably not have security the size of a house."

"They might. And Ray's totally nice and low-key. I've been around him for like two days now."

"Whatever. If you think it's worth the shitstorm, more power to you."

Rob and I finished moving all the junk to the front lounge. People would either have to find new places for their stuff or else store it underneath the bus. Not exactly convenient.

I ran down the bus rules for Lucas and Ray. Once we were moving, I set up a movie in the front lounge. The back lounge was pretty cliquey and I didn't want to subject Lucas to that. Mandy and Oscar and, of course, Ray, stayed up front with us.

I felt good, curled up in Lucas's arms, watching a lighthearted, funny movie about a regular high school student who robbed banks. I tried to act like it was no big deal that the guys hadn't rolled out the welcome wagon. "It's just not their way," I said. But I could tell Lucas thought it was strange. I hoped Mandy's enthusiastic reception had made up for everyone else's rudeness.

When the movie ended, I made Lucas wait in the lounge while I changed into my pj's in the bunk. We took turns brushing our teeth in the bathroom. It wasn't quite as cute as side-by-side brushing, but we did share my bottled water.

Lucas took off his shorts and T-shirt in the bunk aisle then stood there in his underwear. It was like seeing a famous piece of art in person. "Do you not own pj's?" I asked.

"This is how I sleep. Didn't you notice?" Of course I had. "I didn't plan on going to sleep with an audience."

"Just get up there."

"Oh man," Lucas said once we were up in the bunk. "I haven't slept in a twin bed in forever. And never with another person."

"I'm honored, I guess," I said.

"You should be. You're my first."

"Mm-hmm." I knew he was trying to be funny and broach a subject that I wasn't going anywhere near.

We lay facing each other, our legs and feet intertwined. Lucas was on the outside and held on to me for dear life, convinced he was going to go flying out of the bunk. We had so much fun trying to guess which noises belonged to which person. When the snoring started up, he guessed it was Mandy, which made me burst out laughing.

We stayed up whispering and laughing until someone shushed us. He propped himself up on his elbow and rolled toward me for a kiss. "We can go slow," he said.

I wouldn't say slow is exactly how it went, but we didn't go there.

24

Since it was a travel day and we were mostly stuck on the bus, no one was in a hurry to leave their bunks. I knew I'd have the lounge for a while, so I opened my laptop, slipped on headphones, and clicked on Beckett's music file. For several exits I just listened and zoned out, sipping tea, watching the scenery zip past. I eventually talked myself into opening a blank document and attempting to put words to the music.

> You and I were a secret
> And when I agreed to keep it
> I didn't know you meant forever

I stopped and deleted. God, my first attempt at lyric writing and it was so . . . juvenile. Embarrassing. Bad. I reminded myself what Beckett had said about experimenting. These words were about Mike, a boy I didn't even want anymore.

The problem was that it felt like a sad, angry song, and there weren't too many things I was sad and angry about. If it felt like a song about worrying, I'd have a lot more to work with.

Beckett came into the lounge. "Hey." He gave me a begrudging smile and started making one of his gross breakfast concoctions.

"Er, sorry about the overcrowding," I said, shutting my laptop.

"It's nothing we haven't seen before."

"Did Pem say anything?"

"Yeah. He'll get over it, but I wouldn't be in his face about it." He took his breakfast to the jump seat.

At least he was being nice to me again. I wondered if his graciousness would extend to Lucas but somehow doubted it.

A muffled but sharp bang came from the sleeping berth, followed by a string of swears. When the door slid open, I heard laughter, then Lucas shuffled out holding a hand over his forehead.

"What happened?" I asked, reaching for his hand. He was still in his underwear, not that he seemed worried about it.

"I tried to sit up."

"Rookie mistake, dude," Beckett said before swiveling back around in the jump seat. I guess that answered my question.

Lucas put his hand down. "Is it bleeding?"

"No. Just a little red. It'll go away. I learned that the hard way," I said to comfort him.

"It better," Lucas said.

To me, the bigger problem was that he'd woken everyone up. Now they were all coming into the lounge at once, talking over each other and cutting in line to make breakfast.

"You want some cereal?" I asked Lucas.

He shook his head. "Carbs."

Malcolm snorted. "Are you actually standing here in your underwear right now?"

"I can make you some eggs," I said, ignoring Malcolm.

"Like an omelet?" Lucas asked.

"More like hard-boiled."

He nodded without enthusiasm.

By the time I actually got a chance to cook his eggs, we were at the hotel and everyone flew off the bus to get some space.

"Where'd everyone go?" Lucas asked.

"They get cabin fever. People sometimes do laps around the block to get privacy while talking on the phone. Especially the crew guys who have girlfriends."

"Do any of the Melbourne guys have girlfriends?"

"Not exactly." He looked concerned, so I added, "There's no band-crew consorting allowed."

Lucas perked up. "Really? Who came up with that?"

"Pem."

"Why?"

I shrugged. "Why is not really a question I can answer when it comes to anything Pem does."

Lucas rolled his eggs around on his plate to loosen the shells. "I have to say, I thought those dudes would be cooler. I'm such a huge fan. . . . I'd thought maybe we'd be friends."

I sat beside him and looped my arm through his. "Everyone knows New Yorkers are prickly. They hate everybody."

We'd stopped in the middle of nowhere, so everyone just hung out in their rooms until the next morning, when it was time to get back on the bus and finish the drive to Phoenix.

That night Lucas watched the show from the side of the stage. That threw me off a little bit because I felt like I had to direct some attention over there, even though I shouldn't have. But his presence made me kick it up a level, so it probably evened out. He looked so cute, standing there bobbing his head along to the music.

We had late bus call and nowhere we wanted to go, so that left lots of time for signing. Lucas hung back and kept his hood up. It didn't make a difference. Somebody spotted him about fifteen minutes in and started squealing. "Lucas! Lucas! I know it's you! Can you come over here?"

He had no choice but to join me by the parking lot entrance. What started out as signing a couple of things and saying hi turned into a mob scene within minutes. All the fans who were spread out along the fence swarmed to the center like metal shavings to a magnet. Most of them didn't even want to talk to Lucas. They just wanted to verify it was him or snap his picture.

Pem and Malcolm looked on in disgust. Ray got involved to keep people at a respectable distance from Lucas. Finally he had to pull Lucas away and get him onto the bus.

Even though I was overwhelmed, I didn't want to just ditch, so I stayed out. But from that point on, all I got were questions about Lucas. "Are you guys dating? Friends? How did you meet? Is he going on the rest of your tour?"

After I tired of saying, "I don't know," I climbed onto the bus. Lucas was watching TV in the front lounge. I flopped down next to him. "Your life is nuts," I said.

"I know," he replied, smirking.

I elbowed him. "You love it."

"A little," he admitted. "Being on tour is fun. How great is seeing your fans up close and personal every single day? With acting, it's all removed."

"Well, now it seems like we're done interacting with the fans. We're stuck here. What do you want to do?"

"I can think of one thing."

Lucas woke up first the next morning. He repeated his rookie mistake and banged his forehead on the ceiling when he tried to sit up. "Goddammit!" he yelled, holding his head.

I propped myself up on my elbows. "What happened?" I asked, dazed.

"Seriously, this is going to bruise. I'm screwed!"

I took his hand away, and sure enough he'd managed to bang his head in the exact same spot. It was a darker red than last time. "Let's get some ice."

"I have a photo shoot and an awards show in two days. If they can't Photoshop this thing out, the studio execs will lose their minds."

"Will you two shut up?" someone shouted. I hadn't realized we'd been speaking at full volume.

I got some ice out of the freezer and wrapped it in a paper towel. Lucas held it up to his forehead, wincing.

Within the hour, Lucas's bump really started to swell and turn purple. He was completely preoccupied with it; he even called Lisette to have her make an appointment with his dermatologist for when we got to LA. I couldn't believe how unnerved he was. I handed him my concealer.

"We're not even the same skin tone," he said. I gave him a

strange look. "What? You think this is the first time I've put on makeup?"

The concealer did the trick well enough that he could stop staring into a mirror. He was right; it wasn't the same tone, but it wasn't as attention-getting as the purple bruise.

Still, when the guys woke up, the first thing Pem said was "Man, are you wearing makeup? That's so high-maintenance."

"But eyeliner is okay?" Lucas asked.

"I wear it onstage. There's a difference between onstage and off," Pem said.

"In your world, maybe," Lucas retorted.

Ray was all fired up for San Diego, our next stop. He'd lived there for a year and put some buddies on my guest list. Unfortunately, that ended with Ray and Lucas getting hammered with said buddies. By the time I got on the bus, Ray was passed out in his bunk and Lucas was slurring at the TV.

I kicked everyone out of the back lounge, which went over so well, and put Lucas to bed back there. At least he wouldn't hit his head in the morning.

In the middle of the night, I was awakened by Jared yelling, "What the fuck!"

I pulled open my curtain to see Ray, hunched over on the edge of his bunk, peeing into Jared's bunk across the aisle. Most of it hit the curtain, but some of it must have trickled in. "Omigod. Ray! Stop it! Go to the bathroom. Ray!" He didn't hear me. He just finished his business and rolled back into his bunk.

"This is so fucked up!" Jared yelled.

"I'm so sorry! Here, sleep in my bunk. I'll go in the back," I whispered.

Other curtains opened up.

Rob: "Chelsea. We can't have this."

Malcolm: "The manny's an even bigger douche than him."

Pem: "They're done in LA."

Beckett: "Go to sleep. Can't do anything about it now."

Jared: "No way. Chelsea, out. I'm sleeping in your bed."

I groaned and climbed down, clutching my blanket, which Jared promptly snatched out of my hands.

Lucas was sprawled out over one of the back lounge couches, still fully dressed, mouth hanging open. I was surprised no one had come back here and drawn on him. It was a bit of an eye-opener to see that even big movie stars couldn't make drunk look good.

25

Lucas fled to Chateau Marmont as soon as we got to LA. We were staying at the Sunset Marquis, since everyone wanted to be centrally located for our day off. There was plenty of time before our show, so Mandy talked me into a random tour of Hollywood called the Dearly Departed Tour. A minibus zipped us around for two hours with a guide pointing out all the sites of some of Los Angeles's most famous murders.

"Are you okay about them banishing Lucas from the bus?" Mandy asked during a rare lull in the guide's spiel.

"No. Their love lives haven't exactly been convenient and nonannoying," I said.

Mandy nodded slowly. "Yeah . . . but then, none of their guests have ever done *that*. I mean, I'm on your side. But they didn't actually say Lucas couldn't come back. Just Ray."

"Are you being serious right now?" She knew as well as I

did, as well as we all did, that no Ray meant no Lucas. "What's he supposed to do? Follow the bus in a rental car?"

The guide launched into an overly detailed description of another grizzly murder. I texted Lucas and got a quick reply: *Working on something. See you at the Wiltern. XX.*

When we took a bathroom break, Mandy decided to broach a slightly less inflammatory subject: her crush on Oscar. "I finally laid it on the line," she said, reapplying lip gloss in the mirror.

"Uh-oh. What does that mean?" I asked.

"You know. I told Oscar I like him."

"Bad boys are your new thing."

"I know. The boys at home are so blah. Anyway, we talked, and he likes his job too much to risk it. He says Pem has his reasons, however weird they may be, and that it's Melbourne's tour, not his, so he's going to play by the rules."

"What an upstanding citizen. It's nice that he's so honorable," I said.

"Yeah. But what's not is that he feels free to entertain all the girls who hang around the bus and venue till all hours. Ironic, considering he was so worried about me hooking up with a stranger."

"You don't know that he's doing anything," I told her.

Mandy gave me a look. And I thought I was the one with trust issues.

I was really nervous for my first real LA show. Maybe it was all that talk about murder, but I didn't think so. Not only was everyone from our stylist to the president of our record label here, but there were also celebrities and press. The guys were on edge, and I knew that we couldn't make any mistakes.

Before we took the stage, I could feel that all of us were more charged up than usual. The crowd was restless, waiting for us to begin.

We started out strong, totally in sync and revved up. Somewhere in the middle of the set Pem noticed people in front looking to the side of the stage. I glanced over, but Lucas wasn't visible. "What are you all looking at?" Pem asked, pretending he was curious to see what was over there too.

There were scattered callbacks of "Lucas Rivers" but nothing we couldn't ignore if we chose to.

Of course, Pem chose otherwise. I looked at Beckett. His mouth was tight. Malcolm looked like he just wanted the whole thing over with. "Lucas Rivers. Seriously?" Pem laughed and went back to his planned banter entertaining everyone with stories from the tour. Pem was most on when he was a little agro.

Right before our last song, Pem gave shout-outs to the people on our team. Then he said, "If you see Lucas Rivers, tell him to go fuck himself!" That met with a lot of laughter and hoots of approval from the audience.

We played the rest of our show really fast. I was so upset with Pem I could barely focus. And I had to figure out how to get Lucas to take Pem's attack as the territorial posturing that it was.

As soon as we were done with the encore, I accosted Pem backstage. "I get you want the focus to be on us, but was that really necessary?"

"If your boyfriend needs an attention fix, tell him to get it somewhere else. This isn't the Lucas Rivers sideshow," Pem said.

"Lucas stayed out of sight during our entire set," I said. "Is it so bad that he likes your band? He's not exactly some loser."

Pem snorted. "Debatable."

"Are you jealous because he has more fans than we do?" I asked.

Malcolm and Beckett looked like they'd rather not jump in but knew that they might have to.

"More doesn't always mean better. And it definitely doesn't mean smarter," Pem said.

I went to find Lucas. He was waiting for me in the dressing room. "You haven't been here the whole time, have you?"

"No, I watched. You couldn't see me?"

I shook my head. "I'm sorry about Pem. You know he just said that for show, right?"

Lucas stood up and hugged me, stroking my hair. "I don't need to be one of the cool kids. As long as you like me." He gave me a kiss. "You like me, don't you?"

I looked into his eyes and nodded, even as I was thinking, *I barely know you.* There was something impenetrable about Lucas; he was always on, saying or doing the perfect thing. And since I wasn't exactly an open book, our interactions did feel a little superficial. Maybe that would change over time.

"You were great." He kissed me again. "I need to get my beauty sleep. I'll pick you up around four tomorrow."

Lucas was presenting at an awards show on our day off and invited me to be his date. Mandy spent the morning with me at the stylist's studio and then helped me do my hair in the afternoon. Without the leather cuffs on my wrists and ankles, the overall effect of the layered tulle skirt and thin cashmere sweater would have been way too ballerina for my tastes. I had my doubts, but I figured our stylist knew what she was doing.

When Lucas picked me up, I noticed that his suit matched my outfit perfectly. It was gray, accented with black and pearl. "How did you do that?" I asked.

"Hey, gorgeous," he said. I tilted my face up for a kiss but he avoided my lips, brushing my cheek with his lips instead. "Don't want to get lipstick on me. Why are you so covered up?"

"How did you know what I was wearing?"

"I didn't. Lisette emailed your stylist a picture of my suit and told her to coordinate."

I was floored. "You decided my outfit? Why didn't anyone say anything?"

Lucas studied my face, puzzled. "What's the big deal? You're my date. Why didn't you choose a different top? People are going to think I'm dating a Mormon."

"Right, I'm your date, not your accessory. Just because I'm going with you doesn't mean I want to be your arm candy."

Even as my anger increased, I was aware that I was over-reacting. But I was nervous about going to this awards show with him, and I would have felt better in something that was more me. Plus, I had this idea that I was letting Melbourne down if I didn't stand out on my own. I was their lead singer. Front women shouldn't blend.

Lucas exhaled, his own anger starting to pop. "Chelsea. I know you're new to this, but this is a big deal. You're walking the red carpet with me. Those pictures will be everywhere. Are you really going to throw a fit and screw everything up?"

When he put it that way, part of me wanted to. Instead, I

turned to the mirror, gathered my loose, feminine waves into my fist, and twisted them into a high topknot. The change in hairstyle added some edge, but it wasn't enough. I wiped off my soft pink lipstick and put on a bright, saturated orange-red instead. I grabbed a pair of giant neon-yellow dangly feather earrings that Mandy had purchased from a costume shop on Hollywood Boulevard.

Lucas's face stayed blank. "Ready?"

I could have used Lucas's arm for support, but I didn't take it. I tottered down the carpeted hallway as gracefully as possible. We passed Beckett. He didn't say anything but shot me an appreciative smile. At least someone liked my outfit.

Aside from the dizzying sensory overload of the red carpet, the awards show was a snooze fest. Lucas presented the award for Best Actor in a Comedy along with his costar, Nina Maras. She'd matured about five years and looked nothing like the little girl I'd seen on TV in Austin. It was a good thing I wasn't the possessive type.

Nina and Lucas had playful chemistry when they presented but didn't seem like they wanted to hang out with each other. "Too much togetherness," Lucas explained.

A couple of Melbourne's rival bands performed, even though there were no music categories. I wondered if we'd been invited to play. It would've been great exposure at a time when we were trying to promote a record.

By the time I said goodbye to Lucas, I was mostly done being mad about the outfits. He and Ray escorted me back to the bus. "When am I going to see you again?" I asked.

"I'm going to try to make it tomorrow," he said.

"Really?" Our next show was in the Bay Area.

"Yeah." He leaned in to kiss me. "I'll call you."

I climbed onto the bus and immediately plopped down to take off my heels. Everyone else was already on board.

"How was it?" Mandy asked. "You looked amazing. I loved the changes you made. So much more rocker. Did you meet any famous people?"

"You know, we're famous," Beckett said in a mocking tone.

"Nina Maras. She's in Lucas's movie," I said.

"Dude, she's hot," Malcolm said. Mandy elbowed him. "Seriously. Can he introduce me?"

"If he did, would you stop being a jerk to him?" I asked.

Malcolm thought for a second. "Doubt it."

"Why do you guys hate him so much?" I asked.

"He has that squeaky-clean image. It makes him seem stupid," Malcolm said.

"And he's a talentless pretty-boy hack. Oops, did I say that out loud?" Beckett didn't bother looking up from his phone.

I decided not to mention that they hadn't seen the last of Lucas just yet.

26

Sam spent the night on the bus with us, his eyes glued to his laptop. As we neared Oakland, his typing grew more frenetic. "Saw the show last night. You guys got a lot of airtime. I had my intern monitor Twitter and the text crawler. Said comments went from 'Who's that girl?' to 'I wanna be Chelsea from Melbourne' by the end. Everyone wants to know where to get those earrings. You should Instagram a picture with info on where you got them."

I smiled in disbelief. "That's bizarre. Did you watch Scuttlebutt?" People liked to lump our band in with them.

"Yeah. That's why we pulled out. Pem refuses to play the same stage as them. Didn't you wonder why we had a random Saturday off in LA? Your agent almost lost his mind over that."

"Poor Mark. Why does Pem care? It would have gotten us in front of a lot of people."

Sam grunted and peeled his eyes away from his computer.

"Scuttlebutt has always been like an annoying kid brother. Now that they're more established, Pem thinks it's bullshit that they're always trying to start a rivalry with us. And when he heard they wanted us to play first, he fuckin' lost it. I didn't argue with him, because when we had to commit we weren't sure if you'd be ready for a live TV performance."

Ouch. Faced with a concrete example of how I might have been holding the band back, I felt something very close to mortification. "I've performed a lot on TV."

Sam gave me a look. We both knew performing on a highly produced show specifically made to showcase singing performances was totally different. He tactfully changed the subject. "Michaela texted me to be prepared for a cover story next week. Pictures are all over the place."

I chewed on my lip. A tiny part of me was excited. I was willing to take a little heat if it meant busting out of the guys' shadows and making a place for myself. But most of me was nervous about what I'd unleashed and what it might mean for the band. Sam saw the conflicted feelings on my face. "Can't take it back now," he said.

Beckett, Malcolm, and some of the crew guys came out, and Sam headed to the back lounge to get more work done. Beckett took his breakfast to the jump seat as usual, even though Dave was already off to some hotel. I drank instant coffee from a lumpy mug that a fan had made for him. "Can't you read?" he asked. "It says 'Beckett' and there's a picture of me on it."

Malcolm snapped a picture of me holding the mug. "Must you?" I asked.

"Sings good. Can't read. Sad," Malcolm said as he tapped.

He jabbed at his screen one last time, sending my photo to probably all Melbourne social media feeds.

"Sorry," I said. "They didn't make one for me."

"Awww, poor Chelsea!" everyone said.

"Someone make the girl a mug!" Winston bellowed.

"I didn't mean it like that. Never mind."

"At least we're rid of the d-bag and his incontinent baby-sitter," Jared said.

"They might be back tonight." I ducked to avoid possible projectiles.

Groans all around. "At least the damn bet is done," Malcolm said.

Beckett swiveled around in his chair. "Bet's not over." Everyone turned to look at him, including me. His expression was flat. "I sleep below you."

I was dying. They were about to give me the third degree—I could see it in their eyes. I couldn't believe Beckett knew I wasn't sleeping with Lucas yet and that he'd told everyone. There really was no such thing as a secret on a tour bus. I climbed over legs and feet, making my way to the door with my cup of coffee still in hand.

When I stepped onto the pavement, I was hit with a wall of yells. "There's Chelsea! He must be on the bus!"

About a hundred people, mostly young girls, hung on the fence like they were about to climb it.

"What's going on out there?" Beckett asked as I ran back up the steps.

"I think they want to kill me," I said. Everyone was up and looking out the front window.

"They just want to see the d-bag," Oscar said.

196

"You're scared of a bunch of twelve-year-olds?" Beckett asked.

"Terrified. What are we going to do? We can't just sit in here all day," I said.

"*We* don't have to. They're not screaming our names," Malcolm said.

Sam reappeared. "We're trying to move the show."

"Why? What happened?" Beckett asked.

"Promoters think this is going to get worse and that we should move to a bigger spot," Sam said.

"Can you do that with no notice?" Beckett asked.

Sam shrugged. "Mark's looking into it. Never tried this before."

"There's not that many people out there," Malcolm said.

"It's ten in the morning," Beckett pointed out.

"We can't have this many people on the street. At least if we open up more seats, there's a chance that some of them will buy tickets and get inside," Sam said.

The screams outside grew louder, more insistent. The rest of the bus woke up, none too pleased. "I want to rip my ears off," Mandy said, stumbling into the lounge.

"They're like tiny savages," I said.

"Even when he's not here he's a pain in the ass," Pem said.

Sam's phone rang and he went to the back to take it. We filled Pem in.

When Sam came out, he said, "We can't move today or tomorrow, but we're adding a show in Vancouver. Hopefully Canadian Lucas Rivers fans will stay put. We're putting tickets on sale today."

"This is crazy," Pem said. "Just because there are some

insane Lucas Rivers fans here doesn't mean they're going to follow us around the country. He was seen with Chelsea last night. I'm sure it'll die down."

Sam rubbed at his head, looking agitated. "Mark talked to his counterparts in talent and says we don't understand the passion and dedication of the Rivers fan base. He's your agent, and I think we go with his gut on this." Maybe I didn't understand the Rivers fan base either.

"Chelsea, you have to give me as much notice as you can when he's going to come to a show," Rob said.

"He said he's trying to come today." I thought about telling him not to come. That seemed like the easiest thing to do. But I didn't want to do that to him when things had been strained between us in LA.

"Better get the venue working on additional security." Rob flashed me an accusatory look and then left the bus.

"We should make him pay for the extra security," Pem said. "No, seriously."

A couple of hours later, I got a text from Lucas: *Be there around 5.*

The promoters had been right; the crowd outside now spilled down the block. At least they'd stopped with the yelling. Still, I felt safer staying on the bus. Mandy brought lunch and ate with me.

Once I had to go in for sound check, I stayed inside. That walk between the bus and the theater felt hectic, and I didn't want to do it any more than I had to. I was glad we hadn't moved the show; the Fox Theater was a beautiful venue, decorated in a Moroccan motif with swirly gold details.

Lucas walked into the dressing room just before our meet and greet. "I have a surprise," he said.

"What is it?" I gave him a suspicious look.

"I knew it! I knew you were the kind of girl who loved surprises." Lucas grabbed me and swung me from side to side, trying to get me to laugh. "This is gonna blow you away. You have to come outside so I can show you."

"We have our meet and greet. Can I see after?"

"Cool. And then we'll grab food?"

"How? We're on lockdown, in case you hadn't noticed."

Lucas grinned. "I told you that show was going to be big. Did you check out the pictures?"

I nodded and smiled begrudgingly. We did look good together.

Lucas waited in the dressing room while I did the meet and greet. By the time I got into the room, everyone was already there. I was immediately surrounded by a group of girls. They complimented me on my awards show outfit and said how much they enjoyed my addition to Melbourne. I wasn't naive enough to think this had anything to do with word of mouth from shows, which didn't depress me as much as you might have thought. I didn't need validation about singing; my problem was low visibility. Being with Lucas put me on a level playing field with my bandmates.

Naturally the subject of Lucas came up, and they wanted to know if he was going to see the show. Lying didn't seem like the best idea, but neither did telling the truth. "He's here," I finally said. I imagined the airwaves lighting up with texts and phone calls, causing a stampede of another few hundred girls into downtown Oakland.

But I needn't have worried, because Lucas didn't need any help to cause a stampede.

When Lucas and I got outside so he could give me my surprise, I almost fainted dead away on the spot. Right behind our tour bus was another tour bus. This one was wrapped with an advertisement for Lucas's upcoming movie, *Spring Forward*. The title was scrawled in cursive letters with lots of flourishes across the top of the bus. Below it was a photo of Lucas staring soulfully into Nina Maras's eyes, nearly kissing her but not quite. The whole ad was done in powdery, washed-out tones, but that didn't make it any less garish.

"I don't know what to say." I hoped this was a joke, like when he'd watched his own movie in the hotel room.

"I know it's a little over-the-top, but I got the studio to pay for it," Lucas said.

"That was big of them," I said with more sarcasm than I'd intended.

"But look, this way I can go on tour with you and we can have space and privacy." He said this without irony, even as his fans screamed themselves hoarse and shook the fence so hard it threatened to come down.

"What makes you think, as a girl who's starting to date you, that I'd want to ride around in a bus with a picture of you making out with someone else on it?" I looked hard into his face, willing him to see the absurdity of what he was asking me to do.

"It's just an ad," he said. "It's going to be everywhere in about a week, so what difference does it make? This is one of the things about dating an actor. You just have to get used to it."

He was probably right, but the idea of me being in that bus was crazy. "How long are you planning on being on tour?" I asked.

"Can't we just wing it? It doesn't matter, really. The studio was all too happy to do this. They want me to show up to the premiere in the thing."

"And do you really want everyone to know where you are all the time?"

He rolled his eyes. "Like I said, it'll be bad for about a week. Then that ad goes live and it'll be on tons of buses. Ours will blend in."

There were probably already thousands of posts and reposts of this bus online. We would literally be inside a moving target. The thought made my stomach churn, but I didn't see how I could turn him down after he'd gone to all that trouble. I could only begin to imagine what my bandmates would have to say about this. They might kick me out of the band just for making them look at that bus every day.

Right before bus call, Sam dropped in. He took a quick tour, looking impressed but also weirded out. Having a bus for four people (including Ray and Lisette) was decadent, but it'd be nice not to be in such tight quarters. There was a bedroom in the back instead of a lounge, fewer and more spacious bunks in the sleeping section called condo bunks, with walls that pushed out when the bus was parked—it was very cushy. "We sold out Vancouver," Sam said. "The promoters all know about the additional bus."

Sam looked like he wasn't sure whether to be happy about selling out or annoyed about the atrocious extra bus. Funny, I was having trouble figuring that out for myself.

27

It was Lucas's birthday. The way I found out wasn't in any normal way like, say, him telling me. Instead, I woke up to dozens of fans singing happy birthday to him outside the Peabody in St. Louis. They didn't just sing it once. They sang it over and over again. I nudged him awake. "It's your birthday?"

Lucas rubbed his eyes. "Yeah. Want to give me a present?" He pulled me closer.

Even I wasn't quite sure what I was waiting for. Fooling around with Lucas was fun, but I felt like we were still getting to know each other, despite the fact that we slept in the same bed every night. He didn't pressure me (not much, anyway), and I appreciated that.

We'd spent the past week in our own little world. I was barely with the band long enough to hear the objections they undoubtedly had. Even though that part was nice, I felt cut

202

off from them, like plans and decisions were being made without me.

The *Spring Forward* bus had become a beacon for Lucas Rivers fans everywhere. They came close to shutting things down a couple of times; local police had to be brought in for every city. But the shows all sold out, each of them crazy and amazing. The attention was weirdly addicting, and I was surprised at how quickly I got used to people screaming my name.

Sam was flying in for an emergency band meeting. He also wanted to talk to me privately. This didn't sound good. I tried to get Mandy to snoop, but she couldn't find out anything.

When I got off the bus, there was a fresh surge of "Happy Birthday." Lucas was still in bed, but the fans didn't care; the open doors encouraged them to sing louder.

The band gathered in the production office. They looked like they'd barely woken up on time. Sam came in and closed the door. "The promoters all say that the meet and greets have become clusters. Radio stations and local sponsors want to fit more people in, so we have to change the way we're running them. We're going to sit you guys at a table and have fans line up. Each person will get to say hi and take one picture."

I wrinkled my nose. "Doesn't that lack the personal feel we're going for?"

"If they really want to talk, they can try to catch you guys before bus call."

"This is the way we did it before," Beckett said.

Sam turned to me. "These guys say they feel a lot of fallout from having Lucas around. The crew too. No one feels like they can leave the venue. You guys have kind of left it up in the air as to how long he's going to be on tour. Do you have any clearer idea?"

I shook my head. I didn't feel defiant, exactly, but I did feel like they were harping on the negative. So far there had been no mention of the stronger ticket sales and the fact that Melbourne was being talked about in every media outlet in the country.

"If you could work that out and give Rob a heads-up, that would help," Sam said.

"Is that it?" I asked.

"It's like you committed a white-collar crime, but the jury sentenced *us* to life without parole. You know?" Pem said.

Beckett didn't bother to translate, but he didn't have to. "Can you stick around?" Sam asked me.

When the guys left, Sam pulled his chair closer. "So things are happening. Pacific wants to leverage your new visibility. They've lined up interviews for you in LA and a couple of meetings with companies that are interested in using you as a spokeswoman."

This was so not what I thought we were going to talk about. My mind flooded with questions, but all I could get out was "Really?"

Sam nodded. "You're famous."

We let that idea wash over me for a minute. I didn't feel different, but maybe I wasn't supposed to. Maybe it was because I knew I hadn't truly earned this level of fame. But that was true of a lot of famous people these days, wasn't it?

"Are the guys okay with this?" I asked.

"They don't know about it yet. I wanted to discuss it with you first. Is this a direction you want to go?"

I thought about it. I'd be able to stop feeling apologetic for being foisted upon Melbourne. I'd finally bring something to the table by putting our name and songs in front of different people. "Yeah. I'd love to at least check it out."

"Okay. We'll fly you out tomorrow morning, and the band will continue to Minneapolis. Tomorrow's a day off, and we'll move the show the next day. I'll explain everything to them."

"What if they don't like the idea?" I asked.

"They don't really have a say. Pacific wants this. The record's doing great, but they're always looking to boost sales or wring out another single."

I wondered if *I* even had a say. I also couldn't tell if Sam was excited about this development. I thought he would be, but there was something not quite right in his eyes.

When I told Lucas, he said, "Cool. I'll fly back with you."

"They're going to ask you to lose weight," Lisette said.

I'd become more or less accustomed to her blunt demeanor, but sometimes she still managed to grate on me. "If anyone says that to me, they can suck it," I said.

"It's Hollywood. It's never enough." She turned back to her laptop.

Lucas kissed my cheek. "I knew it wasn't going to be bad. Congratulations." We both knew this development was because of him. But neither of us said anything.

I parted ways with Lucas at LAX. "See you tonight," he whispered before ducking into a town car. I'd decided to stay with him at Chateau Marmont.

"What are we doing first?" I asked Sam.

"Meeting with the team at AEA, coffee with Michaela, and

then a dinner meeting with Bombshell Cosmetics. Tomorrow you're taping *Ellen* in the morning, then you have an interview with *Seventeen,* and then a meeting with Kicks."

"Am I supposed to decide things right in the meetings?"

"I think we're still in the exploratory stage. I'll be in all the meetings with you; Michaela's coming to your interviews. You'll be fine."

Of course Sam wouldn't just turn me over to the wolves, but I wondered how much his presence was to protect me and how much was to protect the rest of Melbourne. And then I wondered why these weren't the same things in my head. They probably should've been. I felt weird being in LA without the band.

I decided to take advantage of the time alone with Sam to nose around about my future. "Is there a plan yet? For after this tour?"

"We're trying to do another tour. International. Mark has dates on hold. We just need Pem to say yes."

"Why wouldn't he?"

"He will. He's in the thick of it, so there's no way we're going to convince him now. Give him a week off the road and he'll be fine. You figure out school?"

I was elated to hear that there was a plan in the works that would keep me out of Lydon. "I already registered to take the GED when I get back."

"Your parents are good with that?"

"I think they'd just let me drop out if I wanted." I'd been so dogged about getting good grades so I could convince my parents to let me get my GED, but now I was pretty sure fame trumped a diploma as far as they were concerned.

Sam shook his head. "You gotta do it. It'll be easier now than later."

"Has Pem said anything about me?"

Sam laughed. "Listen. I think he knows he's stuck with you." That made me feel better, but it probably shouldn't have.

My meeting at AEA eased my mind. They assigned a sponsorship person to me who would also attend the meetings. She used a whole lot of marketing jargon, which I didn't understand. But Sam kept nodding, so I figured I was in good hands.

I ended my stay in LA with offers to design my own line of shoes and to help formulate a lipstick color that would be named after me. Both proposals included full-scale advertising campaigns that we'd begin shooting as soon as the tour was over.

The interviews had gone reasonably well. I had fun meeting Ellen and laughing whenever she asked funny questions about Lucas that she didn't really expect me to answer. *Seventeen* was trickier, but Michaela balked whenever they brought up Lucas, which was about every five minutes.

"I'm not sure about all this. I think all this stuff could be tough for the band to swallow," I said. It was late and we had an early flight to Minneapolis the next morning. Lucas was tired but sweet enough to sit on the balcony with me as I processed everything that had come at me in the past couple of days.

"What could they complain about? Their lead singer's face will be everywhere. Girls all over the world will want to wear and buy stuff associated with you, including Melbourne albums."

"I just don't want to alienate them," I said.

"It's what happens with all great front women. Chicks always get more attention than dudes. That's just the way it is. Besides, the level of recognition that you're going to get will finally put you in a different category than Hollis Carter."

I tilted my face up and kissed him. "Thanks for coming back with me."

"No problem. I'm actually going to stay a little longer. I need to decide some stuff on my house, take some meetings with my agent. I'll fly back to you in a few days."

"Is the bus going to stay on the tour until you get back?"

"For sure. It's your bus. Have Mandy sleep over, keep you company." He played with my hair, twirling it through his fingers.

I already knew Mandy wouldn't leave the Melbourne bus, and the idea of rattling around the other bus by myself was depressing. I wondered if my bunk was still set up. They'd probably turned it into another junk bunk.

By the time I arrived in Minneapolis, I'd decided to stay on Lucas's bus. I felt too awkward about how things were with the band to just go back like nothing was going on.

I went straight to the Myth and stopped by their bus. They weren't there. I was so bored that I helped Rob organize his production office. All his work equipment traveled in a black case that stood on wheels. I hooked up his printer/scanner and plugged in all his chargers. I really wasn't that much help, but I think he appreciated the gesture. He played old Radiohead on the computer and we both sang along while working.

"Don't have anyone else to play with?" he asked.

"Lucas is staying in LA for a couple more days."

Rob didn't look up from his computer but raised his eyebrows. "I'm honored to be your sloppy seconds. Is there trouble in the land of the beautiful people?"

"He just needed to be home. I mean, how many Melbourne shows can a person watch?"

"Plenty. Trust me," Rob said. "Is the bet over, or what?"

"Do you guys bug Pem this much about his love life?" I asked.

"We know a lost cause when we see one."

"What's up with that? He has girls throwing themselves at him constantly. I assume he's had girlfriends in the past." I'd seen him check out enough girls to know he wasn't gay. But as far as I knew, he never went beyond looking.

Rob pantomimed zipping his lips. "You'd have to ask him."

I'd rather cage-fight a wild boar.

Everyone filtered in as we got closer to sound check. When we finished, I grabbed Beckett before he could escape. "What's up?" he asked.

"I want to check in, see how everyone's feeling," I said.

He gave me a bemused look. "And you decided I'm the spokesperson?"

"You're my favorite," I said. Beckett gave a humorless half chuckle but didn't look at me. "Lucas is taking a break from tour."

Beckett looked down at the ground. "Yeah? So you feel like now is a good time to reengage with the band?"

"I feel bad. He made this grand gesture to come be with me on tour while trying to respect the fact that no one really wants him around. I couldn't let him go through all that and then be all 'See ya, gotta go hang with people who can't stand you.'" I crossed my arms and stared at him.

He scrubbed at the back of his head. "I don't know. Maybe that's why none of us has an actual girlfriend."

"I can't help it that you're all emotionally stunted."

"Look, it's not about you having a boyfriend. But he's not good for the band. He brings too much insanity. Every show becomes, in some way, about him. Even your newfound fame—it's all really about him. Is that what you want to be? The girlfriend?"

Sigh. Leave it to Beckett to jump right on the thing that Lucas and I were so careful not to talk about. "No. I want it to be about us. I wouldn't do anything that I didn't think would benefit the band."

"His fans turn our shows into a circus every single night. Our actual fans can't even get to us because they get shoved aside by people who want a piece of Lucas Rivers. Which includes you, by the way."

I felt helpless. I didn't know how to make things right. "What do you want me to do? This is just how it is."

"Maybe you should think about why any person would crave that much attention. It's not normal. And I know it isn't you."

He didn't wait for me to answer. He just turned and walked away.

28

$\mathcal{D}$esperation set in quickly. I called Mandy for company even though I felt ridiculous.

"It's better you're on your own bus. Everyone here wants your head on a platter," Mandy said when I complained about being lonely. We added a date in Indianapolis and an extra show in Cincinnati to make up for my meeting days in LA. This evidently didn't increase my popularity with the band and crew.

"You'd think they'd be excited about more exposure," I said.

"Yeah. They're not," Mandy said. She held the phone away to bicker with one of the crew guys.

"Have they said anything about Lucas not coming back?" I asked.

She sighed. "Only that they hope you're finally ready to

scrape the barnacles off your social boat." I didn't have to guess who'd actually said that.

Even Malcolm, who usually took everything in stride, freaked out about all the hangers-on. In Des Moines, he decided to play the show drunk and yelled into his mike, "Lucas Rivers has left the building! If you're trying to catch a glimpse of that ass, you're shit out of luck!"

That was the low point.

The good news was that I had plenty of time to work on my song. Since I was alone on the bus, I didn't even need headphones. I tried writing in a notebook to see if that would free up my thoughts. It didn't. Lines were crossed out as soon as I wrote them. I forced myself to move away from the specifics of my life and write more generally about emotions, but then there was nothing to anchor the story.

I thought about the songs that our fans loved most. What they all had in common was that they were detailed enough to be unique stories but general enough to be relatable. Even (shudder) "Parietals" had that going for it. Who couldn't relate to the thrill of sneaking around, breaking rules, to be with the person you were into? After all, that's what had made it the perfect song for me and Mike Malloy.

My usual resolve to forget Mike ever existed broke down as the Detroit show neared. I wondered if he'd see me as this totally different person. Even though I didn't want to be with him anymore, I wouldn't object if he were to spend months or even years wallowing in regret.

During the next few days, as I tried to write my song, I relived that awful chapter again and again, which only increased my hysteria. I filled and emptied the trash bin many times, and balled-up paper littered every corner of the bus.

I hoped Lucas would come back to the tour before we got there. I knew it was shallow to want a celebrity boyfriend as a security blanket. There was so much that I was unprepared to deal with.

"Don't think about it," Mandy advised. "Why would you even want people from school to accept you? I'll try to help with your parents' circus, but if my family comes I might have my hands full. You know they don't understand crowds."

"What if Mike shows up?" I knew she couldn't really have the answer.

"So what if he does? Ignore him like always and move on," Mandy said. I must not have looked convinced, because she leaned forward and gave me a squeeze. "I mean, say he does come bearing roses and a sweet apology. What's that going to do? It's two years too late. You're dating Lucas Rivers, who makes Mike Malloy look like yesterday's dog food. Why you're even wasting your time thinking about high school, I have no idea."

"You're not nervous at all?" If you asked me, going home could be even weirder for Mandy, since she'd definitely be back for senior year.

"I didn't say that, but I'm loving my summer. I have the best job, and I'm not going to let haters bring me down over some ancient, made-up drama."

I groaned and felt guilty once again that her only fault in said made-up drama was staying my friend.

How could Lydon High ever have been my real life?

My phone rang as soon as I remembered to turn it on. "It was a still from our publicity shoot. You know I'm not into her, right?" Lucas said when I answered.

"What are you talking about?"

"You haven't seen? Go get online."

I passed the ghost town of the sleeping berth and went out to the lounge. "What am I about to see?" I waited for my laptop to start up.

Lucas sighed. "Me kissing Nina. It's a still from our publicity photo shoot. I swear."

"Why do you think I'm going to be upset about this?"

"Because. The way it's cropped and blurred out, it looks likes a paparazzi shot. All the headlines say I'm cheating on you." He blurted it out, like saying it was going to be the hard part.

I searched for their names together and the picture loaded right away, right there in the search results. "Yeah, I see what you mean." I felt my insecurity and pitiable dating track record taking over, ruling out any rational thought.

"I'm coming to see you. You're in Cincinnati for one more day, right?"

"Maybe you shouldn't—"

"I want to. I have to."

I could already feel myself starting to shut him out. Whether he'd been with Nina or not almost didn't matter. That everyone thought he had was bad enough.

Our show that night was fantastic, which was totally bizarre since I performed entirely from muscle memory. I almost wasn't even there, I was so absorbed in thinking about Lucas and going home.

"That show was killer," Pem said. "Whatever you were doing, definitely do it again." That wouldn't be a problem.

If my bandmates knew anything about Lucas and Nina, they were being discreet. Only Mandy had any interest in the subject. We had a night in a hotel, so I got a break from feeling like the tour outcast. "Why would Lucas do that?" she asked. "Do you think he can tell you're still scarred from Mike?"

"I am not!" My shrill voice gave me away. "Lucas doesn't know anything about that."

"You haven't told him?" She eyed me like I'd neglected to tell him about a terminal disease. "I'm just saying, maybe he senses that you're not completely available."

Her reaction threw me. "So you actually think he did it?"

Mandy's cheeks colored. "No! I'm just trying to understand what the reason might be *if* he did. But I'm sure he didn't. He's obviously smitten with you."

"He's coming tomorrow. I should probably hear him out." I realized that in some ways, I'd expected this to happen. Not that I deserved it, but it was kind of a setup for failure to date someone who could have whatever he wanted whenever he wanted it.

Mandy put her arm around my shoulders. "I just want you to finally put the Mike Malloy debacle behind you. You deserve that."

Lucas arrived just before our meet and greet. He burst into the dressing room. "Can we get a minute?"

Beckett looked at me with raised eyebrows and I gave a

215

quick nod, so they left. I stood up and clasped my hands in front of me. "I didn't hook up with Nina. I don't even like her," Lucas said.

"Okay," I said. Even if I'd had a gut feeling, I probably would have ignored it. Since when had my gut ever been right?

"Okay you believe me, or okay get the fuck out?" Lucas asked.

I laughed despite myself. "A little of both, I guess."

Then he came and stood close to me, rubbing my arm and peering into my eyes. "I'm sorry that's out there, but it's not what they're saying it is. If I wanted to get together with Nina, I would have done it a year ago when we were on set every day." That was supposed to make me feel better. "I want to come back on tour."

"For how long?" Maybe focusing on facts would help me manage this confusing situation.

He stepped in to hug me. "As long as you'll let me."

After the show, which he watched dutifully from side stage, Lucas went straight to the bus. He assumed correctly that no one was thrilled to see him back and stayed out of the way.

Beckett caught me on my way out of the shower. "Everything okay?"

"I'm sure it will be," I said. It meant so much to me that he cared enough to ask.

"Okay." He searched my face for more. "Hometown show tomorrow."

I groaned. "I just want to get it over with. How do you play in front of people who have known you your whole life?"

Beckett laughed. "We'll do you proud. I promise."

When I got on the bus, Ray was passed out in the lounge, and Lucas was beside him, reading smoothed-out pieces of notebook paper. My lyrics. I went over and grabbed them out of his hand.

"What is that?" he asked.

"My really bad attempts at writing a song." I smiled so he'd think I was just embarrassed.

"Is any of that stuff real?" he asked.

"Of course not."

29

It was lunchtime when I ventured out to the front of the bus. Ray was playing video games and Lisette was working on her computer.

"Is he awake?" Lisette asked. I shook my head. "We traveled for twelve hours to get to Cincinnati yesterday. We should have hired a private jet. That was so not worth it." She gave me a cool stare. I guess it was kind of my fault that she was back living on a bus instead of a cushy room at Chateau Marmont.

I texted Mandy to see what she was doing. She replied with: *Home to do laundry and eat. B back soon.*

I had no desire to go home. Being in Detroit was hard enough. I didn't want to do anything to break the rhythm of being on tour. Hanging out in familiar surroundings would make gearing back up too difficult. I got dressed, then went to the other bus. "Anyone want a no-holds-barred tour of Detroit?" I asked as I walked up the steps.

"No," Pem said.

"Pass," Malcolm said. "We've been here like five times."

"Fine, your loss," I said. "What are you doing?"

"I have a call with Sam in ten minutes," Pem said. He gave me a wary look so I knew they'd be discussing my stuff. "Have you listened to *Horses* ten times yet?"

"Yup. Ten times straight through, no interruptions."

"And?"

"Patti Smith still has not grown on me."

Pem groaned.

"Sorry. I think it's overwrought and contrived," I said.

"Everyone from Courtney Love to Bono has cited that record as a major influence." Pem looked at Beckett like there was something Beckett should be doing to change my mind.

"Just because it's weird doesn't mean it's good," I said.

Pem stared at me, but Beckett shrugged. Apparently my music taste was beyond fixing.

"I'll take a tour," Beckett said.

"That's okay. I wasn't serious." I smiled at him.

"Oh, if Malcolm doesn't want to go, there's no tour?" Beckett elbowed me.

"Fuck it, I'll go." Malcolm stood up. "Just let me change."

"I was totally kidding," I called. "There is no tour."

"Come on," Beckett said. "We've never seen Lydon."

"Consider that a win," I said.

Even so, an hour later I found myself telling the runner to slow down as he passed my house.

"Nice," Beckett said.

"Cute," Malcolm said.

We drove by my high school.

"This tour's fucking boring," Malcolm said. He balled up a sweatshirt and used it as a pillow. Within minutes, he was asleep.

"I told you," I said to Beckett.

"Maybe you can introduce him to some of your friends."

I guess I'd never explicitly said that Mandy was my only friend. It seemed a little late in the game to be correcting his assumption that I had others. "I don't know anyone who's his type," I said.

"Malcolm has a type?"

I laughed. I decided to bring them by Ford's Fast Five. Beckett shook Malcolm. "We're visiting Brian and Linda."

"Oh God." Nonetheless, Malcolm sat up and blinked himself awake.

When we walked in, my mother was helping Mrs. Carlson, my precalc teacher, pick out swim goggles. "Honey!" she said when she saw me. She turned to Mrs. Carlson. "These guys are in the band Melbourne. Have you ever heard of them?"

Mrs. Carlson nodded. "I hear you on the radio all the time. And I'm so happy to see something good finally happening to you, Chelsea."

"Uh, thanks, Mrs. Carlson." I ignored Beckett's and Malcolm's questioning looks and steered them to the counter, where my father rang up another customer. "What a surprise!" he said.

"Just giving a quick tour of Lydon," I said.

"What do you think?" my father asked.

"Very quaint. Big on charm," Malcolm said.

My father grinned. He loves a bullshitter.

I was about to show them around and wow them with my vast knowledge of sporting goods when my mother waved us over. The two people she was talking to turned. Mike Malloy and Caryn Sullivan. Why did Lydon have to be so damn small? My breathing went shallow.

"Chelsea, come here," my mother called.

I trudged over with Malcolm and Beckett trailing behind. I wanted to make a run for it. At least Mike and Caryn would be too starstruck to be nasty. "Mike. Caryn. Meet Beckett and Malcolm," I said. My mother looked ecstatic that I was the conduit for this epic meeting between famous and popular, but she slinked away just like a mom of a cool girl would.

"I'm such a huge fan," Mike said. "I'm the reason Chelsea even knows about your band."

Beckett gave Mike a look that was hard to read. "Wow. Thanks."

"We're coming to the show tonight!" Caryn was all excited, even though I could guarantee that she didn't own a single Melbourne album. "Is Lucas Rivers here, or is that just a rumor?"

I was grateful that Beckett and Malcolm remained expressionless. "He's here."

"So that Nina Maras thing was made up?" Caryn squealed. "I also read that you're coming out with a solo album."

"What? No, that's not true." I shook my head at Beckett and Malcolm. The confusion of talking to Mike and Caryn more than I had in the past two years combined was short-circuiting my brain.

"Are you going to play 'Parietals'? Chelsea can sing the hell out of that song," Mike said.

Now Beckett was giving me a look. "It's part of the encore," I snapped.

"Cool." Mike smiled, deliberately clueless as always. "You moved to the DTE Pavilion, right? That's a big deal." We'd been scheduled to play the Fillmore, but Mark had managed to move us to the larger DTE.

"Why don't you give them passes?" my mother called from the register.

"Because you're bringing everyone you've ever met," I called back.

Mike shrugged. "If you can scrounge any up, hit me on my cell. You still have my number, right?"

I didn't bother hiding my cringe as he and Caryn left the store. Malcolm took one look at me and said, "I'm just going to put this out there: You have the worst taste in boys."

"I never dated Mike," I hissed in a furious whisper.

"Why don't you have anyone on your list?" Beckett asked when we got in the car. "Even Malcolm does."

"Who?" I asked.

"Rochelle and Caitlin from Grosse Pointe," Malcolm said.

"My parents are taking all my passes, plus yours and Pem's. It's easier than fighting with them," I said.

Beckett studied me but let the subject drop.

When we got back to the venue, he and Malcolm went to their bus and I went to mine. I missed hanging out with them and didn't want our afternoon to end.

Lucas was waiting for me and wasn't happy when I told him I'd shown Beckett and Malcolm around my hometown. "I would have gone," he said.

"Lisette said to let you sleep. It was boring anyway." I held out my hand to him. "Want to come to sound check?"

"No thanks." He ignored my hand. "Seen one, seen 'em all."

For the meet and greet, we sat at a long table and the fans passed, single-file, said hi, and snapped a picture. It was like they were on a conveyer belt. This was the first time I'd heard Rob give his spiel at the beginning. They were in the hall, but I could hear him clearly. "Everyone will have the opportunity to take one group shot. I know you all have a favorite band member, but to be efficient we're only allowing pictures of everyone together."

I turned to Malcolm. "Why is that a rule?" I'd just assumed everyone wanted a picture with the whole band.

"So all the pseudo fans don't hold everyone up waiting to get a picture with Lucas Rivers's girlfriend."

Midway through the meet and greet assembly line, my parents got tired of waiting. They didn't just jump in front of the line themselves; they brought an entourage of about twelve people with them. The next person in line was about to blow up, so I touched her arm. "Sorry. My parents. I'll get rid of them." I stood up and matched my mother's maniacal grin. "What. Is this?"

"Honey, everyone wants to see you!"

I nodded at my parents' friends, most of whom I knew (though I did notice a couple with a little boy whom I'd never laid eyes on before). "Okay, but you can't just cut."

My mother didn't even notice everyone glaring at her. "We

want a picture!" Their posse gathered around the table shep-herded by my incredibly intrusive parents, and Rob snapped a picture. My mom put her arms around the shoulders of the people I didn't know. "We met these nice folks at breakfast. Their son, Noah, is a real Beckett fan, right, Noah?" My mother staged the next photo so that Noah, who looked to be about ten, stood in front of Beckett and started shooing the rest of us out of the way.

"It's one picture with all of us. That's it." I turned to Noah's parents, who probably had no idea what was going on. "Sorry, we have all these people to meet and we need to do it quickly." I gestured down the length of the line shifting with restless fans. Rob finally took control of the situation. "Okay, we need to keep going."

When the meet and greet was over, Rob shook his head. "Your parents are a piece of work." That was putting it mildly.

Miraculously, our show was going smoothly. I'd decided to pretend we were in another city. But then my eyes landed on Mike Malloy. He and his crew had floor tickets and were disturbingly close to the stage. Once I knew he was there, I couldn't take my eyes away from him. He sang every word with me just like he had back then. My heart started to palpitate.

A few people in that area held signs. Fans occasionally made them to proclaim undying love for one of the guys, but it was by no means a regular occurrence. I squinted to see what they said.

One read:

lucas: dump chelsea! date me!

Another read:

entrapment is for losers.

Shit. I was totally rattled and felt like I couldn't get enough air into my lungs to sing. I spotted Lucas at the side of the stage. Before Beckett could start the next song, I said, "Hey, everyone, say hi to Lucas!" and pointed to him. He took a bewildered step forward, looked at me, then straightened up and strode out onto the stage.

The crowd went nuts, although there were some boos.

He took my mike and opened his mouth like he was going to sing. "I'm totally messing with you. I can't sing at all. Hello, Detroit!"

More ecstatic cheering.

"I've always wanted to do that. You're beautiful! Thanks for saying hi!" Lucas gave me my mike back along with a peck on the cheek.

My eyes went round with disbelief. I hadn't expected Lucas to make that big a spectacle of himself. I thought he'd just wave and duck back into hiding. Pem and Beckett both looked like they wanted to flay me alive.

I hadn't planned to do it; I needed to get the focus off me and there was no way to do that when you were onstage. We continued our set, but from then on many people, including the girls from my high school, kept their eyes on the spot where Lucas had been hiding. Their distraction freed me up again.

We started the second song in our encore, which was sup-posed to be "Parietals," but Beckett launched right into the

225

guitar line for our last song. Pem looked at him with an angry, questioning expression. Malcolm fell into line with a shrug.

"Thanks for the shout-out, babe." Lucas was fully visible now, and some girls in the front were having a group meltdown. He blew them a kiss, then pulled me to him, dipped me low, and gave me a long, energetic kiss. The girls screamed. I was speechless when we stood back up. He grinned. "Now everyone can forget about that stupid rumor." Yeah, maybe not everyone.

30

"They're in the production office," Winston said when I asked him about my parents after the show. "Yo, you better stay out of Pem's and Beckett's way tonight."

Duly noted.

My parents had Lucas cornered. My mother gazed at him with an adoring fangirl expression. "So, young man, what are your intentions with our daughter?" my father asked with a serious expression.

I couldn't see Lucas's face, but he stammered an incoherent reply before my father burst out laughing. Rob was pretending to work, but he couldn't contain his laughter. Anything that had the potential to make Lucas miserable had the band and crew's full support.

A nice girlfriend would have intervened, but I was maxed out from my parents' earlier antics and the show itself. Lucas could take this one for the team. I fled to the bus.

Mandy latched onto my arm. "Holy crap, we survived."

"We're not out of the woods yet," I muttered. "Bus call's not until two. Did you talk to anyone?"

"I took my brother out for ice cream and got swarmed by everyone wanting hookups. Even Dane. He was willing to pay and everything."

I wrinkled my nose at the thought of my old boss coming to the show. "Did your parents come?"

"No. Too afraid. But how amazing is it to come back and be all 'In your face!'? That has got to be the most delicious feeling. It was for me, and I'm not even in the band. I'm only cool because I get to hang out with you. Talk about a turn of events!"

"Uh, that's not exactly how it went." I glanced out the window and saw Lucas leading my parents toward the bus. "Hey!" I flashed Lucas what I hoped was an irresistible grin when they got on the bus.

Lucas's smile was more of the nervous and baffled variety. Mandy, sensing trouble, slipped off the bus but not before getting mauled by my parents.

After they finished grilling Lucas about "showbiz" (which I gathered they'd been doing for almost an hour now), my parents looked around. My dad marveled over the hydraulic doors and the wonders of bus plumbing while my mom deemed everything in the kitchenette "adorable." When we got to the back bedroom, she asked, "Who sleeps in here?"

Lucas looked at me. "Lucas does," I said.

My mother raised her eyebrows. "And where do you sleep?"

"In one of the bunks." I turned to Lucas. "We need to get out of here."

"Is there a party? Can we come?" my father asked.

I shook my head. "We have a tour meeting. You know, tour business."

My mom got teary-eyed and I almost felt bad until she turned to Lucas and said, "I am so happy Chelsea finally has a boyfriend. After the number Mike did on her, I wasn't sure she'd ever get her confidence back. As a mother, you always hope your child will meet that special someone."

Now Lucas looked even more scared than before. *"Mom."* I dragged Lucas off the bus.

"Should I even ask?" Lucas stared at me.

"Probably not," I said.

Ray and Lisette stood outside, smoking. "Can you get a runner?" I asked. "We're going to get food. Wait a sec. I'm going to get Mandy."

On my way to the other bus, I spotted all my bandmates and some of the crew guys piling into cars. "Where are you all going?" I asked.

"Royal Oak. Our friend's DJ'ing," Malcolm said.

"You're going all the way down there?" The Royal Oak Music Theatre was at least half an hour away.

"His show is unbelievable. You should come."

I thought about what Winston had said. "You sure? Don't Beckett and Pem have a contract out on me?"

"Yeah. But that's not gonna change if you stay behind. Might as well take your medicine like a big girl."

So I rounded up Lucas, Lisette, Ray, and Mandy and followed the other cars to the Royal Oak.

Once we arrived, someone came out to escort us to a roped-off VIP section in the front of the floor. The set was already in full swing, and behind us the audience jumped and flailed in unison.

Atom, the DJ, hovered high above the stage in his booth—a long white counter that blended into the backdrop so that he was the center of one enormous video screen. Colors and shapes flashed and swirled, at times moving so fast it felt like we were speeding through a tunnel of light, at others erupting like a psychedelic volcano. White strobe lights and lasers shot all over the inside of the venue. The bass thumped so hard my heart felt like it was beating in time to the music, making it impossible not to dance.

I'd never been to an EDM show. Atom's expression reminded me of a little kid who knew he was getting away with something naughty. We were his puppets and he liked it. He was a little god up there, ordering an assault on the crowd's senses, removed from us but controlling our every move. If he bounced, we bounced; if he waved his arms, we waved back. Just as the song's tension ratcheted up as high as it could, it went plunging down into the drop. The crowd went insane.

Lucas stood behind me with his hands on my hips, completely mesmerized, until Ray, probably the only person in the place not into the show, came over and tapped him. Lucas nodded and motioned toward the lobby so I knew where he was going. Lisette followed them. I kept dancing and caught Beckett's glance a couple of times. I liked the way he moved: smooth and restrained, not flashy. Mandy and Malcolm passed a water bottle back and forth. Even Pem was upbeat.

I worked up the courage to go to Beckett. I braced myself for a scathing comment, but instead when he leaned down to talk into my ear he asked, "You like it?"

I nodded, relieved he didn't hate me. I gestured for him to bend down again. "Totally. I just think it's funny how pleased he is with himself up there, all untouchable."

"What do you mean?"

"When we perform, it's more of a collaboration with the audience. Even though we're manipulating them in a way, it's not so blatant."

"Yeah, but don't you like the way this feels? For me it's hard to get lost in other bands' music because I'm always analyzing. This is so different, I can just go along for the ride."

We'd stopped dancing to carry on this conversation. I could imagine how strange it looked—the only people standing still in a sea of writhing bodies, our heads glued together. So when Lucas tapped my arm, I stepped back from Beckett like I'd been caught doing something wrong.

"Let's go outside." Lucas's expression was neutral. "Ray can buy us drinks."

I followed him out to a bar area, where Ray and Lisette sat on stools. We could still hear the music pulsing from inside. "What were you guys talking about?" Lucas handed me a red plastic cup. I took a sip. Rum and coke.

I didn't get a chance to answer, because Mandy, Beckett, Malcolm, and Pem came out of the theater. "Hey, we need to talk about the stunt you guys pulled onstage today," Beckett said. Uh-oh. Here it was. "We don't want attention directed at Lucas any more than it already has been. If you want him on tour, that's your call, but you can't bring him onstage."

Letting Beckett down stung in a different way than disappointing Pem. Though the latter wasn't pleasant, at least I could partly attribute it to his sparkling personality.

"Man, it was just a quick hello. It's not like I came out and break-danced," Lucas said.

Malcolm snorted. "That would actually have been more interesting."

Lucas flipped him off.

"The Lucas Rivers Corporation and Melbourne are two things that should never go together," Pem said. "Like socks and sports sandals or kilts and underwear, you know what I mean?" He stared at us.

There was no point in trying to justify what happened. "I'm truly sorry," I said. "These jerks I went to high school with were pushing up on the barricade and I was already so nervous. I just needed a reset button."

"You need to figure out a different one," Beckett said.

"It did the job, didn't it? She got the pressure off and took a minute. Personally I think it was brilliant." Lucas was defending me, but he was also using me to annoy my bandmates. I had to shut this conversation down.

"It won't happen again. Chalk it up to first-hometown-show jitters," I said.

"Those people were not good to her," Mandy added.

"Yeah, what was up with the signs?" Malcolm asked.

"Trying to bring Chelsea back down to size," Mandy said. Her eyes lost focus. God, she was really drunk. I grabbed the water bottle out of her hand and dumped it in the trash. She didn't even notice. Whatever was in there, it definitely wasn't water. "Maybe they realized that they're going to peak in high school and that she's just getting started."

"Anyway, let's move on." I glared at Mandy, then glanced around as if someone from our school might overhear her.

It was quiet for a moment. Lucas had been toying with a sugar packet on the bar and gave it a light toss onto the floor. "Hey, Chelsea. I dropped a little bit of you on the floor."

It took me a minute but then I got it. "Awwww," I said at the same time as everyone else either groaned or laughed condescendingly. In these moments, I totally understood why the Melbourne guys found Lucas disingenuous. He lived for theatrical moments, sometimes to the point of being cringe-worthy. Occupational hazard, I supposed.

"And why am I reading all this crap about you recording a solo album?" Pem asked.

"I don't know. I just heard about it today." I hadn't seen the stories myself, but everyone kept asking about it. No real person had been quoted, only "a source close to the Melbourne camp."

"Oh, that was me." We all turned to stare. Lisette waved and smiled like she was getting an award. "It makes you seem like you have more game."

"No one gave you permission to do that!" I snapped. Lisette got under my skin on our best days. Like Ray, she had trouble with boundaries when it came to Lucas.

"Relax." Lucas tugged on my shirt. "She thought it would add more intrigue to your story."

"I don't care! That wasn't her call to make." Everyone was watching me unravel, but I was past worrying about it.

Lucas patted my hand, which came off as totally patronizing. Lisette shot me a self-satisfied smile. I couldn't believe Lucas would overlook her stepping out of line like that. He turned back to her and Ray.

Later, as we stood up to go back in, I had a chance to talk to

Beckett without everyone overhearing. I asked him why he'd skipped "Parietals."

He looked at me intently. "It seems like you have baggage with that song, and I didn't want to make coming home worse for you."

I was momentarily speechless. Beckett was too observant. "Thank you." Words were so inadequate sometimes.

He kept looking at me like he could see right into me. "Anytime."

I reached up and gave him a hug, which was bold, since we hadn't been close lately. He slid an arm around me but pulled away when he noticed Lucas staring at us.

The next morning we arrived in Columbus. And just when I should have been able to breathe a sigh of relief, Mandy barged onto our bus. Everyone else was still asleep. "I need to talk to you," she whispered. "I screwed up."

This wasn't going to be good. Mandy was jittery, all over the place. "What happened?" I asked.

"I had sex last night." She wouldn't look me in the eye.

"With Oscar? Why's that bad?" I mean, I knew it was against Pem's rules, but come on.

She rolled her eyes. "No. He's too obedient. Only groupies and hangers-on for him." She leaned forward. "I slept with Malcolm."

"Oh." Slightly bigger deal. "Was it . . . I mean, are you glad?" I was wide-awake now.

"I threw myself at him. That much I remember."

I knew Malcolm well enough to know he wasn't going to

turn that down. "Malcolm's not going to say anything. Even if he did, I don't think Pem's worried about onetime hookups."

Mandy bit her lip. "Are you sure?"

I wasn't sure. I was only saying what seemed reasonable to me. But what was reasonable to me and reasonable to Pem were often in two totally different neighborhoods. "Definitely. So are you happy?"

"If I'd known it'd be that easy, I would have gotten less drunk so I could remember more. I feel like I wasted my one shot." Mandy smiled.

"Did you use protection?"

Mandy gave me a hug. "Of course. No offense, but I'm not an idiot."

When Lucas finally woke, he only spoke in monosyllables. He was upset with me for not sticking up for him with the band.

"I thought you'd be in a great mood today," I said, slipping onto his lap. Chicago was our next stop, and his childhood friend was coming to see us play Lollapalooza. He'd meet up with us right as Lisette returned to LA. Lucas needed people around to entertain him; otherwise he got bored. I was excited to spend the day running around the grounds seeing all the bands I loved.

"I am. Just tired." He pushed me away and stood up. Okay then.

On my way to sound check, Mandy pulled me aside. "We did it again. He said he didn't realize it was my first time until it was too late and that he felt bad. So I asked him if he was offering a re-do and the next thing you know . . ." By the way she was smiling, I didn't have to ask how it went.

I shook my head. "You're pushing it." If Mandy and Malcolm couldn't keep their hands off each other, Pem was definitely going to blow up.

"Can you believe he was such a gentleman?"

I snorted. I was positive those words had never been used to describe Malcolm Ho.

I continued down the hall. "You had your fun, but now you better cut the crap."

Mandy laughed, but I was worried.

After the show, I found Lucas and Ray in the production office playing cards. Lucas still looked pissy. "Were we that bad?" I joked, even though I knew he hadn't watched the show.

"Funny," Lucas said.

"Well, I can't think of another reason you'd be so cranky."

"It's because I know, Chelsea."

I looked around the room as if I'd find some clue hanging about. "Know what?"

"That you're not a virgin," he said.

Thanks, Mandy. "So? Are you?"

"No. I just thought the reason we weren't sleeping together was because you hadn't, and now I feel like you just don't like me enough."

"It's not that. I just don't know you well enough." This wasn't entirely true, but it was as much as I was willing to say in front of Ray.

"You might not have specifically said that you were, but

you definitely gave me that impression. A lot." Lucas shuffled the deck.

"Great. I'm so glad we shared this lovely moment with Ray." I slammed out of the office. I knew when my mother mentioned Mike that Lucas would only be able to contain his curiosity for so long. Exactly one person on this tour knew that story, and she was probably in a closet somewhere with Malcolm. When our buses met up in Chicago, I expected Mandy to do some serious groveling.

31

As soon as I woke up in Chicago, I charged onto the other bus. Nobody was up. I went into the sleeping compartment to drag Mandy out of bed. She wasn't there. I reached into Malcolm's bunk and jiggled him awake. "What the fuck?" he whispered.

"Get up, right now." I went to the front and waited for him, but when the doors opened moments later, Beckett came out. "Hey. Looking for Mandy," I said.

"She's having a meeting with Sam, Pem, and Rob," Beckett said. "Pem wants to fire her."

Sam had flown in to go over the final details of the cosmetics contract with me. I'm sure my dumb best friend was the last thing he wanted to deal with. "What? For what?"

Beckett gave me a look that made it clear that everyone knew how Mandy and Malcolm had been entertaining themselves lately. Malcolm finally came through the doors. "This is all your fault!" I glared at him.

"Not hardly." Malcolm stifled a bored yawn.

"Pem can't fire you, so he's using her to make a point."

"We all think Pem's rule is totally unrealistic and unnecessary. But if I go to bat for her, he's going to get even more pissed, because he'll think it means I love her and that the band will implode. You should talk to him, though." Malcolm finally had the decency to look somewhat concerned.

Perfect. Just as I wanted to kill Mandy, I now had to come to her rescue. I turned to Beckett. "What should I say?"

Malcolm snorted. "Don't ask him. He's the reason we're in this predicament."

Beckett looked away. I wanted to know, but I also didn't want to know. "Where are they?" I asked.

"Probably in a production office, but the festival area is huge. Just wait for them to get back," Beckett said.

All the bands parked in the same lot, and it was starting to come alive. Everyone was in high spirits as they jumped on different band buses to say hi. Touring could be isolating; you got sick of seeing the same handful of faces day in and day out. The bus lot was like the coolest neighborhood block party you've ever been to. When Beckett and Malcolm emerged, they went looking for their friends.

Of course, I had no friends in other bands, so I waited for Mandy, growing more and more desperate for information. Rob was the first one to come back. He shook his head when he saw me. "Dude, it's bad. Pem wants her gone tomorrow."

"Why's he being so insane about this? It was a onetime thing." Well, two-time thing. I followed him onto the bus.

"He's mad because I've been putting all this time into training her. For real, she's smart. She could assistant-tour-manage for me next time, but Pem thinks that Malcolm will break her heart, she won't be able to deal, and she'll go work for some other band. Then our investment is in the crapper, which I agree would be total bullshit."

I groaned. When you broke down Pem's madness, it wasn't always as wildly off as it seemed at first glance.

Rob got a beer and sat down. He wasn't a big drinker and never drank while he was working, so I knew this situation was spiraling out of control. "As a bonus it took two hours and Sam translating to understand the exact nature of Pem's problem."

Mandy came onto the bus, and her face crumpled as soon as she saw me.

"You're not done yet. You need to set up the merch tent," Rob said.

She looked so pitiful that I almost forgot I was mad at her. "Will you come with?" she asked.

I sat next to her as she counted in T-shirts, hoodies, shorts, and sweatpants. "So?" I asked.

"So, the whole thing is majorly unfair. Pem's such a tyrant. You can't let them fire me. I stuck by you when the whole school ostracized you." Her half-baked thoughts tumbled right out of her mouth. She'd never held what happened with Mike over my head before.

"I'll talk to them, but Rob doesn't seem optimistic," I said.

"Chelsea, I swear it won't happen again. It was a momentary indiscretion."

Two momentary indiscretions, I thought. "Speaking of indiscretion. What's up with telling Lucas about Mike Malloy?"

Mandy looked confused. "I did? When?"

I knew her well enough to know that she wasn't faking. "I don't know. Must have been the same night you decided to do the other stupid thing you did."

"What did he say?"

"He feels like I've been lying to him and that he's been tortured into celibacy for no reason."

"I'm sure this is a first for him," Mandy said. I snorted. "What? Personally I think you're insane. He's hot. And rich. And, oh yeah, one of the biggest movie stars out there."

"Ew. That's so not the point. I just don't want to do something I'll regret again."

"Well. Good luck with that." Mandy turned away to fold T-shirts.

"You got yourself into this situation. Don't take it out on me." I knew she was in a bad place, but I didn't think I was crazy to expect a little remorse from her.

"Please, just talk to them," she pleaded.

"Since when have they ever listened to me? How did they leave it with you?"

"They're going to decide after Canada. If you beg, they'll have to keep me."

She was all too willing to overestimate my influence. Anything short of threatening to strike (and ending my own career) and I'd be lucky to even get a word in. Pem was so hardheaded, once his mind was made up it was impossible to get through to him. "I'll do my best."

Our slot was later in the day on the main stage, but we weren't headlining. Beckett was in a great mood. "This is our chance to steal fans. We're not headliners, people aren't here for us,

241

but that doesn't mean we can't win them over. Let's come with everything we have."

His competitiveness would have been contagious if it wasn't directly offset by Pem's misery. "Festivals are the worst. Porta-potties suck, the sound is horrible, if you're not headlining you're dead weight."

"Uh, but Beckett said—"

"Just don't even go there. Yin and yang. Have you learned nothing?" Malcolm asked.

Pem didn't even have time to comment on the Mandy situation, which was a bad sign. When I tried to talk to him he said, "Not today. I just need to get out of here."

I went back to our bus to meet Lucas's friend Derek. They were in the lounge, smoking pot and playing video games. "Say hi to Derek," Lucas said.

"Nice to meet you," I said.

"'Sup," Derek said. I instantly disliked him.

They were best friends growing up in Akron, and Lucas sometimes flew Derek out to LA for long stretches when he wasn't filming. I didn't get the sense they had that much in common. After they finished getting stoned out of their minds, they were ready to see some shows. They wanted to go without Ray as a babysitter, so we were all incognito in hats and dark glasses.

As the day went on, the grounds filled up until it felt like every direction we tried to walk in was the exact wrong one. We were constantly swimming upstream. "I should get back," I said. Melbourne had a signing right before our set.

"Let's get something to eat and we'll walk you back," Lucas said, grabbing my hand. Derek's arrival and probably the pot had put our fight on hold. There were food stands all over the grounds. We tried to pick one with a short line, but it still moved excruciatingly slowly. By the time we got our food, I had to speed-walk. Somebody plowed right into me and knocked me down. My food spilled all over me.

"Oh my God, I'm sorry," the guy wailed. He was a scrawny, hipster type. I was actually surprised he was able to knock me down.

I jumped up, but not before Lucas shoved him. "Watch where you're going."

We kept walking. I grabbed Lucas's arm. "It was an accident. It's a mob scene in here."

The knockdown and ensuing shove attracted enough attention that some girl came up, doing an end run on us. "I told you! It's Lucas Rivers!" Her friend squealed, covered her mouth, and stared at us.

The first girl began grabbing random passersby. "That's Lucas Rivers and Chelsea Ford!"

Soon we were at a complete standstill, surrounded. Lucas tried to position his body in front of mine, but that was ridiculous because he was drawing more attention than I was.

He texted Ray. Derek had obviously been in this situation before, because he put one arm around me and tried to clear a path with the other. It was useless. We moved inches and not always in the right direction. I didn't want to be late, and being trapped like this was making us all panic.

What seemed like hours later, Ray broke through the crowd with Rob. They started shouting at everyone to let us walk. With a lot of pushing and yelling, Derek, Ray, and Rob eventually got us to the signing tent.

The line snaked around the inside. The rest of the band barely looked up as I slipped into the empty seat. At least they didn't see the food stains on my shirt.

Sam and Michaela stood to the side. She glared at me, so I knew my lateness wasn't going to go unaddressed. Her baby bump was showing more, and while it was cute it did not prevent her from looking completely scary.

The signing went on and on. I answered every "Is Lucas here?" with a cryptic smile before turning to the next person.

Even though the day was overcast, the humidity threatened to take us all down. Beckett insisted on giving his chair to Michaela and finished the signing standing up.

As soon as the tent cleared, Michaela rushed over to me. "Are you high, being twenty minutes late for a forty-minute signing? Do you have any idea how unprofessional that is? And you look like a fucking slob. With all the stuff you have going on, do you want to get a rep for being a diva? Because you have not earned it!" She kept hiking her maternity jeans up because her belly still wasn't big enough to hold them up. "Goddammit!"

Okay. I chalked most of that tirade up to pregnancy hormones, because I thought she was seriously overreacting. But when I saw the look on Sam's face, and the way the guys avoided looking at me, I knew what I'd done wasn't cool. The only thing I had going in my favor was that I couldn't possibly be late for the show. I just had to find a new shirt.

Beckett shook his head, took his shirt off, and handed it to me. "You don't have time to go back to the bus. Pem always carries a spare. I'll ask him for it."

Wearing Beckett's faded black Metallica T-shirt felt cozy, intimate. I already planned to steal it.

The show itself was amazingly fun, even in the sweltering heat. We played to an audience easily four times the size of our normal show, even post-Lucas. The stage was a lot bigger too. I felt like I did for our first show, like if I didn't control my adrenaline level I was going to be sick afterward.

There was no sign of Lucas anywhere. While I didn't expect him to watch every show, this wasn't an ordinary one. In many ways, this festival was my big debut to the rock scene. I couldn't believe he'd miss it. Whatever. I willed myself to focus.

Fortunately, forgetting wasn't hard. The sweaty, dirty crowd was completely insane. Girls sat on guys' shoulders, dancing and rocking out. People held up cameras and phones, waved cups, and flung plastic bottles, sending water arcing high into the air. I sang like I was down in the pit going crazy with them.

From the stage, I could see past our audience to other parts of the grounds. As our set went on, more people joined us. I felt like a super magnet, pulling people in. "Here they come!" I yelled into the mike just before the song erupted into the chorus. The crowd exploded.

Afterward I could tell that despite all his doom and gloom, Pem was pleased. In a situation like that, performing in front of a bunch of peers, he'd only be satisfied if we were flawless. I was ecstatic that I'd delivered a performance we could both be proud of.

We all wanted to watch the Wronged, who were that night's headliners. I found Lucas in the VIP area, drinking bourbon with Derek and Ray. Over time I'd learned that Ray's role vacillated between security guard and resident best buddy. He rarely got so out of hand that he couldn't do his security duties, but he came close a lot.

I went to stand with Lucas while the rest of the band and crew stayed clumped together at the other end of the section.

"I love this band." I'd never seen the Wronged play live before, and it felt great to be on the fan side again.

"I can't believe they still perform." Lucas snorted. "I guess as long as there's taxes, divorce, and drug habits, old bands will keep playing together."

Whoa. Talk about not getting it.

Since he was already in such a fabulous mood, I decided to go for it. "You didn't watch our set?"

"Sorry. I wanted to check out another band." Lucas took a sip of his drink. "Where'd you get the shirt?"

I looked down, holding the T-shirt out by the hem. "Beckett. Remember I got food on mine?"

He nodded, expressionless.

"I wish we could stay, but bus call is so early." We had an overdrive to get to our next show, in Toronto.

"Actually, Derek and I are going to stay and check out tomorrow's lineup."

"Really?" I asked.

"Yeah. But you keep the bus. We'll stay in a hotel."

"You sure?" As usual, my polite Midwesterner reflexes prevented me from asking the real question, which was "Are we finally breaking up?"

32

How had everything gone haywire in a matter of days? Nothing looked better in the morning. It felt like a Monday. Everyone was touchy, their moods grim.

Mandy avoided everyone, even me. She kept her head down and got to work. This was her last chance to prove herself, so it was probably a wise choice.

Sam and I had a quick meeting about the cosmetics deal. If I okayed it, our partnership would go into effect as early as the next show. He'd gone over it with the rest of the band as to how it would affect them. Pem was skittish about the tour sponsorship part, but Sam said we'd have control over what went up at our shows. He said Malcolm and Beckett saw how it could be good for staying in the public eye when we weren't on the road or doing promo. Their acceptance put my mind at ease.

"You don't have to cut the rest of the band in except for the tour sponsorship part. You'll be the one doing all the work, so it's up to you."

"Okay." I didn't know what to think about that.

"And this solo record thing is becoming a real problem."

"They know where the rumor started," I said. "They know it's not real."

"Everyone's talking about it online like it's real. Makes the band look bad, like you think you can do better."

"I already said it wasn't true. Can't Michaela release a statement?"

"She's going to, but damage has already been done." I dropped my head into my hands. What was I supposed to do? Lucas thought any attention was good, so he'd never tell Lisette to admit publicly that she'd made it up. I felt exasperated with everyone in that camp all over again.

"About Mandy," I said.

Sam slumped in his chair. "I can't force her on the band. I'd say talk to Pem, but I know you guys haven't exactly become close." He said this like it was because I didn't try hard enough.

"Can't she just stay for the next week? There are only four shows left."

"Pem doesn't feel like just not rehiring her next time makes a strong enough statement. The rules are in place for good reason, and he wants them upheld."

"She's an easy target. If I'd fooled around with Winston or Aaron, he wouldn't kick them out the door."

"Admittedly, she's easier to replace. But that's also why he thinks if he doesn't enforce it now, no one will believe it's real."

"Why is he so anal about everything?"

"He's a control freak, but that's what makes him great at what he does." Sam started typing on his phone, so I knew the conversation was over.

"Where's the d-bag?" Malcolm said when I got onto the bus. He sifted through a stack of colorful drawings.

"What are those?" I asked.

"My next tattoo. I get one for every tour," he said.

Beckett came out. "Did you talk to Sam?" I nodded. "Nothing?"

Malcolm glanced up but didn't say anything.

Now that I knew Mandy was going, I just wanted it to be over with. It wasn't my place to tell her, so I didn't.

When I saw her later and she asked if I'd talked to Sam, I told her I had but I wasn't sure I'd managed to change anything. Tears filled her eyes. "This whole thing sucks. I want to rewind my life to a week ago. Everything was going fine."

"Just wait," I said. "You can sleep on my bus tonight."

"No thanks," she said. "If nobody has my back, doesn't really matter where I sleep."

After tonight's show, Mandy was pretty much catatonic. Beckett and Malcolm scurried over to me just before bus call. "Can we sleep on your bus?"

"Yes," I said, nodding at Beckett. "And no." I glared at Malcolm. "Suck it up. You're afraid of Mandy melting down—which, by the way, you should be—but you can't hide on my bus."

"Thanks. I'll grab my stuff." Beckett ran off.

"Why you being like that?" Malcolm asked.

"Because. You both made this mess. She's taking the fall for it, so the least you can do is put up with a little hysterical crying and spend some time feeling like shit." I gave Malcolm a gentle shove in the direction of his bus.

Beckett blew past with about five bags slung over his shoulders. He couldn't get away fast enough.

"How long are you staying?" I asked when I climbed onto the bus. I gestured to his bags on the floor.

"This bus is so outstandingly cheesy. I'm ashamed of myself for just standing in it. I doubt I'll even be able to sleep tonight," Beckett said. I stared at him, waiting for an answer. "I don't know. When's your boy coming back?"

"Right now, seems like maybe never." Beckett watched me for any sign of emotion. I shrugged. "At least we get the bus."

"Did something happen?" Beckett asked.

"It's more like something didn't happen," I said. He gave me a quizzical look, but I really didn't want to elaborate. I shook my head. "I think he just needs a break. Tour hasn't been as fun as he'd thought it would be."

Beckett looked liked he couldn't care less about Lucas's feelings. "I thought for sure when those pictures of him kissing Nina Maras went public, you'd kick him to the curb. Condo bunks, nice. Are they all clean?"

"They are. But I'm taking that one." I pointed to an upper bunk.

Beckett laughed. "You've got some bus savvy now. Isn't there a bedroom in back?"

"Yeah. I don't want it. You can use it, though."

He gave me a skeeved-out look. "Uh, no thanks."

* * *

We got ready for bed, then picked out a movie. Beckett suggested a Martin Scorsese film and stared at me when I said I hadn't seen any of them. "Yeah. I get it. I'm not as sophisticated as you all," I said.

He smiled and started the movie. "Have you made any progress on the song?"

"No," I said. "I don't think I've lived enough to write lyrics."

"That's a cop-out," Beckett said. "You've been through plenty. You're just not willing to dig deeper. Maybe think about the feel of words. That matters as much as the meaning."

Sitting next to Beckett alone in the dark felt like maybe not the smartest move. Yes, he was my friend, but I'd always been attracted to him. I had no idea if he felt the same way, but I felt an extra charge in the air whenever we were near each other. Technically, I still had a boyfriend, or at least I thought I did, but that didn't stop me from drinking in the heady, heavy feeling of being so close to Beckett.

I barely watched the movie. Instead, I let my imagination run wild, inventing scenarios in which Beckett and I fell madly in love, wrote hit songs for Melbourne, and performed all over the world together. It was way better than anything Martin Scorsese could come up with.

And then my phone rang.

33

"Hey!" I sounded too bright and cheerful for the late hour.

"What are you doing?" Lucas asked.

"Just watching a movie. Um . . ." I put my hand on Beckett's stomach to stop him from talking while I struggled to think of the name of the movie we were supposedly watching.

Beckett misread the signal. *"Taxi Driver,"* he said, loud enough that Lucas could hear him through the phone.

"Beckett's with you." It was a statement, not a question.

"Stuff is going down on the other bus. It's a little tense over there right now," I said.

"Yeah, I know. Mandy screwed around with Malcolm and now the sky is falling. So damn stupid," Lucas said.

"How did you know about that?" Between our fight and Derek arriving, I hadn't had a chance to fill him in.

"Because. I was with Mandy last night. Right before you guys left Chicago."

Something about the way he said "with Mandy" gave me pause. "Oh. Did she seem okay?"

"She was pretty distraught, but I think I made her feel better."

His innuendos were so clumsy and immature, I was embarrassed for both of us. I refused to give him the satisfaction of hearing me get angry. "Are you trying to tell me you had sex with my best friend? Because if you are, you should just come right out and say it."

Beside me, Beckett hit the pause button and shifted to watch me, a look of concern on his face. I waved my hand like it was nothing, then brought it to my forehead.

"I guess that is what I'm saying." Lucas's voice had hesitation in it but not regret.

"Just let me know when you need us off the bus." I hung up.

I covered my face, but I wasn't hiding tears, only wrestling with acute mental exhaustion. "That girl has gone off the deep end."

Beckett reached over and removed one of my hands so he could see my face. "Are you okay?"

"My best friend's on an express to Skanksville, but otherwise I'm great." Now tears were starting to fall.

"You know he's probably lying, right?"

I shook my head. I knew he wasn't. Mandy had been completely unwilling to believe that I couldn't save her job. There might have been part of her that thought I wanted her gone because she made things messy.

"She's not thinking straight. If she were, she wouldn't do anything to intentionally hurt you," Beckett said.

I tried to smile, but I knew he didn't understand. I had this deluge of emotion and nowhere to direct it. Before I thought it through, I lifted my face and kissed Beckett.

I could feel his surprise, but then he kissed me back. At first his lips were soft, reassuring, as if he worried I might just be coming unglued. When he was sure that this was what I wanted, he kissed me harder, burying his hands in my hair. I inhaled the warm, clean scent of his skin. "You smell amazing," I whispered. I hoped that wasn't a weird thing to say, but the thought was fleeting because Beckett pulled me closer, onto his lap.

After long minutes of some of the best kissing I'd ever hoped to experience, I slid my hand under his shirt, trailing my fingers over his strong back muscles, tracing up his spine with my palm. Everything about kissing Beckett felt so incredibly good that I forgot the rest. I started unbuttoning my shirt, but he took hold of my shoulders and held me away. "Let's not do this. It's too messed up."

For a moment, I felt confused. Hadn't he been as into this as I was? Then I realized he was trying to be good to me. I was touched, even if being taken care of wasn't what I wanted in the moment.

We went to bed in separate bunks, but I could still feel his lips on mine.

When I woke up in the morning, every feeling that flowed through me ended in a pool of dread. I was mortified about making a move on Beckett, and I didn't know what to say to Mandy.

Fortunately, Beckett was gone. I walked out to the parking lot just in time to see Mandy climbing into a taxi. I raced over and banged on the window. She rolled it down but wouldn't face me. "How could you? Did you think sleeping with my boyfriend would somehow make me fight harder for your job?"

She started shaking with sobs. "Oh right. You didn't even try! At least Lucas sees that Pem's a lunatic and this whole thing's basically a witch hunt. Pem's never even nice to you and you took his side over mine! And you know who's the only one who didn't? Lucas!"

"You sure he was on your side? Or was he just using you to punish me for not being dumb enough to sleep with him?"

Mandy leaned toward the driver. "Just go, please." When they were out of sight, I started crying too. She was really gone.

I went back to my bus to hide. Not knowing what else to do with myself I opened my computer, only to be bombarded with alerts about Lucas and Nina Maras. Apparently she'd flown to Chicago to enjoy Lollapalooza and "get cozy with her leading man." Unable to help myself, I clicked on the links. In every picture, Lucas and Nina had their arms snaked around each other's waists or shoulders. The captions screamed, "Forget Ford!" or "Lucas Has 'Hard Words' for Chelsea!" I closed down the browser so I wouldn't have a full-blown episode.

I got out my notebook and pencil. I thought about Mandy and Lucas and Beckett, and the words flowed. I filled page after page, stopping only when I felt like I'd picked up every piece of my life and examined it from all angles. I felt wrung out. I had a lot of words and had captured many emotions but didn't feel any closer to a song.

* * *

255

Pem pulled me aside when I was walking into the venue. "I'm sorry. It had to be done."

"She slept with Lucas." It just slipped out because I'd been thinking of little else.

"Oh. That was bitchy. So you're not mad? I mean, how could I have been clearer?"

I put my hand on his arm. "Pem. You were very clear. No one thinks that you weren't."

"Thanks for understanding. Interpersonal drama is band cancer—worse than drugs," he said.

I didn't fully understand, but it was good to remind myself that for a moment last night I was willing to risk my job, my ticket out of Lydon, for a one-night stand.

Beckett found me doing laundry in the basement of the venue. "When you're done with that, want to go see Boston?"

"Sure," I said, against my better judgment.

I tried to cover up and look as nondescript as possible, but even so, Beckett had to guide me past the amateur paparazzi staked out by the venue. Great. When pictures of Beckett and me surfaced online in about ten seconds, it would look like I was trying to get back at Lucas, when the truth was he was already in my rearview.

Beckett and I spent the morning walking around the Back Bay and Beacon Hill neighborhoods. The trendy shops, the stately brick brownstones, the cobblestone streets—it was all so adorably Boston, so different from any city we'd visited. I even convinced him to take a swan boat tour.

The whole time, we joked around and talked about superficial stuff, not going anywhere near the heavier things that had dominated our lives recently and certainly not acknowledging the fact that we'd kissed. I was just thinking how nice it was to be able to go back to normal without having to hash everything out, when Beckett said, "I have to talk to you."

"I bet," I said, plucking some leaves off a weeping willow. "I'm sorry. Kissing you was totally lame of me."

"Not that. Well . . . kind of that. I want to explain Pem's rule and why it's not demented." He was rushing now, determined to get it all out.

"Okay. I'm listening." We continued walking around the Commons. I was only vaguely aware of the passing tourists and frantic businesspeople who passed us on the paths.

"Hollis was my first girlfriend. We dated from freshman year until the end of my sophomore year, which is when the band really took off."

I was floored. This wasn't public knowledge, and they'd never seemed like anything more than good friends. "Okay," I said. I didn't want to jump to conclusions, but I thought I could see where this was headed.

"Yup. We were serious about each other, but we were young. Then, a couple of years ago, she and Pem started dating," Beckett said. Okay, I had not seen that coming. "He was really in love with her, and for a while she thought she was in love with him too. I was okay with it. I'd moved on, met other people, so it wasn't a big deal for me."

"How come you were all so secretive about this?"

"Sam always told us that we'd have more fans if we, and especially Hollis, were single. So we kept it private, which is how they preferred it anyway."

"So they broke up, and she had to leave the band because of it?"

"Pretty much. But there's one more piece. Not that long after they were done, Hollis and I hooked up. It was nostalgia more than anything, and I didn't realize how screwed up Pem was over their breakup. So when he walked in on us—"

"Ouch."

"Yeah. Not hard to do when you live on a bus. Anyway, that happened and, well, one of them had to leave the band and . . . I didn't want it to be Pem." Beckett's pained expression told me he still had a lot of unresolved feelings about this. "Hollis hit the roof when we told her we wanted to replace her. She and Pem fought like crazy about it. I still have no idea exactly what was said, and I haven't spoken to Hollis since the day she left."

"Has Pem?"

"I don't know. I doubt it."

"Oh my God, the bet."

Beckett gave a humorless laugh. "That was Malcolm's ludicrous attempt at getting Pem to get back on the horse, so to speak. He worried about Pem in his own incredibly deep Malcolm way. I mean, there's always some kind of bet on tour but usually not about that."

"The never-ending bet. That thing was doomed from the beginning."

Beckett gave me a curious look.

I ignored it. "Gross. Tell me 'Parietals' isn't about you."

"It's not about anybody in particular." He looked flushed, so I knew he was lying.

I might have confided in him before, but at that moment

I was profoundly disappointed that he wasn't always the fair, considerate guy that I'd made him out to be. Also, I already had a huge inferiority complex when it came to Hollis, and now to find out she came first with the boy I cared about too? It was a lot to swallow.

Pem's insanity made sense to me now. Being in a band was already so hard. There was so much togetherness, so many emotional ups and downs. Adding romantic entanglements on top of that would pretty much always end in disaster.

Once we were in a taxi back to the venue, Beckett asked what I was thinking.

I'd relived kissing him a thousand times since last night but now I knew exactly why it could never happen again. "I feel bad for Pem" was all I said.

Beckett looked away.

We walked into total mayhem. The stage area looked like Bombshell Cosmetics had exploded on it. There were banners along the top and foot of the stage. Bombshell scrims were set up on either side, bracketing the performance area. Video screens, mounted high to the left and right of the stage, had Bombshell ads looping with the intention of having them run while the crowd waited for the bands.

Pem was going ballistic. Rob had Sam on the phone.

When he saw me, Pem stormed over. "How could you okay this? Will you look at this shit? There is no way in hell I'm playing on this stage! Fix it!" He stalked away and Beckett went after him.

Rob handed me the phone. "Hi," I said.

"Is it that bad?" Sam asked.

"It's pretty bad," I said, my voice shaking.

"Fuck. They wrote us a big check. Pacific really wanted it," Sam said.

"Can we get out of the contract?" I asked.

"Not at this stage. Take a picture and send it to me. I need to get on the phone with someone over there."

We hung up and I handed the phone back to Rob. I snapped a picture of the stage and emailed it to Sam, then went to look for Pem. I didn't know what I wanted to say, but I needed to say something.

I found him and Beckett in the dressing room. "Sam's dealing. I had no idea that this is what their tour sponsorship would look like."

"We will lose fans if they see that out there. We have credibility as a real band. We're not made or owned by some corporation. The closest we've come is letting Pacific shove you into the band!" Pem's fury burned a hole through me.

"I'm sorry I let you down," I said, trying not to burst into tears. "I'd back out of the contract if I could."

Beckett wisely stayed out of it. Pem saw that I was upset and backed off an almost imperceptible inch. "It's not all your fault. You don't know what the fuck you're doing. Sam decided to make a money grab. I should have known he doesn't understand the meaning of 'tasteful level of corporate presence.' I thought we were talking kiosk in the lobby, not stage presence."

"Why would Sam do that?" Beckett asked.

"I don't know. Curry favor with the label? What a piece of shit."

Rob came in to find us. "Sam says all the signage will be

Melbourne-specific for the next tour. And the commercials will have Chelsea in them. This was all they could come up with in the short turnaround."

"There isn't going to be a next time if he doesn't make this go away," Pem said.

"They agreed to kill the video screens and side scrims. The banners stay."

"One banner. The one at the bottom. Or I fucking walk," Pem said.

Beckett blew out a long exhale. Rob looked at him. "I'm with Pem."

34

We played the show with both banners. Somehow Beckett convinced Pem to go forward with the show, although he did hold it up for almost forty-five minutes. "Let's live to fight another day," Beckett had said. "Only three shows left. Sam's already working on Philly."

Pem didn't speak to me for the rest of the night. I was used to being overlooked by him, but being pointedly ignored was a whole different level of suffering. If I thought bringing Melbourne to a new audience was going to be seen as a valued contribution, I was sadly mistaken. Pem cared about one thing only: artistic merit. We might not have seen eye to eye on this, but I respected his commitment.

Beckett moved back to the Melbourne bus, so I was alone for the drive from Boston to Philadelphia. "You can come back," Beckett said.

I thought it would be better for us to be apart. "I don't want to get killed in my sleep," I said.

He laughed, but he knew I was right.

At this point, the guys seemed like they just wanted to get through the end of tour. Even Malcolm was lying low and sticking close to the bus and venues. Pem was so tense he could almost have launched himself into space, but when he remembered he had family coming to the Philly show, I thought he was going to start rocking in a corner.

While the events of the past few days had been hard on me, going home wouldn't be an improvement. Before, I at least had Mandy. Now, if it had been up to me, I would have stayed on tour forever.

I walked into the dressing room at the Mann to find Pem entertaining his aunt Kathleen, uncle James, and cousin Evie. "Omigod, Chelsea Ford!" Evie was about thirteen and springy with tween energy. She bounced over and stood directly in front of me. "Mom, she used to be Lucas Rivers's girlfriend!"

"Is that right?" Kathleen asked.

"Guilty," I said. Pem smirked.

Aunt Kathleen and Uncle James both wore suits. They had to go back to work before returning for show time. "Evie is so excited to spend the day with her big cousin, Third!" Kathleen said. Pem chewed the corner of his lip and looked at Evie like she was combustible.

While Pem caught up with his aunt and uncle, I answered every question about Lucas Rivers that Evie could think of. It was a fun time.

When I tried to escape to the bus, Evie caught me. "Are you on the *Spring Forward* bus? Can I come look at it? Please?" Looking at it turned into going on it. She held up a T-shirt that was lying on the bedroom floor. "Is this his?"

I nodded and tried not to laugh as she clutched it to her chest. "Do you want it? He won't miss it."

Evie squealed. "Are you serious? I can have this? Omigod, I'll never wash it." She tore off her cute pink tank top and put on the T-shirt. It hung down to her knees. "Selfie?"

We posed with our heads together, making sure to get at least the top of her new shirt in the picture. She tapped her phone and it went out into the world.

Her phone started buzzing madly. Evie looked at the screen. "Omigod, everyone's so jealous that I'm hanging out with you." She tapped, not even pausing or looking up while she filled me in on her stream-of-consciousness ramble. "My friend Francesca wants to know if she can have one of your shirts. She loves the way you dress. . . . Don't think so. . . . Maddie wants to know where you get your hair cut. . . . Probably in LA, stalker. . . . Everyone wants to know when you started singing. . . . Ava says she thinks you're so cool. . . ."

We went back to the dressing room, where Evie continued responding to envious texts, narrating as she typed. "Hazel says she heard you got into a fight with Kate Martin. . . . Ancient history, move on. We have."

I stifled another laugh, but I doubted she would have cared anyway.

"Ella wants to know when you and Beckett are going to make a video for 'Smash Cut' . . . It's the whole band's song, not just theirs. . . ." She glanced up. "Although I could see the video being just the two of you."

"That's sweet. I'm so glad you guys like that song," I said.

"Yeah, but don't tell Third I said that about the video." Evie was so funny and bubbly that she'd somehow managed to cheer me up. "Okay, girls, last question . . . Natalie wants to know if you wish you'd won *American Pop Star*. Ooh! Good one!"

"No way. Because then I wouldn't be here talking to you guys!"

Evie grinned as she typed. "Excellent answer."

Connecting with fans I didn't know I had was a pretty cool feeling. She put the phone down and studied me. "I think girls like you because you don't try too hard. You have your own style, and it's different from all the other girl singers." It was the best compliment I'd received all tour.

Pem returned from giving his aunt and uncle a tour of the venue. When he saw Evie happily texting away in her new shirt, he gave me a grim smile. All had not been forgiven yet.

I was determined to enjoy the show that night. This wasn't going to last much longer, and I didn't want to take it for granted. The crowd was really into the songs, which helped to lift everyone's mood. I felt the way I imagined normal people feel at the end of the school year. Even though we still had a New York show, I felt like this was the real end of tour. Once we got to New York everyone would scatter. Since the guys were from there, they'd go home and spend the day off with friends and family. Some of the crew might be in my hotel, but it wouldn't be the same.

I wished I knew for sure that the next tour was happening. I'd be a lot less neurotic. If I asked Pem his head would explode, so I settled for visualizing us out on the road, seeing cities in Asia and Europe. For now I focused on the show and reminded myself that even getting to have this summer was a fantasy come true.

When we got to the bus lot, all of my things were sitting on the pavement. The driver told me apologetically that he'd been ordered to return the bus.

I carried my things onto the Melbourne bus, where my bunk was as I'd left it. Coming back actually felt nice.

"Aw man, she's back!" Winston yelled when he saw me.

I gave him a reproachful look. "Last night on the bus. I figured it wouldn't be the same without me."

He gave me a bear hug. "Of course not."

Dave kissed me on the top of my head before getting into the driver's seat. Oscar came on board next. We exchanged wary looks. He'd been the person Mandy was closest to, and I was sure he had thoughts about what had happened between her and Malcolm. I wondered what he'd say if he knew about Lucas. Maybe he already did.

The ride to New York that night was short enough that most of us stayed awake. Everyone packed and talked about their big plans. I felt panic setting in. I didn't know anyone in the city. I could spend the day off seeing the sites by myself I supposed, but that wasn't the way I'd imagined experiencing New York for the first time.

As Manhattan came into view, my adrenaline spiked, making it hard to catch my breath. I'd never been anyplace so big before. New York was always painted as a cold, ruthless city, but seeing all the twinkling lights, imagining all the lives being lived around me at that moment, gave me a warm feeling, a sense that anything could happen. We parked at the hotel on Union Square. I got off the bus and spun in a slow circle, taking it all in. Every direction I looked was a postcard.

All of our things had to come off the bus. People either loaded stuff into taxis or brought it into the hotel. We were all beat, so there wasn't much talking.

Beckett pulled me aside just before I went into the hotel. "Can I come by tomorrow?"

My breathing went shallow again. "What for? Don't you want to see people?"

"What people?"

"I don't know. People you haven't seen every single second for the past seven weeks?"

He grinned. "Not really."

35

When I met Beckett downstairs the next morning, he handed me a little yellow card with a magnetic strip. "What's this?" I asked.

"Your MetroCard. You're going to see the real New York."

The wave of incessant noise and heat on the street almost made me take a step back. We walked in the direction Beckett said was downtown and wandered around the East Village and the Lower East Side. He showed me the Mercury Lounge, the club that gave Melbourne their start. "Our first gig had about fifteen people in the audience. Most of them went to our school."

I tried to see inside, but it was dark. "Mandy would lose her mind if she knew she was missing this." When I thought about what she'd done, it still didn't feel real.

"We can come back and check out whatever's playing," Beckett said.

"Then can we go to the Empire State Building?" I asked.

"You get one cheesy tourist thing. Is that the one you want?" Beckett gazed at me with a solemn expression. I almost forgot what we were talking about.

"I can't choose." At least I knew I'd see Central Park the next day because we were playing SummerStage. It was such a big deal that our whole tour had been organized around this one show. "Can I see where you grew up?" I finally asked.

"Really?" he asked. I nodded. "It's not exactly a national landmark."

"Not yet, maybe," I said, and he shot me one of those amazing smiles.

We kept walking until we reached SoHo. I'd always read about it but never thought about anyone actually being from there. We stopped in front of a gorgeous old building sandwiched in between expensive boutiques and cafés. He pointed up at a window on the fourth floor. "That's my old room," he said.

"Are your parents home?" I asked.

"No. They spend summers in Nantucket. So do my older brothers. I don't live here anymore. Once you go to boarding school, it can be hard to come home, even if no one's in it."

"So they're not coming to the show?" I asked.

He shook his head. "They're waiting for me to grow up and go to college. I deferred Yale two years ago. They're still holding on to hope."

We stood there staring up at Beckett's childhood window.

"Beckett!" We looked in the direction of the voice. I saw a girl walking toward us, arms weighted down with fancy shopping bags. She looked very familiar, tall, model-thin, with long blond hair. I wondered if she was one of Pem's cousins who'd come to the Miami show. When she reached us, she barely looked at Beckett, instead focusing all of her intensity and curiosity on me. "You must be Chelsea." Her icy demeanor impressed me as native New Yorker directness.

"Hi." I looked to Beckett to see if he was going to shed any light on the situation. He stared at her like he was seeing a hallucination.

"Sorry. Chelsea Ford, meet Hollis Carter." He didn't take his eyes off her.

I felt a rush of prickly heat. There was no simple way to describe what I was feeling, but appalled and terrified came pretty close. While Hollis looked somehow more accessible in normal clothes and makeup, she was still a commanding presence.

And then there was the way Beckett was looking at her. I wanted him to stop looking at her like that. His face, normally so closed, opened right up upon seeing Hollis. It was all right there: caring, history, regret.

"It's so nice to finally meet you," I said, for lack of anything better or more accurate to say.

"Likewise," she said.

"Are you here for the rest of the summer?" Beckett asked.

She shook her head. "I leave for the Hamptons for two weeks and then back to school."

"How do you like Vassar?" Beckett asked.

"It's fine," Hollis said in a tone that indicated that she'd rather skip the small talk. She gave me another once-over. "I can't stay and chat. Good luck."

We walked away first, like all of SoHo was her kingdom and she'd banished us. "Whew. So glad I could be there for that touching reunion," I said. "She looked like she wanted to eat my young."

Beckett sighed. "It couldn't be easy for her to meet you."

"She's still in love with you, you know. I mean, there's a thin line between love and hate and all that, but believe it or not I think she's teetering on the love side."

He snorted. "Then I bet she'd really be in love with Pem too right about now." He stopped and grabbed my arm. "I'm not in love with her. Okay?"

I shrugged like it didn't matter to me one way or the other, but we both knew I was full of it. We just weren't ready to call me on it yet.

We spent the rest of the afternoon downtown. Even though I didn't get close, I saw the Statue of Liberty. We took the subway to Brooklyn and wandered around. There was a beautiful carousel right next to the water, which I naturally made Beckett ride with me. Twice. We ate dinner sitting side by side in front of an enormous window at a restaurant that was basically under the Brooklyn Bridge. The sun setting over lower Manhattan and the water was absolutely breathtaking.

After dinner we went back to the Mercury Lounge. We waited in line and paid the cover. Even though everyone seemed to recognize us, they left us alone. Maybe New Yorkers didn't geek out over famous people. But after a few songs, I tugged on Beckett's arm and motioned to the door. The band was too loud for such a tiny space, and their mix was so hot and bright that it was uncomfortable to listen to.

We got out to the sidewalk. "You didn't think they had potential?" Beckett asked. I wrinkled my nose. Snobby, I know. "Oh, that's right. You've never been in a band that sucks."

"And you have?" I asked.

"Believe me, when Melbourne started out we straight-up sucked. I almost feel bad for you that you missed it."

When he put it that way, I was kind of bummed about it. I'd had it easy, slipping into a band as polished and established as Melbourne. I didn't know what it was like to build something from the ground up. Yet another reason to be jealous of Hollis.

After much groaning and bellyaching, I talked Beckett into taking me to the Empire State Building. "Aren't you tired?" he asked.

"Please?" I wheedled. "It's my only free night in New York."

The line wasn't long, which cheered him up immensely. We rode the elevator to the 102nd floor, which is as high as you can go. As soon as we stepped onto the observation deck, a guy got down on one knee in front of a girl and opened a ring box. Everyone stopped what they were doing and cheered as the newly engaged couple shared a tender kiss.

"That is so romantic," I sighed.

Beckett turned to a security guard. "How many times a day does this happen?"

He gave us a look. "A lot. But it never gets old." He started another round of clapping, which I dutifully joined. Beckett laughed at me.

"Do you hate romance or something?" I asked.

"Not as much as you," he said.

"What are you talking about? I just clapped for strangers getting engaged."

"I mean, what happened with you and the d-bag? What's up with you and 'Parietals'?"

"Well, I don't know if you noticed, but Lucas was kind of a d-bag." Beckett continued to stare at me, refusing to let me joke my way out of this. I couldn't lie to him. He'd been so good to me and he deserved better.

The only light on the observation deck came from exterior lights and the city below. The darkness made it easier to open up. I took a wobbly breath. "I had kind of a thing with that guy you met at my parents' store."

Beckett snorted. "As if that wasn't completely obvious. Yeah? So?"

I was thrown by his reaction. "I mean, I don't still like him. It was freshman year." He wouldn't meet my eye, so I moved closer and tilted my head up to look into his face. "I'm being totally honest."

"Okay, Chelsea." He sounded so convinced. I wasn't sure how to continue. "You just seem confused. You kept Lucas around long past his sell-by date when even I could tell you weren't feeling him. You kissed me even though you were in a total state—"

"None of that was about Mike. Well, not exactly." I grasped for the right words. "I don't still want him or anything remotely like that. The part that I'm still traumatized by"—and here I had to swallow whatever modicum of pride I had left—"is that he never wanted anything more with me than top-secret hookups, but I was too dense to know he was using me."

"So your freshman-year boyfriend turned out to be an insecure asshole? Is that different than any other girl's—or boy's, for that matter—freshman-year experience?"

Oh God, I was going to have to tell him the rest. "Could you look somewhere else during this next part?"

He let out a surprised laugh. "Are you serious?"

I nodded, so he leaned back against the wall and watched all the tourists. "We did it, I thought I got pregnant, he bugged and told everyone that I tried to blackmail him into being my boyfriend, the whole school thought I was on crazy pills and shunned me, the end." I took a deep breath. "Okay, you can look now."

Beckett turned back, his expression a mixture of disgust and sympathy. "So that's why you can't sing 'Parietals'? Because it makes you think of him?"

"We sang it all the time, but it took on all-new and humiliating significance after I understood the truth about us. Every time we play it, I die a little inside."

"I think we all do, so you're in good company at least." Beckett sighed and rubbed the back of his head. "What about Lucas?"

"You're right. It would have been more honest if I'd broken up with him earlier." Beckett rolled his eyes. At this point, I had nothing left to hide. Maybe Beckett would think I was pitiful, but he'd also know me better. "He was the first boy who paid attention to me since Mike and was willing to be seen in public with me. I admit that the bar was set low, but can you blame me?"

Beckett looked at me. "What about me? I paid attention to you and ended things with Lauren because of you, and you still got with that poser."

I suddenly got very interested in looking down at Rockefeller Center. Tiny bats dove in and out of the spotlights mounted on the side of the building. "How was I supposed to know that? Besides, what were you going to do about it with Pem's rule? Which, by the way, I completely get now."

He stared at me for a second. I looked up at him, outlined in the darkness, and waited. He reached down to brush my cheek before leaning in to kiss me, something I was not expecting at all. I let myself go with it for a minute, which was probably a minute too long. I couldn't help it. As much as I wished I didn't, I liked Beckett—as more than a friend and bandmate. And he was an insanely good kisser.

There was nothing tentative about us this time. His lips moved against mine, kissing me so deeply and completely that it left me breathless. I wrapped my arms around his neck and pressed against him, not wanting to stop. From the way his hands gripped my waist, I knew he didn't want to stop either.

But we had to. Finally I pulled away and turned to face the window. "I'm sorry, but I can't risk it."

"Can't risk what?" His hands dropped from my hips. "Your place in the band?"

"Yeah," I said. "I want it to work for a lot of reasons."

My heart broke in anticipation of him agreeing with me. After a long moment, he nodded. "I don't think Pem would understand after what happened," Beckett began.

"And I totally see why."

He sighed, frustrated. "I know you think what I did was deplorable. And it was. But when you look at the whole picture, it's not completely black-and-white. Same with you and Mandy."

In my experience, it was always the wrongdoer who said things like that. The thing with Mandy felt pretty black-and-white. Same with what happened between me and Mike. I was willing to bet that Pem saw things the same way.

Beckett and I didn't say much on our cab ride back to my hotel. "Tomorrow we're all supposed to have lunch," he told me. "I'll text you the address when I get home." I nodded and turned to get out. He grabbed my arm. "I want to be with you, but my relationship with Pem is important to me too."

I understood. He'd chosen Pem over a girl once already. "You guys have been friends for a long time."

"It's not just our friendship. Our partnership, the way we write together, it's not something I can just throw away. We'd just have to take it slow. We could come clean eventually."

That wasn't good enough for me anymore. "I don't want another secret boyfriend." He looked at his shoes. "Thanks for showing me New York." I hopped out of the cab, blinking back tears.

36

The next day, I gave the cabdriver the address for a restaurant in Chinatown. The place was a symphony of loud voices, languages, and clanking plates. Families with multiple generations, young professional twentysomethings, and schlubby, middle-aged intellectuals all clustered around large round tables, dining family-style. White-uniformed staff pushed rolling carts around the room, slapping dishes down and marking tickets with an ink stamp.

Malcolm spotted me and waved me over. Pem and Beckett were already seated on one side of the table for four. I sat down and took a sip of ice water, trying to act normal.

"You made it. Behold, Chinatown." Malcolm waved grandly toward the center of the room. "I'm going to take care of the ordering. My Cantonese is shit, but it's better than any of yours."

"End-of-tour lunch," I said. I remembered back to the

kickoff lunch, how nervous and uncertain I'd been. At the same time, it had felt so alive with possibility and more festive with the entire crew and Sam there.

"Cheers," Beckett said. We clinked our glasses together.

Pem poured black tea into tiny ceramic cups with no handles.

A lady pushed a rolling cart to our table and stood by. Malcolm studied the little tins that cluttered the top of the cart. "That," he said, pointing. "And that one and that one." The lady stamped our ticket.

"That one and that one?" I asked. "I'm pretty sure my Cantonese is as good as yours."

Malcolm glowered at me, but Beckett snickered. "Dig in," Malcolm said. He served us pieces of each dish with quick, sure chopstick skills.

I took a tentative bite. "Don't start. We're not getting you a burger," Pem said.

I took a bigger bite. Whatever it was, it was tasty, salty goodness. I ate another one. Malcolm selected more dishes from another cart and we inhaled them. The carts couldn't come fast enough. Waiters replaced our teapot at least three times. I was getting hyper, but the black tea was a perfect balance to the greasy dishes. The whole time, Beckett and I avoided looking at each other.

"Interesting. You won't eat fish, but chicken feet and tripe are right up your alley," Malcolm said.

"What? Are you being serious?"

"Don't think about it," Beckett advised.

When we'd finished stuffing ourselves, Pem folded his arms. "Hollis called me yesterday."

Beckett glanced at me before saying, "Oh?"

"She thinks you guys are, how did she so charmingly put it? Screwing each other," Pem said. He glanced at Beckett. "She's still extremely pissed at you by the way. In case you were wondering."

My mouth dried up. I reached for my water. Malcolm stared, looking back and forth between us. Beckett sighed. "Well. We're not."

"Nothing's going on," I said. Not anymore, anyway.

Pem balled up his napkin and threw it on his plate. He obviously didn't believe us. "I can't go through that bullshit again. Building a band is soul-breaking work, which I wouldn't expect Chelsea to understand. Having it fall apart almost wrecked me. And starting practically all over again hasn't been a cakewalk either. I'm holding on to everything too tightly. I think I need out."

There was stunned silence. After their initial shock, Beckett and Malcolm tried appealing to Pem's senses. "Dude. We can handle whatever it is. We're all adults," Malcolm said.

"All bands deal with stuff. We're not exactly Fleetwood Mac," Beckett said.

"And I don't ever want to be. I really think I'd be just as happy producing and writing songs for other bands. Not to mention, my family can finally stop hassling me," Pem said.

"This is why Sam made the money grab with Chelsea's shit," Malcolm said. "He could tell you had one foot out the door."

"Probably," Pem agreed.

Tears came to my eyes as what Pem said hit me. I'd go back to Lydon to be a high school senior. Just in time for another year of scorn and scrutiny.

And Pem wouldn't be in a band anymore. I was still a fan, and the idea of him not performing, not being on a stage, was too much to process. Getting to watch him work during the past year had been a privilege. Now to hear that he wanted to quit and that it was at least partly my fault? I was devastated.

"It isn't all tragic," Pem was saying. "I wanted to prove to Hollis that we could do it without her, and we did. I feel good about that."

At least somebody felt good about something.

Playing the show that night was surreal, because the only people who knew that this might be the last Melbourne show were onstage. An enthusiastic, unsuspecting hometown crowd packed the intimate outdoor space. Every lyric, every story, took on added significance, but only for us.

I felt desperate to connect, to memorize the audience. If this was going to be my last show ever, I wanted to remember actual people, not a fleeting, anonymous mass. I picked out a guy with a red baseball cap. Beads of sweat flew off of him as he air-drummed, eyes scrunched shut in a state of oblivion. He opened them at the last second and flashed a triumphant, ecstatic smile when our eyes met. Next I focused on an animated girl with a black bleach-striped ponytail. We zoomed in on each other, her intensity rivaling my own while she sang every word with me.

Even with all that going on, I made a point to take in Central Park. With buildings peeking over treetops and the sun setting on a beautiful summer night, playing here was an experience to keep.

Pem got choked up a couple of times talking to the crowd, which almost made me cry. Malcolm hit the drums so hard I was sure the entire world knew his heart was breaking. I didn't dare look at Beckett.

Even though we were falling apart, we left it all onstage one more time.

Sam put the dressing room on lockdown after the show. Even Rob wasn't allowed in. "Beckett, Chelsea, let's have it," Sam said.

Seriously? That's how he was going to jump off? Awkward. "Uh . . ."

Beckett silenced me with a look. "There's nothing to tell. We both want what's best for the band."

"Meaning what, exactly?" Sam asked.

I looked down at my hands, which were clenched tightly in my lap. Better to let Beckett handle this. "Meaning nothing's happening and we're cool," he said.

When I glanced up, Sam's gaze was on me. "You sure it's that easy?" He seemed to want me to answer this one.

"Yeah." I cleared my throat. "I completely get it and don't have a problem."

"Personally I think it sucks that we feel like we have to micromanage each other like this. I mean, at least we all get along," Malcolm said. "Some bands still work together and can't even say that."

Pem made a face. "We get along now, but we all know that bands tear themselves up over stuff like this, and I'm telling you, I can't handle it again."

"Beckett and Chelsea do seem to understand what you're saying and are agreeing to keep their whole situation in check," Sam said.

"We're not just agreeing. It's what we want too." Beckett didn't look at me, but I heard bitterness in his voice. I couldn't tell if it was about me or about getting hammered for his mistake with Hollis all over again. I was dying to talk to him alone.

Pem groaned. We waited. "It's not a simple fix, okay? That's not even the whole problem. I can't deal with Chelsea's visibility. That isn't the right look for this band."

"But now that she's broken up with the d-bag, that should all go away. Right?" Malcolm looked to Sam for confirmation.

"Chelsea has definitely gained her own following, different from Melbourne's, but I don't think that has to be a bad thing. We can choose her projects with a more discerning eye," Sam said.

"Or I don't need to do any." I knew I sounded desperate, but the more Pem talked, the more I felt like this was on me. "I'm happy being in this band. That's enough for me."

Beckett's eyes dropped to the floor. He thought this was how I felt about him too, that giving him up would be as easy as giving up one of my deals. It wasn't that way at all, but it seemed counterproductive to say so now.

"We have a week before we need to decide on Europe. Let's take this week completely off, and then I'll check in," Sam said.

Malcolm went to the door but stopped suddenly and came back. "You're awesome. Bye for now, girl." He swept me up and held me for several seconds. He didn't say anything to the others.

No one else made a move, so I guessed it was my turn. I stood by the door. "Thanks for a great tour, and I'll talk to you in a week." I kept it light, like I was confident that I'd be seeing them again soon. I wanted to see Beckett before my morning flight but knew that he wouldn't initiate meeting up. Anyway, when he finally let himself look at me, his expression stayed blank. So I left.

37

I didn't get out of bed for days. The only Melbourne person I spoke to was Sam. He called the day after I got home. "Pem hasn't been the same about anything since Hollis. He says he's over her, but I'm not so sure," Sam said, trying to make me feel better.

"I don't think he's over that her rebound happened with Beckett."

Sam paused. "Yeah. That definitely didn't help."

"He loves this band. I can't believe he'd really end it."

"It's a little bit throwing the baby out with the bathwater. But it's not over yet."

I couldn't help comparing Pem and Beckett's situation to mine and Mandy's. It wasn't the same thing—with Beckett's screwup the boundaries had been blurry, whereas the lines Mandy crossed would have been completely unmissable from outer space. But I saw how much Pem hurt himself by continuing to punish Beckett.

Mandy understood me and my summer in a way that no one else ever could. When I felt the urge to say something about tour or the people I grew close to on it, my parents would pause whatever police drama they were watching, listen politely, then resume it like I hadn't said a thing.

Still, when Mandy finally came by one night, I wasn't ready to let bygones be bygones. We sat outside, even though the air was thick and unpleasant and I was still in the same pj's I'd put on days before.

"I can't believe I did that to you," she said.

"I can't believe it was Lucas who told me."

She looked at me. "I knew you didn't care about him," she said, sounding small.

"Is that your idea of an apology?" I asked. "We were about to break up, but until then and probably even for a while after, he was off-limits."

She was quiet for a minute. "I'm not saying what I did was right. But your life was so amazing, and all you could think about was this place." She gestured around us. "It was like you didn't fully appreciate what was happening."

"So you thought at least one of us should have fun and it might as well be you?"

"No. Maybe? In a way?" Mandy seemed just as lost as I felt.

"There was nothing I could do," I said. "Even if I'd threatened to quit, I doubt Pem would have budged."

"I believe you now that I heard about Melbourne breaking up."

"You *what?*"

She slid back on the step. "Oh, I mean, that's what I read online."

Of course. Why should I ever find out about anything in a direct way?

I'd tried to stay offline since I got home. The few times I did venture on, I was bombarded by news about Lucas and Nina. If I was ever going to brave it, this seemed like the time. I ignored a link to a photo spread of Lucas and Nina's newly redone Hollywood Hills love nest. Sure enough, dozens of blogs had posts speculating about the end of Melbourne. I read a few but stopped when some of the theories landed a little too close to home. No one knew the Hollis piece, of course, but there was a lot about me falling for Beckett. Naturally they made it sound like I chased him, propositioned him, did everything short of jump him, all because I was licking my wounds from Lucas's rejection. It was all so disgustingly familiar.

When I called Sam he said, "Ignore that noise. Pem hasn't said a thing. But since I have you, Bombshell and Kicks put your contracts on hold."

I crawled back into bed and gave myself another blackout period. I missed my GED test. Not that it even mattered now.

My mother eventually forced me out into the world. "Can't I be homeschooled?" I asked.

"If you don't mind a curriculum of accounts payable, inventory management, and display creation, we'd be thrilled to homeschool you," she said.

"You'll see. Things will be a little weird at first, but everyone will move on, get back to normal," my dad said. But that was actually what I was afraid of.

I ran into Mike Malloy while shopping for back-to-school supplies. "I was hoping to see you," he said. "I feel bad about what Caryn did to you at your show with the dumb signs. I know she put her sophomore lackeys up to it, and I called her out. Now she won't talk to me."

I gave him a disgusted smirk. "She did that because of you. You're the one who convinced everyone that I was trying to trap you."

Mike looked down, to the side, anywhere but my face. "I know," he said finally. "It was my first time too, you know. I was fifteen and I flipped out. It was shitty, okay? I can see that now. I told Caryn the truth."

"You've had years to come clean." I didn't know why I was picking at this particular scab, but I couldn't seem to leave it alone.

He shrugged, helpless. "I didn't think there was any way everyone still believed that."

"No? You thought I was a social outcast for some other reason?"

"I figured maybe you hated everyone and didn't want to be back in the mix."

I sighed. He would never get any less clueless.

"I heard about Melbourne breaking up," he said. Awesome. Yet another person who seemed to know my fate before I did.

"For what it's worth, I thought you were incredible as their singer."

"Thanks," I said. "Like many things, it was fun while it lasted."

In the days leading up to school, I worked on my song, mostly because I had nothing better to do. I started with the words I'd written that morning in Boston, after everything happened. I used the program on my laptop the way Beckett had showed me and recorded my vocals on top of the music. When I was done, I sent it to Pem with a note:

This marks my official retirement from docenting.

My return to Lydon High for senior year had the expected hiccups, as well as some unexpected ones. When I walked into calculus, Mrs. Carlson was telling the story of meeting Beckett and Malcolm at Ford's Fast Five. She stopped midsentence. "Chelsea! What a surprise. I didn't know you'd be back this semester."

Busted, I thought. "Yeah. Plans are still up in the air." From the way everyone shifted in their seats, I could tell that the breakup rumor had spread. I started toward an empty desk in the back.

"Is Lucas Rivers going to visit?" a kid with thick glasses asked.

"Dude," someone else said.

A few people told me they'd caught the Detroit show and enjoyed it. People still stayed away from me, but now it seemed like they were afraid to bother me. I could have felt flattered, but it didn't make eating lunch alone any less awkward. When I passed Mandy in the hall, we said hi, but I didn't rush to her side like I once would have. It was tolerable enough that I could almost imagine this being my life again.

My phone rang in the middle of seventh period. After silencing it, I checked the name. Sam. I called him back as soon as school let out. "I have good news and bad news. The bad news is, Melbourne's done."

I sat down on the curb and covered my eyes. I didn't care if I looked weird. "Doesn't the recipient of the news usually get to choose whether she wants the good or bad first?"

"You make a good point. Here's the positive: Pacific wants to use the last year of your contract. They want you to come out and record a solo album."

After I asked a few bewildered questions, we hung up. My head reeled. I thought I'd feel relief when I knew for sure, but I didn't. I only felt overwhelming sadness and the fear that everything I'd experienced with Melbourne, including my growth as a performer and a musician, was now null and void.

I took a day to call Sam back. "I don't want to be turned into a bubblegum pop singer. I want to work with another band and write songs." I didn't know what I expected him to say. It wasn't like bands were looking for replacement female leads every day.

But to my surprise, he said, "Let me run it up the flagpole." I sent him the song, even though I wasn't sure if it would help my cause or hurt it.

* * *

A week later, I was packing for Los Angeles. Pacific had agreed to the band and found a producer who would cowrite with me. I was flying out to sit in on band auditions.

"But what about school?" my mom had asked when I told her the plan.

"You can't miss this much school and still graduate. Can't they schedule this over winter break like last time?" my dad asked.

"It won't wait that long. Sam says that we have to move now, while I'm still relevant."

"What does that mean? Nobody's going to forget you in a few months," he said.

"I'll take the GED out in LA. Sam already registered me." I watched their silent exchange. "How is this any different than if I was going back on tour with Melbourne?"

My dad sighed. "Melbourne was an established thing. This feels more fly-by-the-seat-of-your-pants. But if this is what's going to make you happy, then you owe it to yourself to try."

It wasn't a total vote of confidence, but I leaped up and hugged them both on the way back to my room. "Thank you. I'll be back in a couple of months. I'll even go to school just for the social stimulation."

My mom swatted me on the arm. "I'm sure the teachers will love that."

In the middle of the chaos, Mandy called. "Congratulations. I knew you'd get a second act."

"Thanks." There was so much I started to say, but I couldn't make the words come out.

She took a deep breath. "I can't fix what I did, but I do want you to know that I'm sorry. I got caught up, and it was horrible that I let a job, let alone any boy, be more important than our friendship." She muffled the phone, but I heard her sniffle. My eyes filled. Neither of us said anything for a few minutes.

"Well . . ." I cleared my throat. "Do you feel like getting a sandwich?"

"Raspberries?" she asked.

"Meet you there in fifteen."

It wasn't that I was able to say more in person. If anything, sitting across from Mandy eating a Jane's Special made me feel like I didn't need to express all the things I felt about what happened between her and Lucas.

"So how do you feel about being back?" I asked.

Mandy shrugged. "It's okay, actually. I almost feel like nothing matters, but in a good way. Our summer was so epic. I mean, we had real jobs with real responsibilities. We saw more cities and met more people in one summer than most people our age have in their entire lives. How much can you come back and worry about people saying stuff about you?"

"I guess. I'm still glad I'm leaving. It hasn't been so terrible, but I feel like the more things get back to normal, the more it'll feel like this summer never happened."

"Well. You don't have to worry about that now." Mandy's smile was a little wobbly, but she hid it by taking a sip of her drink. "Just so you know, I'll never tell anyone about what happened. Not to protect myself but just to avoid giving the gossipmongers any more material."

I nodded, unsure what to say. "Thank you" didn't seem quite right. "Mike apologized."

Her eyes brightened. "No way!"

I wouldn't say it was like old times, but somehow it laid the groundwork for us to return to normal when I got back. And that was really what we both needed. We finished our food and even lingered a little longer.

"Be sure to keep in touch. I might need a merch girl next summer," I said.

"Sweet. I'll be ready." She smiled.

When I got home, I checked my inbox and saw "Pem Fuller" at the top and clicked on it.

Just don't sell out or become a tool. Song's great. You should use it on your album. Congratulations.

Pacific sent a black town car to pick me up at LAX. "I've been instructed to bring you straight to the auditions," the driver said.

"Perfect," I said.

We pulled up in front of the Roxy. I stared at the building for a long time. It looked so different in the daytime without the neon lights.

Inside I paused by the bathroom, thinking about the last time I'd been here. My nerves, the tour announcement, Lucas. It all came blasting back. I shook it off and headed into the club. Sam was already there along with some Pacific A&R staff.

"You ready?" Sam asked. "This is big."

"Sure," I said, not at all sure.

We sat at tables up on a platform, away from the stage.

We all turned toward the door as it opened. My heart stopped. Beckett walked through with his guitar. He grinned when he saw me. "Before I audition, does this band have any stupid rules I should know about?"

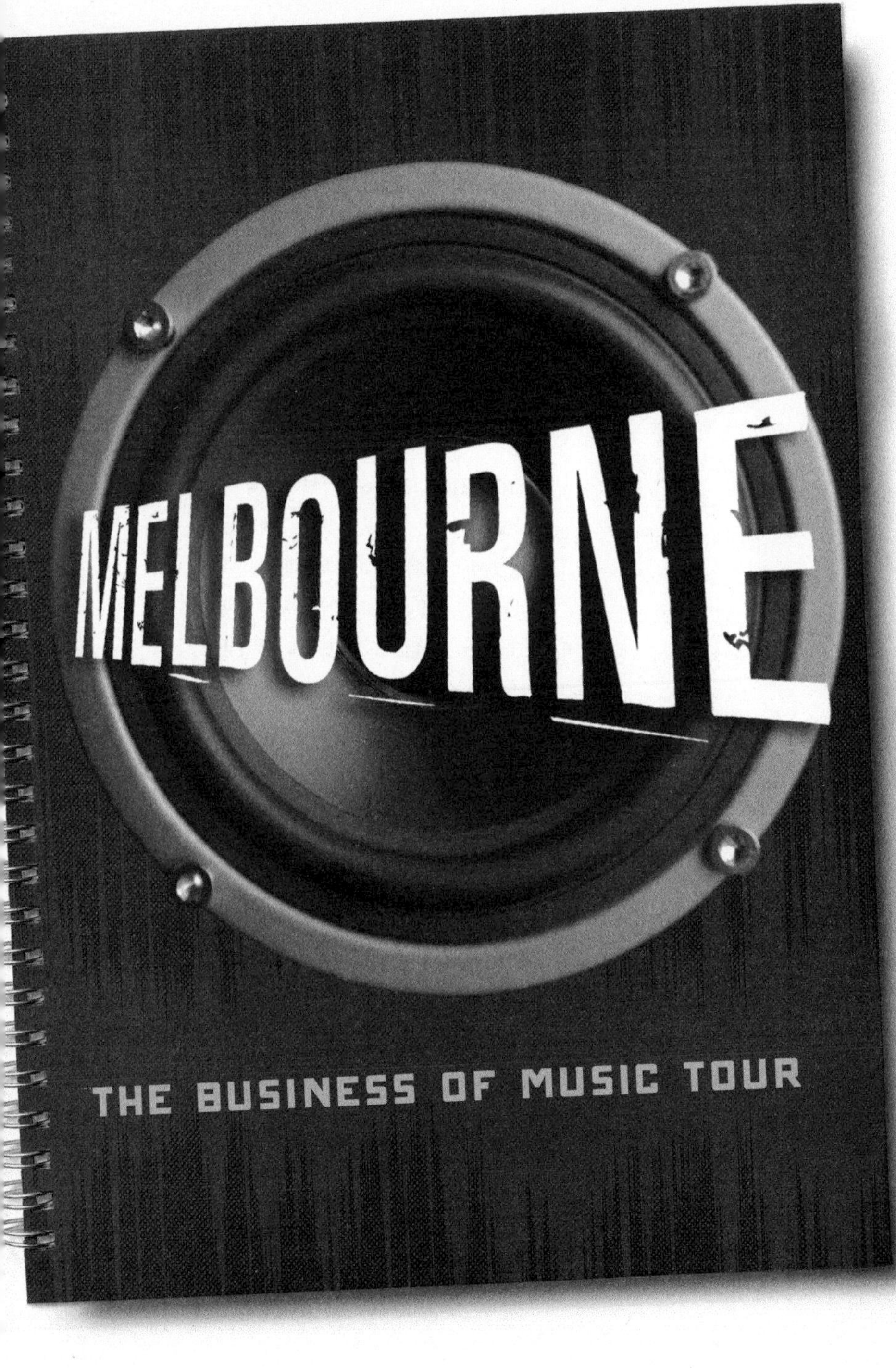
MELBOURNE
THE BUSINESS OF MUSIC TOUR

MELBOURNE

WELCOME TO THE MELBOURNE U.S. TOUR!

We look forward to working with you and thank you in advance for your cooperation and sense of humor throughout the tour!

HOTELS

We will stay in hotels only in cities where there is a day off. Due to tour economics, there are no single rooms available. Everyone will be responsible for paying his or her own incidental charges before checking out of the hotels. Even if you believe that you have no charges, check out at the front desk. This will ensure that no mistakes are made by you or the hotel. It will be your responsibility to resolve any unpaid incidentals disputes with the hotel.

DEPARTURE TIMES

Departure times mean that everyone is ready to depart in the designated vehicle picking up the group. If you miss call time, it is your responsibility to get to the venue.

TRAVEL GUESTS

Tour travel plans are for touring personnel only and do not take anyone else into account. Do not assume it is okay to have a guest travel on any transportation provided by the tour. If you are planning to have a guest travel with you on any bus or flights, please consult the tour manager.

MELBOURNE

CATERING

Local catering is for the artist party, crew, and support band. Do not invite your guests to eat in catering unless permission has been given by production.

TICKETING

A very limited number of comp tickets are available for touring personnel. These tickets are distributed on a first-come, first-served basis. Please have any and all requests submitted one week in advance of the date desired. Day-of-show requests cannot be accommodated. Abuse of this privilege will not be tolerated.

ALL INFORMATION IN THE ITINERARY IS SUBJECT TO CHANGE.
IF THERE ARE ANY DETAILS THAT ARE CRUCIAL TO YOUR PLANS,
PLEASE CHECK WITH THE TOUR MANAGER.

Have a great tour!

MELBOURNE

TOUR PERSONNEL

ARTISTS

Pem Fuller   Bass
Beckett Moore   Musical Director/Guitar/Backup Vocals
Malcolm Ho   Drums
Chelsea Ford   Lead Vocals

MANAGEMENT

Sam O'Malley   Manager

BOOKING AGENCY

Artists and Entertainers Agency
Contact: Mark Gardner

TOUR MANAGEMENT

Rob Chang   Tour Manager and Accountant

CREW

Oscar Lopez   Lighting Tech
Winston Jackson   Guitar/Bass Tech
Aaron Elliott   Drum Tech
Kam Fitzgerald   Monitor Engineer
Jared Pinski   Sound Engineer
Mandy Olson   Merchandise Management
Dave Ryland   Ground Transportation

MELBOURNE

TOUR ITINERARY

6/21 (W) Pittsburgh — Rehearsal
6/22 (Th) Pittsburgh — Rehearsal/Press Day
6/23 (F) Pittsburgh — Stage AE
6/24 (S) DC — 9:30 Club
6/25 (Sun) Nashville — Ryman Auditorium
6/26 (M) Nashville — Day Off
6/27 (Tu) Charlotte — The Fillmore
6/28 (W) Atlanta — Tabernacle
6/29 (Th) Orlando — House of Blues
6/30 (F) Miami — Day Off
7/1 (S) Miami — The Fillmore
7/2 (Sun) St. Petersburg — Jannus Live
7/3 (M) Los Angeles — VIDEO SHOOT
7/4 (Tu) ~~Los Angeles — VIDEO SHOOT~~ *Vegas — private party for cell phone launch*
7/5, 6 (W, Th) Los Angeles — VIDEO SHOOT
7/7 (F) Houston — Bayou Music Center
7/8 (S) Dallas — South Side Ballroom
7/9 (Sun) Austin — Stubb's
7/10 (M) Austin — Day Off
7/11 (Tu) Travel Day
7/12 (W) Phoenix — Marquee Theatre
7/13 (Th) San Diego — House of Blues
7/14 (F) Los Angeles — The Wiltern
7/15 (S) Los Angeles — Day Off

MELBOURNE

7/16 (Sun) Oakland — The Fox Theater

7/17 (M) Seattle — The Paramount Theater

7/18 (Tu) ~~Seattle — Day Off~~ Vancouver — Commodore Ballroom (added date)

7/19 (W) Boise — The Knitting Factory

7/20 (Th) Salt Lake — The Great Saltair

7/21 (F) Denver — ~~The Fillmore Auditorium~~ Red Rocks Amphitheatre (bigger venue)

7/22 (S) Kansas City — ~~Uptown Theater~~ Starlight Theatre (bigger venue)

7/23 (Sun) Kansas City — Day Off

7/24 (M) St. Louis — ~~The Pageant~~ Peabody (bigger venue)

7/25, 26 (Tu, W) — Day Off/Chelsea Meetings in LA

7/27 (Th) Minneapolis — Myth Live

7/28 (F) Des Moines — Val Air Ballroom

7/29 (S) Indianapolis — Egyptian Room

7/30 (Sun) Indianapolis — Day Off

7/31 (M) Cincinnati — Bogart's

8/1 (Tu) Cincinnati — ~~Day Off~~ Bogart's (added date)

8/2 (W) Detroit — ~~The Fillmore~~ DTE Pavilion (bigger venue, pavilion only)

8/3 (Th) Columbus — LC Pavilion (moved from indoor to outdoor)

8/4 (F) Chicago — Lollapalooza

8/5 (S) ~~Travel Day~~ Toronto — Sound Academy (added date)

8/6 (Sun) Boston — ~~House of Blues~~ Blue Hills Bank Pavilion (bigger venue)

8/7 (M) Philadelphia — The Mann

8/8 (Tu) New York — Day Off

8/9 (W) New York — Central Park SummerStage

Song Lyrics

PARIETALS

Lyrics by Hollis Carter

Growing up here's not all it's meant to be
So for just these moments let's be wild and free
We have each other and maybe that's enough
Shouldn't have to stress about so much crazy stuff

Parietals, you have me acting like a fool
Our parents don't know what goes on at school
Keeping us apart, it's pointless and cruel
Parietals, there's way too many rules
Parietals, there's way too many rules

I want to see you, come up to my room
Leave right now you can't get here too soon
Try not to get caught sneakin' around
When you're next to me, we won't make a sound
Maybe we're being stupid
If you hear footsteps, better run

Parietals, you have me acting like a fool
Our parents don't know what goes on at school
Keeping us apart, it's pointless and cruel
Parietals, there's way too many rules
Parietals, there's way too many rules

No movie dates, no long walks home
We're forced into these lies
No parked cars, no empty houses
But when I'm with you time flies

Parietals, you have me acting like a fool
Our parents don't care what happens at school
Keeping us apart, it's pointless and cruel
Parietals, there's way too many rules
Parietals, there's way too many rules

SMASH CUT
Lyrics by Pem Fuller

(CHELSEA)
I saw you coming
A mile away
If you told me then
That this would be our best day
I never would've believed you
I should've walked or maybe run
But then I'd have missed out on all our stupid fun
There was the day I said I loved you
Our moment in the sun
I thought we'd just get better
One minute we were everything and the next you were done

Smash cut to now
I don't know where to find you
I tell myself not to look
But my heart is on the hook
It wasn't my imagination
We had more than just a spark
Unless you tell me why
I'll be forever in the dark

(BECKETT)
We had it all, that wasn't just a dream
You were the sun, the stars
And everything in between
The time I spent with you
Made me who I am
Helped me know the difference
Between being a boy and being a man
I don't know either why we fell apart
But let me tell you this: you always have my heart

There's not one thing I can say
There's nothing we did wrong
We could go our own directions
Because our love's what made us strong

(BOTH)
Smash cut to now
I don't know where to find you
I tell myself not to look
But my heart is on the hook
It wasn't my imagination
We had more than just a spark
Unless you tell me why
I'll be forever in the dark

I haven't given you up **(CHELSEA)**
I wish you'd asked me to stay **(BECKETT)**
We needed more time **(CHELSEA)**
There was more to say **(BECKETT)**
How could we both just walk away **(BOTH)**

(BOTH)
Smash cut to now
I don't know where to find you
I tell myself not to look
But my heart is on the hook
It wasn't my imagination
We had more than just a spark
Unless you tell me why
I'll be forever in the dark

(BOTH)
Smash cut to now
I don't know where to find you
I tell myself not to look
But my heart is on the hook
It wasn't my imagination
We had more than just a spark
Unless you tell me why
I'll be forever in the dark

IMPERFECT
Lyrics by Chelsea Ford

We both know the truth
It doesn't matter now
I got over you and her
Don't bother asking how
I turned the page, I closed the book
Our tragic scene is done
No need to linger, no pieces to find
Stop acting like you won

You tore me down
I struggle to get up
I see you coming near
Feels like you hit me with a truck
I wanted you in my life
How much does that suck
Play it back, remind me now
I'll forget with any luck

My best friend has my back
Or that's what I've been told
Your apologies, your excuses
That shit is getting old
But you know how that saying goes
Revenge is best served cold

You tore me down
I struggle to get up
I see you coming near
Feels like you hit me with a truck
I wanted you in my life
How much does that suck
Play it back, remind me now
I'll forget with any luck

Maybe you're right
Maybe I can forgive
Waiting for the past to change
That's no way to live

You tore me down
I struggle to get up
I see you coming near
Feels like you hit me with a truck
I wanted you in my life
How much does that suck
Play it back, remind me now
I'll forget with any luck

Acknowledgments

I would first like to thank my wonderful husband, Andrew Simon, to whom this book is also dedicated. Without him, *For the Record* would not exist. Thank you for the years of love and encouragement, for routing Melbourne's tour even though I was more demanding than a real manager, and for believing that going to your clients' shows qualifies as a date. I'm happy to be your plus one!

Thank you to my spectacular agent, Adriann Ranta, for believing in this story even before it was written and for pushing me to make it better. Adriann is a total rock star, and I'm so privileged to be represented by her.

I couldn't ask for a wiser, kinder, or more insightful editor than Wendy Loggia. *For the Record* has benefited so much from her talent and expertise. I feel incredibly fortunate to have this debut experience with her.

Thanks also to the rest of the Delacorte team, including Krista Vitola, Angela Carlino, Jennifer Prior, Kerry Johnson, and Anna Gjesteby. Their hard work on behalf of this book is so appreciated.

I'm indebted to Chandler Baker and Michelle Krys, two writer friends who've made all the difference. Without them, the dream of getting agented and published would have seemed impossible. I've also come to rely on many of the amazing writers in my debut author groups, the Freshman Fifteens, the

Class of 2k15, and the Fearless Fifteeners. The support and advice I've found there have been invaluable.

I'm grateful to early manuscript readers, including Andrew (again), Chandler (again), Laura Fallon, Kerri J. Sparks, and Elisa Stumph. Their comments and contributions were essential to this story.

Huge thanks to the sweet friends who answered numerous music-related questions: David Bason, Mark Shulman, Mark Holloway, Maureen Kenny, and especially Patrick Stump. And to all the wonderful guys in Fall Out Boy, thanks for letting me crash your backstage hang all these years. In fact, thank you to all my husband's clients and colleagues who have knowingly or unknowingly informed this project. I have been inspired by so many of you.

I have the loveliest friends, who have been encouraging of me as a writer. A heartfelt thank-you to every one of them, especially Caroline Tse, who designed my website and book swag. Likewise to my relatives in the Chen, Huang, Simon, and Breen families.

I will be forever grateful to my mom and dad, who never said no to any book purchase and instilled in me a lifelong love of reading.

Love and hugs to my beautiful boys, Jackson and Elliott, for their curiosity about my writing and for generally making my life amazing.

Thank you to the readers and bloggers who let me know that they were eagerly anticipating this book. That made me happier than you can imagine. And lastly, thank you to anyone reading this book. I hope you enjoy it.

Turn the page for a sneak peek.

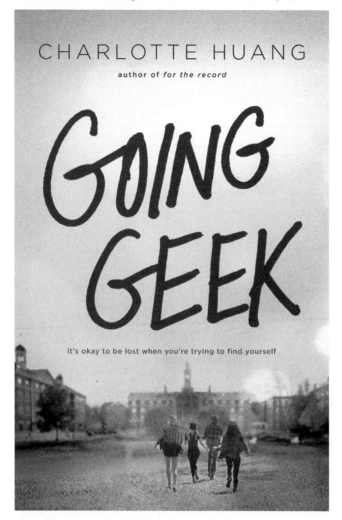

CHARLOTTE HUANG

author of *for the record*

GOING GEEK

it's okay to be lost when you're trying to find yourself

It wasn't supposed to be this way.

Skylar Hoffman's senior year at her preppy East Coast boarding school should have been perfect: amazing boyfriend, the coolest friends, the most desirable dorm.

But it's far from it. A little white lie is causing Skylar's once rock-solid life to crumble fast, and stepping out of her comfort zone has never felt so scary—or necessary.

My phone finally rings, and I snatch it off the floor so fast that Opal actually looks up from her reading. It's Jordana, which, I'm ashamed to admit, is a tiny bit of a letdown, especially since I'm the one who texted her earlier.

"Hi."

"Uh-oh, that doesn't sound good. What's going on?" Jordana asks.

Following good dorm etiquette, I defer to my studying roommate and step into the hall. "Okay, I have to apologize in advance. I'm going to be *that* girl for a while." My voice catches.

Jordana's quiet for a second. "Don't even worry about that. We've been friends for too long."

I take a deep breath. "Well, remember that perfect senior year I was supposed to be having? It has kind of come to a screeching halt."

"Already? What happened?" She sounds genuinely upset for me, which in and of itself makes me want to cry.

I walk toward the common room, which is on the first floor at the front of the house, right next to the kitchenette. Hopefully it has a door that locks. But Jess is already in there on one of the two couches, watching a movie on her laptop. "Aren't you the lucky one with a single?" I ask.

"Yeah, but I haven't given up hope that someone will watch with me one day," she says, not taking the hint. "Until then I have to settle for educating through osmosis." She turns back to her movie. A giant oil tanker takes up most of the screen while a dry voiceover spouts off statistics. Looks riveting.

"Hello?" Jordana's voice comes through faintly over my phone. I glower at Jess and back out of the room.

Outside on the porch I sit down on the steps and rest my forehead on my knees. Even though it's late, the air hasn't cooled much, but a faint breeze stirs the air. "How much time do you have?" I ask.

When I get through the whole sordid story, Jordana is silent. "What? What are you thinking? That I had it coming? That my friends are disloyal jerks—what?"

"Slow down," Jordana says. "Would you believe me if I said all of the above?"

"Kind of a cop-out but, I guess."

"What's up with this Lila person? Do you think Whit would be this spun out if Lila weren't at Winthrop?"

I consider that. "I don't know. Whit always made her out to be a conniving one-upper. I'm sure Whit feels like I made her look stupid. She probably had Lila believing that I was some fabulous A-list party girl."

"Hmm. Maybe she's making a big deal out of it so Lila understands that she didn't knowingly exaggerate," Jordana says.

"You mean so Lila knows that Whitney didn't lie to impress her? Unlike me?" I ask.

"Harsher than I was willing to go, but yeah."

"Maybe." Embarrassment in any form is not something Whitney takes lightly. Ever.

"And Leo?" Jordana asks.

With my toe, I trace an *L* in the dirt below the bottom step. "He's really angry with me. We've never had a fight like this before. The thing that kills me is, I did tell the truth! When I first got here and met everyone, my mom was still doing great. Should I be punished in every way possible just because the film business is fickle and things don't always work out? Is it not enough that my family life is grim and that I had to work a ton of hours at a mostly mindless job? Am I really obligated to tell everyone that my mom's business took a nosedive?"

"Definitely not . . ." She trails off, and I know what she's thinking.

"But if I told Leo, he'd expect me to be honest about it with everyone."

"Why? Is his life an open book?"

"Yes. Because he's perfect."

"Well, that's annoying," Jordana says. My responding laugh is halfhearted at best. "What?" she continues. "It was annoying when he was your boyfriend, and it's even more annoying now that he's holding his perfection over your head."

I straighten. "He's still my boyfriend. And that's not what he's doing. Is it?"

Jordana sighs. "No. From everything you've told me, he doesn't seem like that guy. He just doesn't get it."

"Do you think he's going to break up with me?"

"I don't know, but if he does, that'll be his one imperfect act."

That actually makes me smile. We're quiet for a minute. "Thanks for trying to make him the bad one, JoJo."

"That's what friends are for," she says.

"What about you? Tell me that your year is going better than you thought it would."

"Nope. It's unfolding exactly as expected. Except Joe Brill asked me out."

"That's amazing!" I say.

"I'm going to let you think about that one for a minute," Jordana says.

Realization dawns. "Oh, second grade, nose picker?"

"Bingo."

"Well, that was a long time ago. But this just means college is going to be spectacular for you," I say. It better be. Jordana deserves it.

We hang up, and I force myself back into the dorm. As I pass by the common room I notice that everyone's in it, including a goth girl I've seen around but never met and a girl wearing faded jeans and a gauzy peasant blouse whom I've never noticed before. I stick my head in out of curiosity. Everyone's conspicuously quiet, trying to look busy. I'm about to introduce myself, but then I see that the front window's wide open and realize that they must have overheard every word of my conversation.

"You guys were eavesdropping on me?" Even though privacy is typically scarce at boarding school, it's pretty gutsy to listen in on someone's private phone call so blatantly.

They all exchange glances, each hoping that somebody else will be dumb enough to speak first. "Isn't it kind of better this way?" Raksmey finally asks. "Now you don't have to tell the story a million times."

Unbelievable. "Just so you know, I had no intention of telling any of you any story, ever!"

I storm up the stairs but not before I hear someone whisper, "She's better than Netflix." A few of the others shush her.

As soon as I get to my room, I crawl into bed. Opal is seemingly not completely oblivious, because she makes sure to let me fall asleep before she comes back.